A Circle of Uncommon Witches

ST. MARTIN'S PRESS

ST. MARTIN'S PUBLISHING GROUP

Also by Paige Crutcher

The Orphan Witch
The Lost Witch
What Became of Magic

A Circle of Uncommon Witches

Paige Crutcher

ST. MARTIN'S GRIFFIN
NEW YORK

First published in the United States by St. Martin's Griffin, an imprint of St. Martin's Publishing Group

A CIRCLE OF UNCOMMON WITCHES. Copyright © 2025 by Paige Crutcher. All rights reserved. Printed in the United States of America. For information, address St. Martin's Publishing Group, 120 Broadway, New York, NY 10271.

www.stmartins.com

Designed by Gabriel Guma

The Library of Congress Cataloging-in-Publication Data is available upon request.

ISBN 978-1-250-90554-3 (trade paperback)
ISBN 978-1-250-90555-0 (ebook)

Our books may be purchased in bulk for promotional, educational, or business use. Please contact your local bookseller or the Macmillan Corporate and Premium Sales Department at 1-800-221-7945, extension 5442, or by email at MacmillanSpecialMarkets@macmillan.com.

First Edition: 2025

10 9 8 7 6 5 4 3 2 1

This book is for you. You are a child of the universe, made of stars. I promise, you can do anything.

⸙ ☾ ● ☽ ⸗

The woods are lovely, dark and deep,
But I have promises to keep,
And miles to go before I sleep,
And miles to go before I sleep.

ROBERT FROST
"Stopping by Woods on a Snowy Evening"

The witches' creed is clear: and harm none.
If you dare go against the rule, you undo magic in the world
as it was meant to be.

MACKINNON WITCHES' CREED

((●))

For when the gods of magic were tricked by man, they took back
the magic from the earth and gave its power to only a few families
to guard and grow. To challenge this rule, a witch must enter the
trials and win a blessing. The trials were a measure of strength,
cunning, bravery, and heart. To complete them, the champion
must free the heart from the stone, find the lost story of love,
wake the slumbering giant, and sacrifice what matters most
to break the curse. For power is always waiting, and it would
only take one stubborn witch to set it free.

THE TRIALS OF *BHEANNACHD*
(The Blessing Trials)

ONE

For more years than she knew what to do with, Doreen MacKinnon had been waiting for the day she would turn thirty and find true love or die.

It was the curse of being a MacKinnon; the thirteenth generation of Scottish witches who had been cursed by a rival line, the Mac-Donalds, back during the times of King James VI. Each line blamed the other for alerting the blustering king to their existence, and the witch hunt and trials that followed.

"If Ambrose MacDonald hadn't bewitched Lenora, none of this would have happened," Doreen's aunt Stella always said, usually when Doreen was up to her armpits in research, working on her own to break the curse. "You'll never get anywhere with it, girl, but then again, neither will he," she'd cackle, before returning to pruning the dark violet roses that ran along her drive while Doreen sat on a threadbare blanket in the shade surrounded by books, wondering how anyone could be so happy to have imprisoned another witch.

"Why did he bewitch her?" Doreen asked.

"Oh, he did not," her aunt Kayleen had said during a visit when Doreen and Margot were eight and nine years old. "Stella, you know it wasn't that simple. Ambrose fell in love with Lenora, and Lenora with Ambrose."

"She had a bad picker," Stella argued.

"Still, she *chose* him, and then she left him. All he knew was how she had been spirited away by her family in the night, taken and then gone. Deader than an exorcised spirit," Kayleen said, while measuring out sugar and fermented grapes and hibiscus before pouring all three into her cauldron—a mixer she had purchased from a new store in town.

"You can't have a modicum of sympathy for that man," Stella warned, adding a pinch of lavender to the mix. "He took his broken heart and devastated our family line, cursed us to the bone."

"Broken hearts break hearts," Kayleen said.

"And now we break him over and over again," Stella said, before finally shooing the girls out of the room.

"All these years later, and I still don't get it," Doreen said to her cousin, Margot, some twenty years later. They were sitting in their family's herbal apothecary shop in the small town of Pines, waiting for customers or time to hurry up and pass them by. "Why won't anyone tell us where Ambrose is?"

Margot shot her a look. "He's in the Dead House."

"Which is a myth."

Margot snorted. "Yeah, and so's the curse."

Doreen blew her too-long bangs away from her face. "The curse *can* be broken. And you know it."

Margot shook her head.

"You do, and yet you're really going to marry Dean Whitmeyer?"

Margot sighed, not bothering to look up from the soul cards she was sorting. "I love him."

"But you don't know if *he* loves *you*."

Margot didn't reply. She wasn't about to lie to her best friend and cousin, and she couldn't rebuke the truth. What Margot had chosen instead was to accept that she was marrying a man under her spell. Or enthralled, as Stella put it, but a *thrall* always made Doreen think of a B movie with a vampire rising from the grave, his black hair slicked back, eyes bulging as he sank his fangs into the neck of the first unsuspecting blonde who came his way. *"I vant to suck your blood."*

Though what Margot was doing felt almost as bad. *"I vant to steal your love."*

Doreen pulled out her final resource from beneath the table. It was a notebook adorned with a unicorn flying across a rainbow on the front, the cover bent and worn from age and love, and a last-ditch effort to convince Margot to make a different choice. She turned to a dog-eared page, and slid it under her cousin's nose, over the cards.

"I know what it says," Margot said, shaking her head at Doreen. "I wrote it."

"Are you *sure?*"

When Margot made no move to glance at it, Doreen took it back and began to read out loud instead.

" 'I, Margot Rose Early, being of brilliant mind and even better body, do hereby promise to never give up on myself or true love. Unlike the aunts and mothers before us, I refuse to believe this hogwash of a curse. This jinx of a whammy will not take my sanity or my life or my heart. I am the goddess of my destiny and may no curse mess with me.' "

"We were kids, Doreen."

Doreen huffed an exasperated breath. She leaned over and grabbed Margot's arm, forcing her cousin to look at her. But she dropped it when she saw the tears in her eyes.

Margot was strong, fierce, and determined, and Doreen was always convinced it would be her who would smite the curse and restore the balance, once and for all. When they were small, Doreen and Margot had created a spell that enabled them to get into the magically locked attic of their home and steal Stella's books on their history and craft. It was a spell they would use many times while researching how to break the curse and grow their powers. Doreen, the mimic, was able to duplicate any spell, and Margot, the creator, capable of crafting any charm from thought.

Doreen had never considered Margot would give up.

"Oh, Margot."

Margot sniffed and turned back to the cards. "I don't want to *die*, Doreen. This is my best option, and I do love him. I can be enough for us both. You'll see."

"You're wrong, and what we're forced to do is wrong," Doreen said.

"We have a choice," Margot said. "That's more than most get about their fate. Maybe we should try to be happy instead of wasting our time dreaming we can change it."

Doreen remembered vividly the day she had learned the truth. She was seven and had developed her first crush on a boy named Lucas in her first-grade class. Doreen always thought he was so mysterious, mainly because he ignored her no matter how often she studied him. But one day, during a field trip, they'd ridden the bus to the science museum in the next town over and gone over a bump. He'd looked back at her, grinning his gap-tooth grin. In that moment, it hit her—a bolt of lightning to the soft spot under her belly. She wanted to jump up, climb over the seats in the bus, and brush her fingertips against the curve of his smile.

Her stomach quivered and he blinked, and a change slowly came over his face. His eyes widened, his mouth trembled, and he got out of his seat. He moved toward her as though she were the only person on the bus. He bumped into Dave Sanders, knocking his bag to the floor, climbed over Suzie Macintosh and Lennie Brown in the seat in front of Doreen, and dropped into the bench beside her.

"Doreen," he said, her name on an exhale. He smelled of caramel Pop-Tarts, and his eyes were so green she thought they might have been dipped in food coloring.

"Hi, Lucas," she said, smiling and ducking her chin, shocked he seemed to feel exactly what she was feeling.

His hand reached up, and he ran a finger over the hair falling into her face, tucking it behind her ear. "Hi," he said. "Want to split a grilled cheese with me at lunch?"

For the rest of the day, they stayed side by side, holding hands as they walked the star walk—a dark room filled with projections of stars—studied the mini tornadoes produced by controlled gusts of air inside glass domes, and made water flow back and forth in the crank tank to study the tides. It was the single best day of her life.

Until she got home.

"Who was the boy?" Stella asked. She stood in the doorway, waiting, her arms crossed over her chest.

"My new boyfriend," Doreen said, grinning so wide she was afraid her cheeks might split in two. She hadn't officially asked Lucas to be her boyfriend, but some things were simply destined.

Stella sighed. "It's time."

She ushered Doreen into the kitchen and sat a glass of milk and single biscuit in front of her. One of Stella's secrets were her beloved biscuits. She only made them for birthdays and special occasions.

As Doreen gobbled the biscuit down, Stella drummed her painted red fingernails on the table. "You can't have a boyfriend."

"I'm not too young," Doreen said, rolling her eyes, dusting crumbs from her lips. "Maisie Newnan and Sally Jones both have boyfriends, and so do Sam Haven and George Miles."

"No, love, you don't understand." Stella sat at the table holding a tin can with a smiling dog on its front. "You can't have them because it's not real."

"Of course it's real, I like him."

"I mean it's not real for *him*."

Doreen frowned, confused.

For years, any time Doreen had shown any romantic interest in members of the same or opposite sex, Stella had found a way to subvert it. She'd pulled her from library programs, preschool classes, and their one failed attempt at choir. Doreen had assumed she was either bad at the programs or Stella was just that grumpy. But now her trembling knees told her *this* might be something different.

"My girl, you're cursed. *We* are cursed. You have no hope of finding true love, because every person you ever show interest in will fall under your spell, your thrall. Your only hope is to accept that what you have will never be real. I'll bind the boy; he won't bother you again."

It was then that Doreen understood Stella's ruthlessness. That her aunt would do whatever it took to protect her in whatever way she saw fit.

From the beginning, there were signs of disquiet in the love lives of the MacKinnon women. Doreen knew it in how no one ever spoke about love. Not in the ways people in storybooks would. There was no such thing as "happily ever after" or even "happily ever now." While there were aunts and cousins who married, they didn't see them often.

"Marriage is a cage for those of us unable to escape the lie," Stella would say while baking her biscuits on a Saturday morning.

"What's the lie when it comes to love?" Doreen asked Margot later, while they were lying in their twin beds in their attic room. "Love is why we're here."

"Stella says we're here to balance the imbalance in the world and change it," Margot replied, unable to suppress a yawn. Margot thought her mother, Stella, was grumpy and lonely, though she never dared to speak those words out loud. At least not then. She also thought her cousin Doreen thought too much. Margot didn't have half as many words thinking in her head as the ones that came out of Doreen's mouth.

"I don't want to change the world," Doreen said. "I want to hold hands and dance under the stars and laugh so hard we cry and then dance some more."

"We do that," Margot said, thinking it wasn't like Doreen was missing out when she had Margot.

"Yeah, but it's different than if, say, Lucas and I were doing it. If he held my hand I would burst into a firework, fly into the sky, and fall back down like a hundred shooting stars."

"That sounds painful," Margot said, before rolling over and falling asleep. And it did sound painful, but it also sounded like the most beautiful thing Doreen could think of.

It was no surprise, though, that when they confronted Stella for more details the following day, Margot was accepting and Doreen, angry.

After what happened with Lucas and Doreen, Stella invited both girls out into the garden to help cultivate the herbs they would need for her full-moon tea readings.

"Do you remember the story I told you," Stella asked, as she cut the lavender and placed it into a stainless-steel tray shaped like a crescent moon, "of how the bee got its stinger?"

Margot looked up from where she was chaining daisies, pausing her knot. "The bee fell in love with a stingray, but the stingray couldn't fly. It needed to live in the water."

"Right, and then what happened?"

Doreen dipped her palm into the lavender tray, letting the flowers tumble from her fingers. "They realized they couldn't be together and the stingray was so sad it tried to make a deal with the gods of the ocean, but the gods were tricky, as they so often are, and they cursed the bee and the stingray instead."

"By giving the bee a part of the stingray, a piece of its heart," Margot said.

"And yet when the bee tried to use it, thinking it would lead it back to the stingray," Doreen said, "it died, and they were never together again."

"So the bee lives on land and in the air, and the stingray is stuck in the water," Margot finished.

"Neither are better off for it," Stella said, before she handed each girl a pestle and mortar containing a scoop of dried lavender and a pinch of her own blend of herbs she liked to call Hella Stella. Stella shifted back onto her heels from her kneeling position, watching them get to work. "We're a bit like the bee, girls. We got stung by a very big jackass."

"Jackasses are donkeys, not stingrays," Margot said.

"Right, well, we would have done better with the jackass. Now we carry our own curse."

"That's why you don't believe in love?" Doreen asked, her eyes locked on her aunt's and the answer to a question Stella had been avoiding like a snapping alligator.

"I believe in love, but love does not believe in us. We are cursed so that love can no longer see us; only desire and infatuation can meet the wise women of our line."

"Cursed like the bee?" Doreen asked.

"And the stingray?" Margot said.

"Cursed worse than both," Stella said, with a huff that might have been a sigh. "We are the bumblebee. Many years ago, a stingray fell in love with one of us. And when she could not stay with it, the stingray cast a spell on us all. Because of it, our stingers will kill us if we don't use them by the time we reach maturation, or the age of thirty."

"Wait, is Ambrose the stingray? Also, I thought the gods gave the bee the stinger?" Doreen asked, still stuck on the word "kill."

"How do we use our stingers?" Margot asked.

"We must sting another with desire, infecting them so they fall in love with us, and we commit to that union. I suppose poisoning them like we did the stingray so long ago."

"And if we don't, we *die?*" Doreen said.

"We're dying from the day we're born," Stella said. "Or most of us, at least. This just gives us a firm deadline."

"But what about the people we sting?"

"Oh, this kind of poison isn't so bad," Stella said, with the wave of a hand. "Most people don't mind it."

"Is that why my mama died?" Doreen asked, her voice small.

"Your mama died because it was her time," Stella said. "Not all women die in their own time; your aunt Goldie refused to sting, and she never made it past twenty-nine. Neither did my great-aunt Stephie, or our cousin Valerie, or cousin Pauline."

"You stung," Doreen said. "Or else Margot wouldn't be here."

"I was once young and foolish," Stella said. "I did not think love songs were written for me, or that I could ever be the main character in a Jane Austen novel. I did, however, think I was powerful enough to protect myself. I was not, and I failed, much like my mother failed to protect me. Which is why I won't fail the two of you."

"That's why Margot's dad isn't around?" Doreen asked.

"Why none of them ever stay?" Margot added.

"Living a lie is like living a secret that poisons you from the inside out," Stella said. "It's not something those who are pure of heart can bear for long."

"So you make them leave?"

"Yes, and who could blame us? They aren't meant to stay, child. We have enough autonomy to make the choice to enthrall for the chance to have children. But when it leaves you all wondering about your fathers and wanting something we can't give you, then it's not much of a choice."

"What's autonomy?" Margot asked, her brow furrowing.

"The ability to live our own life."

"Oh," Margot said, sharing a look with Doreen. Later, after they did a magical scry to locate their fathers and came up empty, they would pull out a dictionary and look up the word *autonomy*. Both would agree they did not, in fact, have the right to self-govern, as Stella governed them and everyone else in the family as far as they could tell. The idea of it was nice, though.

"We'll never find love?" Doreen asked, the story adding into a truth she did not want.

"Not like those fairy tales you love," Stella said, taking the mortars from them and pouring the ground herbs into little perfume jars with bellies as round as the stone gnomes in their front yard. "We have each other, and we have our power, and most of us have realized that is more than enough. The love we have is not one that can be stolen, and the truth is that love is its own curse. Honestly, the stingray did us a favor."

"What happened to him?" Margot asked.

Stella glanced over her shoulder, down the road, and back to the girls. "He got what was coming to him. We pulled his stinger out and made it so he can never sting again."

And with that, she put the jars in a wicker basket and carried them over to her car, leaving the girls to wonder what was so bad about love that it would need a curse to take it away, and why they both felt so heartbroken at the loss of something they'd never had.

The following day at school, Doreen broke up with Lucas and

subsequently spent the next three years pining over him in secret as she watched him move on without a second thought.

She and Margot continued to gather information about their line. The curse wasn't the only thing that made the MacKinnon family different. They were witches, the thirteenth line, and therefore prophesized to be the most powerful. It was why their aunt Kayleen said that the other cousins refused to play with them at family reunions. Why the people in town were extra skittish around them unless they needed something from the shop. In the way that you smell rain in the air, people felt power sloughing off the two of them. Little sparks, unseen, but still curdling the air, especially when they were together, and Doreen and Margot were always together.

They had been born atypical, and Doreen was as well versed in the occult as any MacKinnon could be. Her powers to cast came in handy, and she spelled her own memory to hold each important piece of data related to the MacKinnons and the MacDonalds. But her data was incomplete. The family didn't believe in breaking the curse any longer. Not after so many of them went mad or died trying. There was Aurora who altered her beloved Arthur into a fox and killed him for seducing a cat. She wore him for the rest of her life as a hat. Then there was Bella who fed her beau her blood, hoping to cure him. It turned him anemic, but she was convinced she'd changed him into a vampire and staked him in the end.

With each attempt, they only failed to destroy the curse once more. It was because of this no one could tell Doreen what she really needed to know: *What happened three hundred years ago?*

That answer had vanished to the ages. Stella refused to budge on talking further about the family stingray, and no other resource had provided Doreen with answers.

If she could just find the truth, she knew, deep in her bones, she could figure out how to break the curse. She had a litany of information at her disposal, an arsenal of answers from her research.

And somehow, none of it helped.

So, in the end, on an aggressively sunny day, Margot said "I do." Dean couldn't take his eyes off her. One month later, she turned thirty and moved into a townhouse with Dean. They celebrated with strawberry cake and champagne.

Margot didn't die.

But she didn't come back to the apothecary shop, and she stopped returning Doreen's calls. She knew Doreen didn't approve, and it was easier not to be around the person who reminded Margot that she had made the choice to settle, the one who she had disappointed the most. Margot was happy, or at least trying to be. She had chosen her path, and it was never a path Doreen would follow.

On October thirty-first, Doreen turned twenty-nine.

And with her birthday, the clock began ticking toward her death. Doreen continued to search high and low, scouring occult shops, annoying any relative who would accept her call about the curse. For eleven months she did everything she could to find the answers she needed. She did not date, she barely ate, she never checked in with friends. She didn't have many of those anyway.

She was a MacKinnon and she was a witch. Certain people might have relied on her skills in the apothecary shop to help cure them of unwanted lust, insomnia, and prematurely graying hair, but they didn't necessarily *like* her. She wore all black, her hair was the color of spilled blood, and her eyes were the shade of burnt honey. Doreen unnerved most of the people of Pines, but she didn't mind. After all, she had a mission. Friends would only have gotten in the way.

Though she did sometimes daydream of them. Of people who liked her just the way she was, and wanted to help her, not ignore her like her cousins, or scoff at her like her aunt. When those particular pipe dreams arose, Doreen reminded herself that she didn't have time for them. Not when there was a curse to break, and herself to save, all while the clock was counting down.

The problem was Ambrose MacDonald.

The MacKinnons had locked him away in a slumbering state, where he would live on trapped, unable to be with those he loved. A curse for a curse. It didn't make a lot of sense to Doreen; it just seemed mean. None of the aunts or cousins would answer questions about the curse, not truly, and especially not about Ambrose. The MacKinnon women were often intentionally vague. They carried secrets like a rain cloud harbors water. From each other, from the outside world. It was the way it had always been. This, in fact, was their motto.

Safe as secrets. As it ever was.

They didn't particularly like to speak of the curse at all once they made their choice, outside of passing on the information to the next generation.

Months after Margot married Dean and disappeared from her life, Doreen sat in the attic surrounded by boxes of books. She reached up and pulled down the last notebook. The one with the unicorn flying across the front. Her heart pinched, but she ignored the pain. She opened it and her eyes tracked down the page to something that had not been there the last time she'd seen it.

There was a Post-it Note written in Margot's handwriting, just beneath her cousin's oath. On it were four words.

The Dead House exists.

Doreen's breath came faster as she read them over and over. Margot must have tucked it in before she got married. Or could it have been after?

She called Margot, holding her breath as she waited for her cousin to answer.

"You found it?" Margot said, by way of greeting.

That was the way with them, closer than sisters, no greeting necessary no matter the passage of time. Doreen exhaled in relief that the tether between them hadn't been cut simply because Margot abandoned her. Her temper sparked, thinking of it, and she shoved it aside. She didn't have time for "a mad," as Stella called her often ill-timed anger.

"Of course I did," Doreen said. *How are you? I love you. I'm so lonely without you.* She could have said any one of those things, but a wall had cobbled together and solidified in the absence of Margot, and Doreen didn't know how to vault over it. Instead, she said, "Are you sure?"

"I made a family vow after the wedding. I can't speak of what I know," she said. "I wrote the truth. You can't give up. It's . . ." Margot swallowed the sob, but Doreen heard it anyway. She felt it curling into a ball in the back of her own throat. "It's not what I thought it would be. Nothing is."

"I'll come get you," Doreen said, one foot out the attic door, one hand already reaching.

"No, Dore. I made my choice. Autonomy, remember?" She took a deep breath, and Doreen could almost see her, brushing a hand down her striped shirt with the sleeves rolled halfway up, pressing at the curls falling forward from where she pulled them too loosely on top of her head. "It was never okay, what Stella did to you with Jack, but it's not too late for your happy ending. Don't give up."

"Margot," Doreen said, tripping over her words in her hurry. She could feel Margot slipping away as the reminder of Jack pinged in her chest. She didn't need to be reminded of her ex and the mistake she made with her heart, or how Stella nearly broke it. "Let me come to you. Or come to the shop. Work with me, take a little of your old life with your new."

"The answers are still out there, Doreen. That's all I can tell you. I . . . I have to go."

She hung up, leaving Doreen to her tears and sorrow.

Doreen cried until there was nothing left except the promise of the soggy note she held in her hand.

The Dead House exists.

A memory stirred in the back of her mind, like a string unfurling from a tightly wound ball of yarn.

If the Dead House existed, *he* existed. Ambrose MacDonald. The answer Doreen had spent her life searching for, hoping for—how to break the curse, change her fate, even to save Margot—was out there.

As she sat in her little apartment drying her eyes, under the gloam of a rare supermoon, with the veil between the worlds thinning, Doreen stopped dreaming if her life could change and started changing it.

She stood up and crossed to the window and called his name.

Ambrose, she sang to the whispers of the unburdened wind, *I'm coming for you.*

TWO

The Dead House did not exist on any map. No uncloaking spell, no revealing incantation or scrying could bring it into Doreen's reality. But there was that small memory, curled up like a child hiding during a game of hide-and-seek, just out of sight.

Only one witch would dare to alter Doreen's memory.

Stella.

Doreen sat beneath the supermoon a few short hours after speaking to Margot, preparing to open herself up to that which had been hidden from her sight. This night was typically a night of celebration. For charging crystals, casting, and calling down the moon.

The trees on the estate of the MacKinnon family weren't like other trees. Oh, they *looked* like the rest of the deciduous plants you might find growing in the forest. There were tall ones, squat ones, full and flowy ones. Romantic weeping willows with their roots tracing zig-zags underneath the ground, stately pines with their erect spines staring down at the more compact, sophisticated magnolias. Nothing was

amiss if you glanced at them as you passed by, not that you could—
the MacKinnon estate was all-knowing—but it was what might happen
if you climbed into any one of these ordinary-appearing trees.

Branch magic is old magic, started by the goddess of the Celtic
broadleaf forests of Scotland, Ireland, and the United Kingdom.
Thousands of years ago, one single tree was planted from a special
seed. This tree was less of a tree and more of a portal. Meant for use
by witches alone, it had the ability to carry the witch anywhere they
wanted to go. Unfortunately, the goddess soon discovered that witches
traveling from the tree would end up trapped where they landed. On
another continent, a lonely island, or even in the otherworld. She decided to plant a handful of trees throughout the world so there was
always a way to find your way home. Over time the trees were forgotten, except by a few old witch families who kept the locations guarded,
and who planted new seeds in a few precise locations. Eventually, the
MacKinnons even built their family home near one, and over the years
they watched as the roots of one special tree spread and infected the
others on their property.

Today, many of the trees on the MacKinnon estate were magical, ready to spirit them away to any number of exotic locales at first
daydream. And because it wouldn't be prudent for children to start
disappearing on MacKinnon land, the wards were strong, and the way
was shut . . . unless you were a MacKinnon woman.

(It should be noted, there were rarely males born into the Mac-
Kinnon family, and on the few occasions they were, they were never
magical. Whether it was a byproduct of the curse, as Margot believed,
or simply, as Stella stated, "Women are stronger and we are strength,"
Doreen couldn't know for sure.)

Doreen looked up at the moon, and she brushed each of her
seven chakras with a charged amethyst, opening herself up to remembrance. The wind sighed as the earth beneath her warmed, and

Doreen whispered the four words Margot had gifted her with: "The Dead House exists." No sooner had the words left her mouth than a haze in her mind shifted, and the forgotten memory arose with new clarity.

When Doreen was twelve and Margot thirteen, the branches were traversed and the estate filled with aunts and cousins under the light of the full moon. Picnic blankets and tents spread across their yard, leaving it looking more like Burning Man than a family reunion. Bonfires were scattered across the land, altars erected, and circles drawn. Into each circle went the eldest MacKinnon from each corner of the family line.

These women chanted in unison: *Welcome, Mother of all life, gale in the air, spark in the fire, sapling in the earth, droplet in the endless sea. Come into me, into us, bring your knowledge, protection, and love. Be true to Me, we honor that which you have created, we are true to you. With harm to none, so it shall be.*

While they called down the moon and one of her goddesses, Margot and Doreen were eavesdropping on two aunts who'd had far too much wildflower wine.

"It's not fair that we don't get to see the Dead House when we've traveled all the way here," Aunt Sweetie, who was neither an aunt nor very sweet, bemoaned to her sister Helena as they sat on the picnic table nearest to the house, unaware of the two girls hiding beneath it.

"They won't let anyone near it, and there's no getting our hands on the Secretum Veritas either," Helena said, hiccupping softly as she built a crown from fallen sycamore bark and fat maple leaves. "All secret truths are hidden away. It's Stella's domain."

Sweetie swayed, shifting her elbows forward, and a hunk of petals rained down on the girls. Margot handed them up, and Sweetie thanked Helena, while Doreen tried not to laugh. "Don't you think she might have too much domain? I heard she keeps a sharp eye on her two girls, terrified that the thirteenth line has the power to undo us all."

"Hogwash," Helena said, while Margot elbowed Doreen. "She's just overprotective, is all. After how she lost her mama, who wouldn't be? She knotted that grief to herself like it was a cape to keep her warm. Can't put it down, won't take it off. She's just doing what she thinks is best. Trying to give them as much of a childhood to dream about as you can with our situation."

"Yeah, right, Stella the benevolent." Sweetie snorted, the bench creaking as she shifted her weight. "Keeping the Ambrose witch hidden from us all."

Doreen and Margot exchanged a look. *What witch?* Margot mouthed. Doreen shrugged and pointed back up to the aunts.

"I've heard he was a fine specimen," Helena said. "You think it's true?"

"I think he's like the Order of the Dark Shadows, the *Sgàilean Dorcha*. A myth that sounds like it must be real. If he exists, he is the Sleeping Beauty in the Dead House. Ambrose MacDonald is on ice, and there's no way to get the key." Doreen wrote the name down in the journal she always carried with her, while Margot stared on, her eyes wide. "I tell you what," Sweetie continued, "I think she's given up. We've all given up. Destined for heartbreak, the lot of us."

"She doesn't view it like that. It's power, not being chained to love," Helena said, the soft timbre of her voice coated in sadness.

"I don't know that I believe *that*," Sweetie said, her voice dropping to a whisper. "I think there's more to life than power and family. It's why I want a peek inside the Dead House. The secrets kept there are our answers to the curse, and I have to hope that life is meant for more than this."

"You mean more than your five paramours and fifteen dogs."

"Flip that equation around, darling Helena, but yes."

They broke into giggles at that, and Doreen and Margot crept out from under the table, slinking toward the house.

"The curse *can* be broken," Doreen whispered, her voice caked in excitement.

"*The Dead House*," Margot said, slipping her hand into Doreen's and tugging her forward.

"And the Secretum Veritas," Doreen said, squeezing her palm.

Behind them, the chanting MacKinnons levitated into the air, fireworks filling the sky as the other witches shouted with joy. Neither Margot nor Doreen looked back; they were too busy focusing on the future.

"That's where our answers await," they said, looking at one another with hope before running inside.

But no matter how often or hard they tried, Margot and Doreen could never remember the name of the Secretum Veritas. There was a book, they later were told, rumored to contain power, but you could only call it to you by giving up what you valued most. The one time they'd tried to summon a key for it, thinking they could outsmart a silly old book, Stella appeared at the door of the attic.

"Do you want to lose one another?" she'd shouted, her face a molten purple. "Calling that book will rob you of what you most love, you fools."

Terrified, they'd helped her scatter their rose quartz circle, apologized profusely, and spent the rest of the day collecting thyme and tearing up at what they might have done, had Stella not found them in time.

But times, like the seasons, change. Doreen had lost everything that mattered to her. Margot was gone, the clock was ticking down to her death, and Doreen refused to ever do to another man what she'd nearly done to Jack just to save herself.

She knew what to do now that the memory was made clear. And there was only one reason it had been hidden to begin with—Stella was working against her, trying to control her actions and keep her on the path she preferred for Doreen.

It was time to go against Stella, call the Secretum Veritas, find the house, and wake Ambrose MacDonald.

It was time to break the curse.

In the middle of the country, surrounded by rolling hills and towering trees that never failed to shed their sap and needles, the town of Pines existed. Green, lush, and quiet, it was a calm place, but it was never a *silent* place.

Especially not for Ambrose MacDonald.

Birds chirped, tweeted, cawed, and occasionally quacked from beyond where he was suspended in a state neither here nor there. Rain thrashed against windows that rattled, thunder cracked, and the world around him shook. He could not touch the world, but sometimes, he could taste it.

It was honey, sweet but bitter, pressing against his lips. There would be a waft of jasmine, and the sound of steps coming to and from nowhere.

He didn't always smell or know or hear things. At times, he lived in the dark. At other times, he thrashed against the darkness. Fought the terror that clawed down his throat and ripped away pieces of his memory, gnawing on them over and over. Those heartbreaking memories showing him Lenora in the meadow, dancing beneath the stars, writhing with passion in his arms. He tried to hold on to them, but they shifted to smoke, wafting out of his grasp. Instead, he was wrapped in soaked muslin, dipped in a hundred petals of rose, sprinkled with anise and a poison so sweet it curdled his blood. Then he was no longer in his body. Or any other body that he recognized. He was here, but not. Time was here, but not.

Every so often, he would hear words whispered over him. Or under him. Or from somewhere near him. A chant sung low, an incantation that soothed him to his soul. Other times, he was awoken to the sharp words of a language he no longer could claim to know. Sounds more than words, and they opened him up like an ax slashing into a melon, splintering it wide. Images would flood in when this happened, of the world around him, of those he had loved—who were now lost. Of time moving on, and finally of him. Trapped forever. Cursed. By the witches MacKinnon.

So, he bided his time and he waited, knowing that one day, he would take his revenge.

Doreen went deep into the woods and drew her circle with fresh salt from the Dead Sea. She laid a line of herbs inside it and used her wand to clear the air, keeping the circle closed to prying eyes and ears. Then, placing the bloodstone in her bra, over her heart, she set about making a fire, using fallen wood, along with leaves and twigs. She had her fire steel, and struck it over the kindling until it caught, blowing gently as she placed it into the wood. The flames began to catch, crackling in the air as they sparked. She pulled a small cauldron from her bag and gently sat it in the fire, before adding the vial of moonwater she had collected.

Once the water began to boil, she removed the bloodstone and dropped it in, adding a lock of her own hair and the last of the herbs.

She sat in front of the cauldron, her eyes closed, and breathed deeply, drawing in the smoke, and opening herself up to that which she sought. Her head swam, and the ground beneath her shifted from firm to air, her bones light, her thoughts clear.

"Sometimes, you just have to be willing to believe," Margot used to tell her. "Allowing what you need to find you is half the battle, especially when you spend most of your life being told you'll never have what you want."

There was a lot that Doreen wanted, but did not have. Her mother. Margot by her side. True love.

A pair of eyes flashed into her mind, and at first Doreen thought she knew them. Jack Morgan. The man she almost married. Her hands shook and she dropped the spell. Doreen took deep breaths, trying to shake off the memories pressing in.

"It's not real, it's not him," she said out loud. She wasn't going to look into the past, not right when she was trying to change her future. She didn't want to think of Jack, of Stella and the sharp sting of betrayal she'd suffered.

Doreen knew what she wanted. She wove the spell back into place and asked for words hidden from sight, hidden from her. She offered the pain of the heartbreak she'd suffered so long ago with Jack and cast the spell.

She raised her hands high, and the words lifted off the page before floating down into her palms, running up one arm and down the other. Doreen had stolen the spell from the book like a thief in the night, cracking a vault on the first attempt. This spell came with a warning. Magic, like so much in life, was born of give-and-take. Doreen did not mind the giving if she could finally get what she needed. The words faded into her skin, and the knowledge settled deep inside her. She opened her mouth and spoke the name: "Ambrose MacDonald."

The wind howled, lightning split the sky, and thunder rumbled so deeply across the forest that it shook the ground beneath her. Doreen did not so much as twitch a single muscle.

"*Show me,*" she commanded.

The sky darkened from violet to navy to a deep charcoal, the stars overhead blinking out one by one. Doreen opened her eyes and saw the sheen of a single star lighting the world. It was all that remained in the skies, illuminating a path into the forest.

Her pulse quickened, her heart beating rapidly in her chest. She stood on shaking legs, and her hands trembled. She was clumsy in clearing her circle, nearly knocking the cauldron over twice as she sought to disperse the fire and circle. It took her three times as long as it should have, and when she stepped onto the lit path, a vibration rocketed up her arms and nearly blasted her back. She planted her feet, took a deep breath, and began to walk. One slow and forced step at a time, into the woods, toward a house that time had *almost* forgotten.

October usually came calling with its chilling bite. The month of shawls and cardigans, of gourds and pumpkins, spiced ciders and steaming-hot cocoas. There should have been a chill in the air, but instead the wind blew hot as Doreen walked out of the woods onto Willow Road. The street was mostly abandoned. Not even desperate teenagers came here to vandalize or throw rowdy red-Solo-cup parties. Willow Road had been a "residents' row" once upon a time. Home to multiple asylums that ran out of money at the turn of the century, the people had been displaced after a cut in funding, and the buildings shuttered one morning without fanfare or warning.

Doreen found the street quiet and peaceful. She walked to the end, following the last of the light, and came to a stop in front of a home that stood out like a redhead in a sea of blondes.

The town of Pines, Georgia, featured tasteful Craftsman-style houses these days, in shades of neutral grays and navy and dark green. This house sat far enough back from the road for the weeds and trees and bushes to grow over its lower half like a bushy, determined beard, and it was hard to say what style it was. From the corner of her eye, Doreen thought it was a seventies-style Mediterranean home, but when she looked again, it was a gray brick building without windows resembling a castle dressed as a prison. She blinked and it was a ranch house, and when she looked at the home from under her lashes it was a Victorian. The house clearly couldn't make up its mind on what it was, but that wasn't its fault. Doreen knew a spell when she tasted one.

She spit out the flavor of ash and brine water. Her lips tingled as though they had been stung by a family of bees. This was no simple magic.

But she was no simple witch.

Doreen had always been clever, though she hadn't been strong. That was Margot's lane. Margot, who stood up for her when other kids taunted her for being too strange because she only wore black and would rather be inside with a book than speak to them. Margot, who taught Doreen to stand up straight, stare people in the eye when they intimidated her, and repeat their mantra in her head, *"I am magic."*

Margot was no longer by her side. Doreen had failed her in not being more active in helping break the curse before she got married. Doreen had been too complacent, refusing to go against her family because she was happy with her life, with Margot and the shop. That was gone. Now Doreen would have to be the strong one.

"This is a MacKinnon curse, and I am a MacKinnon witch."

She pulled a small athame she had named Delores from her bag and slid the blade across her palm, wincing.

Doreen walked up to the house, digging deep to push forward as the feeling of a hundred snakes slithered over her skin, the sound of a thousand bees buzzing in her ears. She was gasping, out of breath, and shaking when she reached the front door. The door shifted from brown to red to rotting, the handle a glimmer that never seemed to be where it claimed. With a sigh, she closed her eyes, opened her fisted hand, and smacked it on the wood. At her bloody handprint, everything went utterly and totally silent.

W hen Doreen opened her eyes, she was looking at a black door without a handle. The house itself was as gray as the sea after a storm. The space for windows was outlined with pointed arches and bricked in. The roof was steeply pitched, and delicate wooden trim ran along front-facing gables. It was a Gothic masterpiece, and she couldn't suppress the excitement that rose like bubbles in her even as a wicked shiver wracked its way down her spine.

Her handprint stood out, the blood soaking in to reveal a pale outline of her palm and fingers. MacKinnon blood. MacKinnon magic. She took a breath and pushed at the place where her hand was outlined. The door creaked open halfway. Enough for her to slip through.

The light of the moon followed her in, its sweeping rays sufficient for her to see the room she entered. The walls were blue, the color of a cerulean sea, and when she brushed a finger across, she touched soft fabric. Velvet. An intricate design of vines formed a pattern beginning at the door frame, where a single line stretched out and branched across the walls. As her eyes adjusted, she realized the spell kept the house hidden and locked away, and whatever was inside bolted in. A binding spell woven into the very fabric of the home.

The floors were a faded dusty wood, and there was a single velvet chair in the corner. If there were other rooms aside from this single one, she could not see them. It was a cage. Ornate and beautiful, with thick crown molding along the ceiling, at the base of the floor, and framing the arched windows that showcased nowhere.

In the center of the room was a storm.

A cyclone of mist and sand and wind and rain. Lightning sparked inside it, in a flash of brightness before the wind cut through and a dark mist swarmed within. In that brief moment, Doreen saw into the storm, to the man suspended inside.

Like Margot, she'd assumed that if he did exist, Ambrose Mac-Donald was locked in the curse like Sleeping Beauty. Perhaps it was the child who'd first heard the story still writing it in her mind. But this was no easy sleeping curse. This was a nightmare.

She'd only been able to catch a glimpse of his features. Furrowed brow, somber, thick slashes over closed eyes. His lashes had been dark and long, and his mouth pursed in pain. For three hundred years he'd been fighting the storm that raged around him, and it struck her that when she set him free, he might turn whatever rage had been building just as long directly on her.

She stared at the swirling black mist, and her gaze dipped to his left hand. It was held out, as though reaching for help. As though he were begging.

"And harm none," Doreen whispered. This was the opposite of the creed she followed. This was torture.

She decided it didn't matter. She needed his help, and he needed hers.

Doreen was all in.

She wasn't sure how to break him free, having never come across a binding quite like this. Her instinct was to cast a circle, to see if she could pull the magic into it and buy enough time to yank him out.

"Kill me."

Doreen's breath caught in her chest as she looked up to where Ambrose was suspended. She met his now-open eyes. They were aqua, bright, and focused on her. He let out a low moan. His pain shook the house, and the storm grew more punishing.

"Kill me. Please." He gasped as whatever the spell was doing to him escalated at his words.

Doreen knew what it was like to feel hopeless, to feel defeated. She had never known what it was to feel broken, but she understood as she stared at him what it looked like, and she *hated* the sight.

She was clever, but she'd never considered herself strong—until she threw down her bag and ran as fast as she could toward the storm. She dove into it, her cut hand still bleeding, and slammed it into Ambrose MacDonald's chest. His hand came up and wrapped around hers. On instinct, she twisted her hand so their fingers were entwined and looked into his aqua eyes.

The storm exploded around them, wind and rain slamming into the walls and shredding the wallpaper, sending the single chair crashing into the door. Ambrose collapsed to the floor, and Doreen threw her hands up, sending the storm toward the single sliver of a skylight in the far-right corner of the ceiling. The glass shattered and the wind, rain, and lightning rushed out as the spell broke apart.

She crouched down on the ground next to Ambrose. Her heart raced, her hair was soaked, and the cut on her hand wouldn't stop bleeding. The cost of expending so much magic had the edges of her vision fraying, but she forced herself to stay as steady as she could. He rolled onto his back, looking up at her.

His dark hair hung in thick clumps down to his shoulders. His eyes glowed that strange green and blue, and up close she saw there was a black circle around the outside, as though trapping the color in. He had sharp cheekbones and a defined jaw covered in thick stubble. His mouth was drawn into a frown, his lower lip fuller than the top.

"What have you done?" he rasped, his deep voice low and dangerous.

"I think the words you're looking for," Doreen said, meeting his eyes, "are thank you."

She crawled to her bag, reaching in for a bandage and doing her best to quickly dress her palm. She could feel his eyes on her but didn't look over. She needed a moment to gather her thoughts without his features burning into her mind.

"You're not her."

She looked up. "I'm not who?"

He didn't answer.

She picked up the bag and crossed back to him. He jerked away from her, flinching like a wounded deer caught in a sniper's range.

"Who are you?" he asked, his voice a deep rumble that made her stomach dip.

"I'm Doreen MacKinnon," she said, then hesitated and shifted back a step. "You're Ambrose MacDonald, and you're going to help me break the curse you put on my family."

He froze. Then he burst out laughing.

"No."

"Excuse me?"

He tried to stand and staggered, falling back to the floor.

"You're not in much of a bargaining position," she said.

He locked his bright but shadowed eyes on hers, and it was her turn to resist flinching. "I could kill you."

She lifted a brow, praying he couldn't hear the pounding of her heart. She reminded herself she was safe; he didn't know she was a mimic. "I could call the storm back and return you to its heart."

He swallowed and dropped his head to the ground. She blew out a quiet sigh of relief.

"Doreen," he said, and the way he rasped her name had a chill prickling along her arms. "Daughter of Frances, niece of Stella." He nodded, as though to himself. "I dreamed of you. The one they do not see, the one they turn from."

She shivered at the wonder in his words and reminded herself he was a witch. *The* witch.

"When my insides were being turned out, when my eyes would bleed into my mouth, when a thousand bees were stinging my face, the pain would overtake me, and I would dream. Of you, of the others in your line. I saw you looking for me, and I saw them keeping you in the dark. I wonder why."

Her stomach rolled at the truth in the accusation. This witch knew her family did not trust her. Not only had her family locked him away, they had tortured him, and now his words did the same to her.

The unfiltered menace in his voice left her shuddering. "It turns out I didn't need them to find you," she said, grateful her voice didn't shake. "I don't dream. I'm the only one in my line who doesn't." She tried to speak as matter-of-factly as she could, as though she wasn't speaking with a person who could fillet her insides with a snap of his fingers. "But I do plan, and I refuse to die by your curse, so you *will* tell me what I need to undo it."

He laughed. This time the sound was a weak hiss. "I fear you are—what is the modern term?—screwed, then. I have spent centuries watching the world, losing everything I ever loved all because of your family." He rolled his head to face her, and she had to force herself not to get lost in the study of him. This witch who was ancient and broken.

He'd drained himself of expression, and staring at Ambrose was like examining a painting of a dragon slayer come to life after he fought a great battle and lost.

Doreen needed a win.

"If you help me, I promise you your freedom," she said, holding her palms up. "I will make sure no MacKinnon witch ever curses you again."

"How can you promise such a thing? Your ancestors lived to torture me. Who do you think that chair was for?"

She glanced to the broken pieces of the velvet armchair scattered across the ground and swallowed back revulsion.

"Stella likes to throw poisoned darts," he said, almost—but not quite—pulling off sounding bored. "Her mother, Victoria, used to pull the wind from the room so I would lose consciousness, but just before I'd expire, she'd flood it back in. Poor Victoria, she was the only one foolish enough to leave herself open. She bled for an hour when the wind cut through the overhead window and brought glass down on her. That was almost a good day." He paused, his breath steady even as his words shook. "The women in your line have been tormenting me for three hundred years."

"You did curse us first," she said, the knee-jerk defense of her family rising before she could stop herself.

"I fell in love with one of you," he said, his voice a near growl. "That was the first curse; the rest has been nothing compared to that betrayal."

"Boy, she must have done a number on you to have the Torture Curse be less traumatizing than falling in love." She looked up at the ceiling. "I bet you did it wrong."

"Did what wrong?"

"Falling in love. It's not a curse. It's a hope."

"You are a fool."

"Excuse me?"

"To think such a thing . . . What do you know of it? Love is not hope; it is destruction and madness. It cost me everything. Your kin cost me everything."

She narrowed her eyes. "I am the thirteenth generation in the line of MacKinnon witches. I am the cleverest of my line and I am not giving up. If you really won't help me . . ." She shrugged. "I can return you to your storm and your curse."

The corner of his mouth curved into a feral half smile. "You're the color of a new dawn's snow, and you've bled your magic to the point of harming yourself." He sat up, stretched. Doreen realized the coloring in his cheeks had returned to a deep rust, and his eyes were bright. He stood in a fluid motion and crossed to her in two languid strides.

Doreen shrank back before she could stop herself. She'd thought him weak, even terrified, but as he towered over her, water dripping off the cuffs of his black shirt, flexing his hands at his side, she realized she'd made a terrible mistake.

If Ambrose MacDonald could survive three hundred years twisting, quite literally, in the wind, he was stronger than any witch she'd ever met.

"Now," he said, "why don't we stop wasting time and you tell me—"

He was cut off as the door to the Dead House flew off its hinges. Stella rushed inside, her hands out and the storm riding on her coattails. Words flew from her lips, arrows aimed for Ambrose.

> *"Winds of my daughters*
> *Blood of my blood*
> *Salt of my bones*
> *Hear my words.*
> *Wrap this man*
> *Hide him away*
> *Seek our vengeance*
> *Do as I bade."*

Stella called for the cage of a storm to return to Ambrose, her eyes barely registering Doreen.

Doreen thought of her hard work, of all her dreams of true love and a life worth living, and they dissolved like water into mist as she realized what Stella meant to do. If she succeeded, Stella would make certain Doreen never found Ambrose again. Stella would win, again, and Doreen would be truly damned.

She could hear Stella's whisper in her mind, the same thing she always said to Doreen, a refrain she'd heard year after year: "You're clever but not wise, Doreen MacKinnon."

Margot thought Doreen was more than clever; she believed in her. Doreen had gone against her family, her coven, breaking the bond they had forged. She'd lose everything if her aunt prevailed at trapping Ambrose.

She'd likely lose her aunt and Margot forever if she did what she needed to do.

Doreen gave a resigned sigh. Sometimes there was only one way forward. She climbed to her feet, shook out her aching arms, and lunged in front of Ambrose at the last millisecond, as the storm wrapped itself around her instead of him.

THREE

Inside the cyclone, Doreen lost track of time. She could hear her heartbeat and the rushing of her own breath, but she did not know where she began and the vortex ended. A blast of cold rushed through her, followed by a heat so intense she screamed, but no sound escaped. It took all her effort to keep her thoughts in her head. Static roared inside her. She knew her name and lost it, knew her purpose and it disintegrated. Soon she would know nothing.

She feared she could not suffer through another minute of being inside the deathly dervish, and yet Ambrose had spent *centuries* surviving it. The air smelled of burning sulfur, her mouth tasted of ash, her skin crawling.

Doreen wanted to die.

She thought of her life so far. Of days spent with Margot, hiding in the forest, pilfering Stella's supplies from the new shipments to the apothecary, working on spells. Of growing up laughing when they managed to pinch some of Stella's wine or beloved Brie. She thought of the mother she never knew, who left her behind because she wasn't worth staying for, and the man who she'd wanted to give her heart to but who could never hold it. Each memory cut deep into her bones, and she tried and failed to scream them out.

A bright light flashed inside her mind. The air turned warm, and a lullaby cut through the noise. A melody she knew but had forgotten, like a teddy bear she'd set down one day as a child, before stumbling across it unexpectedly and realizing she'd been missing a best friend.

Suddenly the pain stopped. A gentle hand was wrapped around her arm. It was connected to a muscular forearm. She tracked it to a broad shoulder and wide chest.

Ambrose was breaking into the spell. If he got inside, he'd be trapped just as she was. His face pressed in, those blue-green eyes finding hers. He looked down at her hand and ripped the bandage off. He dug his fingers into the fresh cut, and she screamed. When the blood came, he pressed her hand to his and yanked them both out.

Doreen stumbled, the world spinning around her. Ambrose tucked her against his side, and she sank into him. Forgetting, for a moment, where she was and what was at stake. He was holding her in a way no one ever had before. As though he cared, as though she mattered. She realized she did—she was the only one who could keep him safe.

Stella let out a cry that sliced into Doreen's soul. "Doreen Antoinette MacKinnon, *how could you?*"

She straightened, staggered, and raised her head to meet her aunt's incredulous gaze.

"How could *you?*" Doreen said, her voice as dry as dust, one of her hands still captured in Ambrose's as she took a single step away from him. "This family is built on secrets and lies. Is a curse worth torturing someone for three hundred years? Is it worth all the pain we cause, all the loss?" She didn't wait for Stella to reply. "I refuse to die because you're so invested in this feud that you've damned us all."

"You've damned yourself more than anyone could by freeing him," Stella said, pain and rage merging on her familiar face. A rare glimpse of worry and something else, something calculating, flashed in her aunt's eyes.

Doreen refused to be another chess piece for her aunt to move around on the board that was her life.

They stood, facing one another, suspense building as Doreen tried to pull herself together.

Stella gave a heavy sigh, and raised her hands, flicking the palms out. "Get out of my way, child, so I can undo the damage you've wrought."

"I don't think so," Ambrose said, his voice low and lethal.

Doreen's hand tingled where Ambrose's was pressed against hers, and she shivered at the determination in his voice. "The cage is open," he said, his tone firm. "Now it's my turn to play."

He whispered an incantation too low for Doreen to hear, and suddenly the wind was back. It wrapped around them, shifting the landscape as a cyclone opened. Through it, Doreen saw a path leading into a field. Ambrose gave her hand a single squeeze. He raised a brow at Doreen, who looked at Stella.

"There will be no coming back from this," her aunt said, and now it was grief Doreen saw reflected at her.

Doreen met Stella's eyes. Swallowed down the regret. She had tried to find happiness, first with Jack, and then with a family of her and Margot. Her aunt had been the cause for both to break.

This was the only way for Doreen to change her fate.

"I know," she said, before she stepped forward and pulled herself and Ambrose through the open portal, leaving Stella and life as Doreen knew it behind.

D oreen and Ambrose walked onto the path and into a forest the color of emeralds. They were surrounded by hills and tall trees, and she breathed deep, pulling in a heady scent of pine and cedar. A breeze stirred through the air, and she thought she heard music riding the wind before it died down, and with it, her panic rose as the portal closed behind them.

"Shit. Shit shit *shit*." Doreen began to shake all over. She ran her hands through her hair, squeezing her neck at the base. "Stella will disown me for this."

"And that's a bad thing?"

She spun on her heel to face Ambrose. He towered over her, his eyes hooded as they took her in.

Her stomach tightened and she cleared her throat, refusing to be intimidated.

"Stella's my family."

He looked down at the tatters of his clothing before meeting her eyes. "You have a horrible family."

"Only to you."

"History would argue the point. You know nothing of your line, and I remember it all. Torturous and villainous. Family is a casualty of living, but yours is particularly heinous. Besides, she threatened you, her own blood." He looked up at the sky, a shudder rolling through him. "For years she tortured me with a smile on her face."

"I'm sorry," she said, knowing the words were inadequate. "I can't make up for centuries of pain, but to be fair, that's what your curse inflicted on us. It's horrible, truly. But you responded in kind. Do you care how many of us died? That I have no mother or father, that those of us lucky enough to have a parent end up with a partial one who lives with a broken heart, unable to give their children what they themselves never had? That we are never whole, never fully loved? That we are just echoes of who we could have been, and we live with that knowledge every day that we face a mirror? Do you even realize what you stole from our lives?"

"You all had a choice, which is more than your family gave me," he said.

She glared at him, not wanting to weigh if there was any truth to what he said. Doreen was completely on her own. Partnered with the most powerful witch in the world. A man she couldn't trust and who could turn on her at any moment.

"Though you can't help who you're born to," he added, his voice low, as though he didn't mean to say that part out loud.

Her jaw clenched. "I saved you."

"Why do you think I haven't killed you yet?"

Doreen grunted at him. She needed to find a way to regain the upper hand.

"I need to get out of these clothes, and we need to set our terms," she told him. He looked as distrusting of her as a speck of lint facing a dryer sheet. The wind rustled the leaves, bringing a new chill to the air. She inhaled deeply, accidentally breathing him in. He smelled of magic, his own blend of it, like fresh earth and summer rain. He was as distracting as he was dangerous. She refused to be preoccupied by anything other than the task at hand. Dry clothes. Answers. Breaking the curse. Simple.

"There's a town just over that hill," he said, after a long moment. "Do you have any money on you, or should I summon the clothing and save us the trouble?"

"Summoning makes stealing sound fancy, when really it's just being an asshole," she said, forgetting to think before she spoke. It was another of her biggest flaws, according to her aunt Stella.

She'd just insulted the most powerful witch in existence. She lifted a hand, preparing herself to fend off an attack, and the corner of Ambrose's mouth gave a slow twitch. Doreen blinked. She couldn't look away. The hint of his smile knocked her knees together. Or maybe that was the adrenaline leaving her, since he didn't seem insulted or ready to engage.

"I need to sit," she said, plopping to the ground as the weight of what she'd done rolled through her. "How do you know there's a town there?"

"I was trapped in my body, but not even your line could trap my spirit."

"Astral projection?"

"Not quite. More like mental . . . glimpses."

"Ahh, that's why you sound like you're speaking the King's English." She cocked her head. "Your accent is posher than any I've ever heard."

"I've witnessed centuries passing. I've listened and learned."

"Sounds lonely."

"I was alone, but I learned long ago that being alone and being lonely are worlds apart. I saw you, and your strength. I saw you struggle." He squatted in front of her, holding out his hand. "May I inspect the wound?"

She hesitated, looked at her palm. "It's fine."

"If it gets infected, it will hinder your plans immensely."

"It's not the seventeenth century anymore. I'm not going to get gangrene, and I've had my tetanus shot, thanks."

"Stubborn."

"Brilliant," she said, still not trusting him to inspect anything on her. "And it just needs a salve, which I can make from the herbs beyond that little bush there." She hesitated. "What did you see when you watched me? Which sounds super creepy, by the way."

"I saw you not give up, and I saw Stella fight to box you away."

He gave a curt nod, leveled his gaze to hers, and stared so deeply into her eyes her head swam. "You won't give up, and neither box nor cave could hold you, I do not think. I am glad you broke me free of mine, but I do not trust you, Doreen MacKinnon."

"That's funny," she said, blinking and shaking off the feeling of being seen. It made her shoulders want to sag in relief, but she didn't know what to do with the feeling from him. "I thought we were about to become besties."

"But you did save my life."

"Twice."

"For your reasons."

"Yes."

"I'm a means to your end."

"You're a means to *an* end." She forced a smile and tried for a bit of false bravado. "And just so you know, if you want to try and end me, I'll put you down before you can say the words *chauvinistic penis*."

His brows quirked. "Charming," he said.

"Not really. But I'm quite happy with myself."

His lips twitched and she waited for another barb. Instead he brushed his hands down his solid, wide chest. She refused to follow their path on principle. It was unnatural that he should be so fit after being tortured for so many years. She really thought she'd like him better if he looked more like a waif than a six-foot-two lumberjack.

"We're in agreement, then," he said, shifting his weight, stretching out one long leg. "Neither of us trust the other, but we will use one another for as long as it's beneficial."

"You mean I'll keep saving your life if you tell me how to reverse this curse? Yes, we're in agreement."

He looked down, bent to pick a single leaf, and ran a finger down its side. The leaf curled into a ball and when it unrolled again it was a caterpillar. He set it down in the grass and watched it scoot forward.

"Whoa," she said. She had never seen anyone perform such an intricate spell so quickly or with such ease.

He stared at the ground for so long, Doreen wondered if he'd forgotten she was there.

"I don't know how to undo the curse," Ambrose said.

"Wait. What?" She took her eyes from the caterpillar and stared at him. "You set it; you must know how to undo it."

"I had no desire to ever break it." He paused. "I am not sure I do now."

"Are you *kidding?*"

"Love is terrible, Doreen. Losing it is worse than ever having it. You don't know."

"I never had a chance to know, because *of you.*"

He took a slow breath, scratched at his chin. "The Keeper is the only one who might be able to help."

"What is a keeper?" she asked as she watched the caterpillar begin to munch on a green leaf. "Is that caterpillar eating himself?"

"It's a simple energy transfiguration spell, and yes, he is." Ambrose stood up. "The Keepers are guardians. I'm not surprised you don't know of them. Don't know about transfiguration; can't recharge. You live in the shadows. Knowledge just outside your reach. Your power must have terrified them." He glanced down at her. "It's why you can't hold your magic."

Doreen stared up at him, both grateful and irritated his giant form blocked the sun from her eyes. "I broke through a *centuries*-old spell to save you."

"It depleted you."

"Forgive me for needing a moment to catch my breath," she scoffed.

"You don't need to catch your breath. You're letting what you cannot do interfere with what you can."

"And what can't I do?"

He leaned down, held out a hand. She hesitated once more.

"Stubborn or scared?"

Sighing, she put her hand in his. A current, strong, steady, and bright, flowed from him into her. Every zapped ounce of her energy returned, filling her up until she was so full, she thought she might rocket off the earth.

He'd transferred his energy to her, without even having to snap his fingers.

Ambrose lifted his brows as she gaped at him. Then he released her hand and sat down on the earth, his bare feet pressing into the dirt. He dug his fingers into it and drew in a deep breath. Light, twinkling and bright, floated up from the earth, along with bits of water, sparks, and dirt.

He closed his eyes and leaned back, inhaling deeply through his nose. The light settled into him, the elements resting, smattering across his skin. Every ounce of power he'd given to her, he'd recouped, and more, if the vibrant color of his eyes was any indication. The aqua nearly glowed.

"You deplete yourself when you don't have to," he said, his low voice rumbling through the air before it dropped down into her. Its vibrations ran deep into her bones.

Doreen didn't know what to say. What he'd done was unbearably kind. And worrisome. She'd studied under her aunts, learned from her cousins, read thousands of books, articles, and grimoires, yet he'd shown her in one move she knew next to nothing. "I've never been taught to replenish myself like that."

"They don't want you to know," he said. "Your villainous family has you as locked up as they did me. You look a little like your mother did, but you look even more like the one who should have been able to free me." He looked up at the sky. "Lenora. You are not her."

"You saw my mother?" Doreen asked, her heart giving a single painful squeeze.

"I did."

"What happened when you saw her?"

"She died of a broken heart," he said. "I told you love is a terrible thing."

"Because of the curse?"

"No, because of pride."

Doreen's jaw ground too tight and she forced it to relax. "How?"

"She left you. Frances didn't trust herself or her magic." He shrugged. "She did not come here, did not torture me. Once she was gone, I could not see her any longer. That is all I know."

"You know nothing."

He did not respond, simply stared out into the distance.

"And Lenora?"

"I loved her."

"Oh." She was the one, then, the reason he cast the curse. "I think I may have heard her name before."

A muscle ticked in his jaw, and he rubbed a hand over his heart before flicking his eyes to her. "They rarely say it. They do not honor the dead."

Doreen did not disagree. They didn't say her mother's name either. It hurt Stella too much, that was what Margot thought. Stella and Kayleen didn't try to contact their lost loved ones with the Ouija board like Margot and Doreen did or whisper their names when they lay their heads down to sleep in hopes they were listening somehow. The aunts and cousins did not look back, and they didn't look to the future either. Not like Doreen. "Why would Lenora be able to free you?"

"It is what she said, your ancestor who set the original spell."

"Ah."

She stared at his hand, how it pressed into the ribs that protected his heart, and he looked down. He dropped his hand. "I do not know how to help you."

"What about the Keeper?"

"They may help. They may not. Regardless, they are the only one with the power to do so."

Doreen stretched her arms to the sky. Every fiber of her being felt like it was floating out from her body. Recharged. What a divine sensation to be so full of life, of power. She did not trust Ambrose any more than he trusted her, and yet he had shown her something no one else had.

He didn't know she was a mimic, that she could duplicate any spell she read or saw. Now that she'd seen how Ambrose could refill his power, she could do it too. She now had the power to refill herself, and he might think he knew what she was capable of, but Doreen was beginning to think even *she* didn't know what she might be able to do.

"Okay." She nodded as she tugged her lower lip between her teeth. "You say you can't break the curse, but you know someone who can help me. Will you take me to them?"

He furrowed his brow for a moment, staring at her mouth before answering. "They keep a record of time, spells, and magic. They are . . . not always wise to trust."

She wrinkled her nose. "You sure you can't just tell me what to do?"

"I do not know how."

"Or want to."

"That is irrelevant, as you said. I owe you."

"Worried about a life bond, are you?" All witches knew that to save another was to bond to them, to owe a debt. The way Ambrose mostly avoided getting close to her made it clear he'd rather turn himself into a caterpillar than be tied to Doreen—though it might not be for very long if she didn't break the curse and save her own life.

She looked beyond Ambrose to the pristine blue sky, and found her gaze inevitably drawn back to him. "After we see this Keeper and get what I need?"

He glanced at her face, studying her. His pupils expanded as his gaze dropped to her mouth again. Doreen narrowed her eyes at him. Had she managed to glamour him? Could Ambrose even be enthralled?

"I leave, and you *will* let me."

Clearly not. She swallowed, finding the idea of his going peculiarly disappointing. But this is what she wanted. To be free, to find true love. To live. Not to be saddled with a potentially sociopathic ancient witch.

She held out her hand. "You have yourself a bargain, Ambrose MacDonald."

"And you have yourself a bridge of hope," he said, referencing her earlier words to what she believed love was. "Let's *hope* it doesn't crumble beneath you when you attempt to cross."

A mbrose didn't want to keep looking at the witch. She was stubborn, foolhardy, and, gods help him, more beautiful than the night sky during the winter solstice. She didn't look as much like Lenora as he'd first thought. Her hair was brighter, her voice raspier, and she moved like she was always ready for battle, whereas Lenora moved like she was ready to be attended to.

He'd really enjoyed attending to her.

Doreen MacKinnon also smelled of the magic of a full moon. Not the burnt charcoal of the moon itself, but the light scent of rose and bergamot. Ambrose was trying to ignore his physical reaction to her, because what he really needed was to get away from her. As fast as possible. He did not trust this witch, but he could help her if it meant achieving what he'd dreamed of for three hundred years.

Kill her family. Slowly. Painfully. And with pleasure.

He could never tell her the truth, that he knew how to break the spell. He would never consent to what it required, the cost of breaking it. He didn't want her to die—he didn't *really* want anyone to die—but he had no choice. She didn't know the price of love. How it could and would destroy you.

Ambrose dropped her hand after they shook on the deal and turned to the town beyond them. The Isle of Skye had not changed much over the centuries, and yet it had completely transformed. That was the funny thing about time. The landscape might shift, but the heart of a place, when firmly planted, beat steady. He could leave now. Leave *her*. But he wasn't ready, and if he stayed with her . . . He could take every last MacKinnon down, using her as his bait.

"There's a knitwear in Portree," he said. "It's a bit of a walk over the hill and along the cliffs, but you should be recharged well enough to make it now."

"Portree?"

"Yes."

"As in . . ."

"Isle of Skye."

"Scotland."

"Of course."

Doreen blinked at him. "I didn't bring my passport."

Ambrose let out a laugh, his first true one in centuries, and watched Doreen's eyes light up. He wondered what would make that look of wonder deepen across her face and tried to banish the thought. It lingered like a kiss. He told himself it was chemical; she did look a bit like Lenora, after all.

"I've not got any coin, but the Keeper may. We'll get fresh clothes and, if we're lucky, your answers."

He went to step forward but stopped when she spoke. "I always get lucky," she told him, with her head held high, before stubbornly marching past him.

Ambrose MacDonald sighed, and found that once again, when it came to a MacKinnon witch, he could only follow.

FOUR

Doreen's feet were killing her. She hadn't dressed for a trek through the Scottish countryside with an ornery ancient witch when she'd left the house. She had thought she would find Ambrose, ask him the right questions, get the information she needed, break the curse, and be done with it all. She did not think it would involve freeing a trapped witch, going against Stella, stepping through a portal, and climbing over indescribably beautiful rolling hills and roots that were as large as an SUV.

Or going on a quest to find who she was calling Real-life Gandalf. Doreen blew out a breath, climbed over another root, then a boulder, and finally arrived at the top of the hill... right as storm clouds formed overhead and rain broke free.

Fat, freezing drops tumbled quickly down. They made the earth beneath her impractical shoes soggy. She stepped over another root and stumbled, falling to the ground. Ambrose let out a low curse and crossed to her. It seemed like every move she made left him grumbling.

His warm hands circled her arms as he helped her up. His touch was far gentler than the expression on his face, which, if Doreen were reading it like a sentence in a book, might state *I'm going to shake you until you break.*

It was the furrow in his brow, the pinch of his lips, and the way his eyes narrowed. His gentle hands spoke a different language. Doreen preferred the look on his face to the unfamiliar etymology of his touch; it was the latter she didn't know what to do with.

"I'm fine," she said, untangling from him.

"You're a bloody disaster," he said, his hand clenching. "You can't recharge, can't walk . . ."

"I can send you back to that dungeon of a cage," she said, his annoyance at her inspiring the strong urge to spell him on his ass.

He shifted a step closer. "I don't think you will."

"Oh, no?" She crossed her arms over her chest, wishing she were taller, or at least had the higher ground. He was too damn tall.

He gave his head a shake. "Your aunt is a sadist of a witch, but you clearly don't have that streak."

Doreen thought of Jack and swallowed hard. Maybe she did, maybe she didn't. "There are other things I can do to you."

"Sure, but the thing is, I've had everything done to me already and I'm still standing. I don't want to be cursed again, and I don't want to be tied to you."

"Feeling's mutual."

He didn't so much as glance her way. "I want to be free as much as you do," he said. "Though I have my doubts you can do much in the way of freeing me."

She snorted. "I already have. Remember: me, you, the Dead House of your demise?"

He rubbed at his temple. "Can you even perform a summoning spell?"

"Of course I can." She paused, brushing the soaked locks of hair back from her face. Gods, he was cranky. "What do you want to summon? A better attitude?"

He looked at her, barely, his eyes skimming her face in what she took as disinterest. "Who, not what. The Keeper," he said. "There's no way we will make it to the Forest of Forgetting with you falling over your feet. The Keeper will be less inclined to help us from a summoning than if we knock on their door, but I can't carry you, and at this rate it will take us a week to get there."

"Perhaps I should have left you in the cage, after all," Doreen said and stretched her aching back. Though he wasn't wrong, much as she hated to admit it. If they kept walking, she was going to end up with blisters on her blisters and cracks in her bones. "I'll need something of this Keeper's. You don't happen to have a lock of their hair on you?"

"You mean did I keep a lock of hair in my pocket for three centuries while being tortured?" His nostrils flared. "No, I did not."

Doreen winced, and bit her lip.

"It must have been awful," she said, looking away. She didn't want to empathize with him, but facts were a hard thing to dismiss. "Stella has a way of drawing things out. Of stretching a simple punishment for making a potion for the wrong ailment into a year of silence." She wrapped her arms around her midsection, trying to infuse warmth. "I made a mistake once, and gave someone voice, when she wanted me to take it."

"Why did she want their voice?" he asked, his eyes eventually, reluctantly, finding a way to hers.

"They were saying things about us in town."

"What kind of things?"

"That we eat little children and kidnap puppies," she said, the corner of her lip curling up. "That we kill our own and use their plasma to curse our enemies. You know, the usual."

"Why didn't you take their voice as punishment?"

Doreen reached for a twig, peeling back the dead bark on it. "The woman was sad. Lonely. Bitter. Not because of us, but because of a bad romance. I gave her back her voice because she didn't know she'd given it to him. After, she wasn't sad anymore. She got out of the relationship, and she stopped talking about us."

"Bad romance?"

"She was stuck with a horrible man. He made her feel small. Some people like to do that."

"Yes," he said, looking up at the sky, the corners of his mouth turning down. "They do."

"Let me guess," she said. "Stella once turned you into a frog, shrank you down?"

"I was thinking of my father," he said. "He was exceptional at making his words into weapons, even without the power of a spellcaster. Stella never got into transmorphiguration. She preferred sharper, pointier methods. Though it sounds like she made you feel small, too. She certainly did her best to keep your power minimal."

"You don't need to tell me what I already know about Stella," Doreen said, and studied his profile, waiting.

He sighed. "Hastings."

"That was your dad's name?"

"No. Hastings is a name the Keeper cannot ignore. A connection to who the Keeper once was. Try using it for your summoning spell."

Doreen wanted to ask him about his father, but banished it as a foolish thought. It wouldn't do to forget who Ambrose was, and who he wasn't. He was a problem and a solution, not someone she should waste her compassion on. Instead, she nodded and set about gathering twigs and leaves. He didn't offer to help. She lay them in a circle around the base of a thick yew tree. Doreen hadn't taken many supplies with her when she'd gone to confront Ambrose, but improvisation was her strong suit.

Ambrose watched Doreen pluck flowers from around the base of another tree and lay them against the trunk of the yew. "You don't need casting materials?"

"These work," she said. "The ritual and intention are what matters. The words and my ability to manipulate energy and see beyond the borders of this world are what guide me. I mean, yeah, certain elements amplify spell work, but it's the witch who really matters." She looked up at him, from where she was crouched. "You of all beings should know that."

"In my day we were precise with our work and words. Sometimes when you concoct, you can step into the wrong element."

"You make it sound like you're going to hang out with a bad crowd instead of performing a summoning."

"Maybe you summon the wrong crowd."

Doreen snorted. "Can you grab some of the pine needles for me?"

He crossed his arms over his chest. "Why?"

"I need them."

"You just want me to grab them so you don't absorb the poison and I do."

She huffed a breath out. "The needles of this tree aren't poisonous. Wait. *Can* you safely ingest poison?"

He lifted a single eyebrow. "It won't kill me, but it will hurt."

"Interesting," she said.

"Don't even think about it."

"I would never," she said, unsure if she was telling the truth. She thought of what her family had done and winced. He had a right to assume she'd trick him or want to watch him writhe in pain, but it was the opposite of who she was. She didn't hurt, she helped. She would not forget that. She stood to gather the needles, but he was already moving toward them. Grumbling, but helping.

She walked to the tree and stared at the purple-and-red bark. It shimmered before her, a sign this tree was more than old. It was as ancient, if not more so, as the witch behind her. She gathered two handfuls of berries.

"As a cursed witch, thanks to you, I don't have a long lifespan. Unless, of course, I decide to enthrall some poor human and take their chance at happiness and love." She turned to him, the question popping out before she could swallow it down. "Can you be enthralled?"

"By you? Definitely not."

"Okay." She rolled her eyes so hard she got dizzy. "I'm cursed to die, but you can't enthrall me either."

"Half your line chooses to die rather than marry."

"You still say that as if they had a choice. We die if we *don't* marry. No action required on our part."

"You're not choosing the marrying path."

"I guess I would rather die than settle."

"Death or love?"

"Life or death," she said, wiping her brow with the back of her soaked sleeve and huffing at the ineffectiveness of it all. "When you don't have love, you don't have anything."

"That's true in more ways than you know," he said. "When you have it, the world is open. The air is easier to breathe, the skies are bluer, the sea is sweeter. Food tastes better, but you don't need it. Songs sound sweeter but you only need the sound of the other person's voice to know true music. Life is worth living, if you have true love." He dragged a hand through his hair, scratched at the stubble covering his jaw. "It's also no longer worth living when it is taken from you. Without it, life is hell. The landscape menacing, void. Worse than feeling nothing, you feel everything. The pain and devastation, the cold emptiness. It is a torture far worse than any the daughters of MacKinnon inflicted on me, than anything anyone ever could."

He stood still, his breath rising and falling in equal measure. His one hand was clenched into a tight fist again, the other clutching a bunch of needles. Doreen was afraid to inhale, to breathe in not his scent this time, but the ruin seeping out of him.

"She must have been something, Lenora," she finally said, when she thought it safe to speak. "For you to do what you did."

"She was everything."

"I'm sorry."

He gave a single, curt nod. His hand released, a slow unfurling that left her sighing. He glanced over. "You aren't entirely without. Is there not someone in your life you love?"

Doreen crouched by the tree. "Yes, Margot. She's my best friend. Or was. She got married, and now . . . that's gone too." She looked down at her hands. "You've been spying on us for centuries. You should know this. My mother chose to have me, but not to marry. Death was perhaps more preferrable to her than staying for her daughter. You lost sight of her; so did the rest of the family. Margot was the only one who wanted me for me." She cleared her throat, finding it too clogged for comfort. "I have one chance at finding the real thing, and I have to believe it's worth it. Even with the cost of losing it."

Emotion flickered across his face, there and gone so quickly she wasn't certain if she'd imagined it. He took three steps to her, and lay the needles down, overlapping her berries. His movements were quick and skilled; he may have been out of practice, but he was not without knowledge.

"Do you really believe the curse, all of this, was worth it?" she asked him, her voice growing quiet. "It . . . it didn't bring her back."

Ambrose lifted a shoulder, rolled it back. "An eye for an eye, Doreen MacKinnon."

"You spent three hundred years locked in a tempest because of a curse."

"Losing her was worse. What your ancestors did to her and me was unforgivable."

"Either way." She swallowed. "Just remember, until you and I fix this, or I turn thirty, I'm not so easy to kill."

"There are pains worse than death, Doreen."

"Perhaps. I simply want to remind you that while I don't yet need to poison you or try to kill you in your sleep, you can't harm me, either, should you decide to try."

"I make no promises either way," he said, his eyes tracking her every move. Doreen wondered if this was what a rabbit felt like before the dogs were released. "What do you mean, you're not so easy to kill?"

She shifted, pressing her palms into the dirt, seeking a connection to it. "I mean your curse gave us thirty years of impeccable health and not a day more."

"Impeccable or impenetrable health?"

"The latter."

"Interesting."

"I guess." She stood and stepped back from the tree, turning to him. "It is what it is."

"Your ancestor . . ." He rubbed his chin, his fingers brushing the stubble back and forth. "She only ever wanted to be impermeable."

"Lenora?"

He nodded. "Understandably. She didn't need to tell me how she needed to be made of steel to be a part of your family. I think it made her feel she needed to be impenetrable to them, and the world. It turned out her instincts were correct."

"You think she was miserable because of—what, her parents?" She tilted her head, curious.

"Because they did not approve of me, or perhaps, her. She bent for no one's will but her own, and they could not tolerate that."

"Is that why you cursed us this way?"

"I repaid your ancestors for what they took from me."

"An endless curse that robs everyone of true love in our line was a rational way to go about it?"

He glowered at her.

"Why can't you break it?"

"I am here"—he waved a hand toward the needles—"helping."

"Yes, I suppose you are." Doreen sighed. "I'm almost done."

"Good."

She scooped up the little caterpillar leaf and put it in the pocket of her shirt, then stepped into the circle. "Ignore him, Hastings," she whispered to it.

Doreen hadn't been thinking when she said the name. Not about the circle, or the earth beneath it. She certainly hadn't thought about the blood soaked deep into the core of Scotland, a country which had witnessed the persecution and death of thousands of innocent women and witches over the centuries. It didn't matter. The dead heard everything.

Ambrose gave a sharp shout right as the earth opened and swallowed Doreen whole.

It is argued that ergotism caused the witch trials," a breathless voice said. "What fools they all were, but it did prove me right, didn't it?"

"You're a stronger fungus than ergot," Ambrose said, his tone dryer than dust.

"Oh, hush," the crackly first voice said, a childlike laugh following.

Doreen was slow to open her eyes. Her head was pounding, and every bone in her body ached. She managed to get one lid open enough to survey the scene before her.

A small person sat by a roaring fire, their back to Doreen. The fireplace was the largest she had ever seen. As tall as Ambrose, and as wide as four of him. There was a large stack of wood to the far left of the fire. The being on the stool was hunched over, holding gloved hands up to the flames.

Doreen tilted her chin down, and looked to Ambrose. He was standing at her feet, his hands on his hips, brow drawn. He was imperfect. The scowl on his face was as constant as the curls at the edge of his hair, behind his ears. She couldn't stop staring at the way the black strands tucked in on themselves. She wanted to slip her finger into the edge of the curl, unfurl it and roll it back up. She wanted something to soothe the panic in her bones away, to chase the pain back into the shadows. But she was on her own.

Doreen pushed herself up into a seated position. Her clothes and hair were dry, and she was grateful for that. She took a shaky inhale, and Ambrose did not so much as blink in her direction.

"No one's tried to cross here in a small forever," the creature from beside the fire said. The voice was indecipherable. It sounded young, but as Doreen replayed the words in her mind, then the voice was brittle and old. The being shifted, their hood hiding their features. "You could have been spirited beyond the hedgerow, child, gobbled up by creatures no longer remembered by time."

"I wasn't," Doreen said, her voice strong as she summoned a strength she did not feel. "Unless you're one of those creatures."

The sound came again, high and full. A delighted laugh that left her shuddering.

Finally, the creature turned around, throwing the hood back. The face was made of shadow and echoes. A person no more, here sat a ghost. An impossible apparition. One born of a ghost story Doreen's aunt used to tell her when Doreen was a girl. One only spoken of by the aunts or cousins when too much moon wine had been consumed.

The Queen of the Order of the Dead was the leader of the *Sgàilean*

Dorcha. A legion of ghosts. The queen was known for her eyes as fathomless as the deepest ocean's floor, with pearls where their pupils ought to be. Given to her by the gods of death as payment for a curse the queen set a thousand years before. It was the pieces of others' souls that gave her long life. She kept enough of the souls of the living she possessed to alter her into something beyond death.

The Keeper.

Her aunt Stella had told her of the queen, and immediately deemed the idea "obnoxious nonsense. To think there are spirits so clever as to have a dominion over themselves, let alone the living and dead, is utter hogwash."

Yet here sat a spirit as real as Ambrose.

Ambrose cleared his throat, and Doreen realized she had been gawking. "I didn't think you were real," she said, unable to keep the shock from her voice.

"I exist in this reality," the spirit said, its voice both ancient and ageless. "You exist in this reality. We are both of us real."

"So you're a real soul eater?"

Ambrose made a sound resembling a human garbage disposal. "Ada is the Queen of the Order of the Dead, and she's not one for insults."

The creature stood and shifted closer, her body moving out of alignment with her shadow.

Doreen remembered what Margot used to whisper when they stayed up too late telling ghost stories. The Queen of the Order of the Dead did not move like any other creature on the earth. She was made of bones, but they were not *only* hers. She was constructed of ashes and tears and the bits of soul she borrowed . . . or stole. She could appear the size of a giant one day, or the size of a child the next. Her arms might reach the floor, or she might have one leg twice the size of the other. Regardless, she moved with elegance, as though her mind was reminding the rest of her body to pretend to be water. To flow with an ease the bones should not allow.

"You don't know your history, do you, girl?" Ada said, rolling her shoulders back one after the other, an audible *pop, pop,* echoing in the cavern. Doreen swallowed the gasp rising in her throat. "You don't know about me or from whence you came. Yet you managed to penetrate my cave."

Doreen fought a shudder at the hiss that followed, the sound bouncing off the walls. Something in the undulation of it reminded her of the warning of a snake before it struck.

"This is a cave?" Doreen asked, doing everything she could to keep her voice steady as she made a show of taking in the dark stone walls and floor, the dripping of water from the stalactites hanging overhead. She would have guessed right away . . . if not for the distraction of the mostly terrifying ghost in the room. "Which cave?"

She knew enough of her history to know that under Scotland ran a series of caves, reputed to be used by witches for centuries. They were where they hid from King James VI when he persecuted them in a baseless effort to prove his masculinity.

"I won't be sharing that," the queen said, her shadow snapping its fingers while her body remained still outside of the creaking of bones. She sounded like a rocking chair whose bolts no longer fit inside the joints. "This is my sanctuary."

"I'm in a sanctuary for a bedtime story meant to frighten misbehaving witches," Doreen said, her mind still reeling.

"The *Sgàilean Dorcha* will get you if you don't watch out," Ada said, something close to a smile pulling at the angles of her face. A strange buzzing settled over the tops of Doreen's arms, skittering up to her face and over her scalp. "Yes, though it's not a warning, it's a promise."

"We need your help," Ambrose said, stepping in front of her so he cut Doreen off from Ada's line of sight. Doreen let out a breath she didn't realize she'd been holding as the sensation faded from her body.

"You want to make a deal with me, Ambrose MacDonald?" Ada asked, her voice echoing around them like a bell rung in a canyon.

Ambrose didn't respond. His mouth thinned and his eyes dropped to the floor before he responded, "I do not wish to bargain today."

If the Order truly existed, then there must be truth to the nightmare stories Doreen had been told as a child. Which meant everything about them could be true, and *that* was a terrifying prospect. Margot had once told her, "There are worse things than being cursed to not find love, Doreen. We could be like the queen of the *Sgàilean Dorcha*, cursed to steal the souls of the living. She takes them, slipping in and possessing without care or thought."

Margot somehow always knew so much more than Doreen, though neither knew near as much as they wanted. Like Doreen, Margot's life was filled with considering the magic most people preferred to forget. Or it had been, before she gave in to the curse.

Doreen wanted to call her now; the urge was nearly all-consuming. Ambrose turned to face her, his gaze pressing into Doreen. She took a long measure of the terrifying spirit peering around the giant of a man.

"The Queen of the Order of the Dead consumes souls," Margot had said. "She's a reverse necromancer. It's because the spirits are bound to her through the ancestral lines, it must be—magic is thicker than blood, but better when it comes from it."

It felt like Ambrose was waiting on her to speak, and Doreen had never been one to lack the gumption to ask what she wanted to know. "What do you want from us?" Doreen asked Ada, with Margot's warning ringing in her ears.

"Answers," Ada said. "But you don't have them yet."

"That's pretty cryptic," Doreen said.

"You want to break your curse?"

"Of course."

"Don't want to die? Don't want to marry for less than love?"

"Yes."

"That makes you *an* answer."

Doreen's eyebrows drew together. "What was the question?"

"Your ancestors settled. Why shouldn't you?"

"Others have died rather than give in. That's not exactly settling." But that wasn't a question. She started to ask again but froze as Ada's face of shadow and bone shifted. Her pearl eyes flashed, and beneath them, sharp cheekbones that did not quite match and an angled chin lifted. Regal even in death, she gave Doreen a look that made her swallow hard.

Doreen looked to Ambrose, who met her gaze, his expression shuttered. "And so death came for them," he said, his tone betraying a hint of urgency. Doreen understood. Do not linger with a taker of spirits unless you want to be stolen too.

"*How* do I break the curse?" Doreen asked instead, as the same itching sensation creeped back over her skin. Her mouth twitched outside of its own accord, a spasm trying to take over her entire face.

"You could let me in," Ada said, shifting closer.

Static roared into Doreen's mind. A haze drifted over her eyes and her head grew heavy. Her body sagged; her thoughts slowed. A resounding *thump-thump* knocked across her consciousness.

Margot's voice drifted out from the attic of her thoughts: "We can never let our guards down, Doreen. Remember. You are the best of us."

She dug her nails into her palms until blood pooled beneath her fingertips and her mind cleared. "No," she said, her voice ringing out louder and clearer than any rung bell.

Ambrose growled and Ada let out a sound that might have been a sigh or a scream. "Then you have to go about this the hard way."

"I don't think this one knows what the easy way is," Ambrose said, but he moved closer to her. If Doreen didn't know better, she'd almost say he was protecting her.

"It's good, then, that she has you as her shadow," Ada said, letting loose a laugh that was all edges and corners. The sound scraped its way down Doreen's spine.

"We will be rid of each other as soon as we can be," Doreen said, and Ada laughed harder. "I won't make a deal with you. I don't have any answers."

"And I can't make a deal if you won't give me what I want . . . but there is another way."

Doreen leaned forward, stopped. Wracked her mind for any other bits about the Queen of the Order of the Dead, but Margot's voice was no longer there. Only silence remained.

"Which is?" Ambrose asked, shooting an annoyed look in Doreen's direction.

Ada's cheeks pulled back, revealing a decaying row of teeth mummified beyond time. Doreen shrank away as she offered a poisoned grin and said, "If you need something from the gods, there's always the trials."

The Trials of *Bheannachd*
(The Blessing Trials)

There was once a complete history and knowledge of spells given to all witches as their birthright. It started with a handfasting.

When witches came of age (exactly what age was determined by their particular coven), they completed a ceremony where they were bound with the knowledge of the ancestors and the history of their magic; the bridging of this connection was witnessed by the village. However, time has a way of changing how things are done, though time might argue people have a way of changing laws and they therefore change everything.

The binding of magic to witches changed because of the latter. More specifically, due to avarice.

Avarice Maoileanach was a greedy man. He came of age in a time when great battles were fought, and power was the ultimate conquest. It was a time not unlike this one. There are always loopholes in magic. Things meant to be safety measures that inevitably are perverted by entitled mediocre men, typically, and set by the powers that be to test witches and determine whether they have become too greedy. Avarice was aptly named, and he was the downfall of magic.

In the beginning, magic was plentiful. It grew on the vine, like wisteria or grapes or honeysuckle. You only had to create your offering to draw more in. A bit of blood and hair, a few wistful and poetic words, a gust of wind and fire and you'd be right as rain. Magic was used to create, to bring art and peace into the world, to aid in the growth of community for the better. It was a gift from the Ultimate Powers and was not meant to destroy.

But Avarice wanted more. Of everything. To ensnare his enemies, enslave those he desired, to rule everyone and everything.

The Ultimate Powers did not need the competition in the form of an overzealous and maniacal male witch. They saw through him and decided to offer him a trial... of sorts. If he could complete the challenges they set forth, he would gain the power to transform himself.

The trials lasted for thirteen days and thirteen nights. Avarice was taken through the door of truth, into the Forest of Forgetting, and beyond to the lost city of words.

The trials were a measure of courage, heart, strength, and cunning. To complete them, the champion must free the heart from the stone, find the lost story of love, wake the slumbering giant, and sacrifice what matters most to break the curse.

He did not pass a single trial.

Avarice lost his magic and his power, and whatever the gods saw in him angered them enough that they took back half of their power from the witches of the world. No longer would there be handfasting to the ancestors' truth and power. A history of magic was lost, the knowledge returned to its source. Witches had to write down their spells lest they lose them, creating the first of the grimoires. Magic flowed from line to line, but sparingly, like a sprinkle from a failing rain cloud instead of a gush from a geyser.

Over time, the trials were largely forgotten. Only a single witch succeeded at discovering and completing them.

Ada Rose made a choice. It was a selfish one, and a selfish choice is often any witch's undoing. For when you choose to go against the rule "and harm none," you undo magic in the world as it was meant to be.

The gods guarded the trials with the utmost care, for one never knew what could happen if such power landed in the wrong hands. Witches carried on recording their magic, and new powers grew on the vine, daring and different—and waiting for the right time to strike.

But power is always waiting, and it would only take one stubborn witch to set it free.

FIVE

Teeth terrified Doreen. It wasn't just that they were exposed bone, which was a bit unnerving when she thought too long about it—it was that they were mountainous. She'd had visions as a child about teeth that turned into volcanoes, which erupted and festered and boiled. When Ada, with her cloak of smoke and face that refused to reveal itself, said the word *trials*, Doreen saw the jagged mountains of her waking nightmares.

"What trials?" Doreen asked after forcing a swallow.

"The blessing trials. They are the only way to break an unbreakable curse. Which is what you carry. There are ways to demand knowledge, to gain the answers to any question. Though there is a price that comes with the asking."

"You have questions," Doreen said. "Why don't you take the trials?"

"I traded my chance for a request of a different sort."

"What do you mean?"

"I chose to stand before the gods and ask for power. For the power to find a soul."

"And?"

"The power granted to me turned me into this. If you seek an audience with the gods, I suggest you choose better," Ada said. Doreen turned her head, unable to stare at the misshapen form of Ada any longer. Her gaze fixed on the nearest wall, which shimmered in a hundred shades—a rainbow of color.

"Margot said you were a necromancer," Doreen whispered, the words tripping off her tongue.

"The strong and cunning Margot," Ada said, her voice deepening. "It must have been hard for her, seeing as much as she did."

"Seeing?"

"The truth of her life."

"She didn't see a way out; she chose to marry."

"She chose to believe in love," Ada said, a wistful tone creeping into her voice. "For now, at least."

"And you are a necromancer over the living as well as the dead?" Doreen asked, fear spiking in her that Margot could have been possessed by the creature. That, perhaps, Margot's bad choices weren't only her own.

"She has dominion over her own soul. I am a seeker and keeper of souls, a whisperer to the ones that come from me and mine." Ada's voice shifted, dropping into sotto voce. "I think you should let me speak to yours. Will it listen?"

"Enough," Ambrose said, his voice cutting in, bright and disorienting. "Ada, what of the trials?"

"The centuries have made you less fun, old friend. The language of the lost is there, on the wall. Those who wish to speak it will find it waiting, and if you follow, you will find your way. But remember . . ."

She paused, and her next words echoed in the cave. "The truth is the spell. The spell is the truth."

"That's not cryptic," Doreen said, but she stood, moving closer to the shimmering stone wall. It undulated before her. "How do we read something that isn't there?"

The air moved around her; fabric brushed the tips of her fingers and she shivered. She knew it was Ambrose, invading her space like he owned the air.

Before he could open his mouth and tell her, because she was fairly certain the pedantic witch lived to talk down to her, she reached out and pressed a fingertip into the wall. With a pop, a fissure grew and spread, down, up, over, and sideways—a spiderweb of cracks spilling across the wall.

The cavern shook from the force, and Doreen stumbled back, turning from the wall. Ambrose caught her, the skin on her arms tingling where his hands gripped her. The urge to lean into him was there, and she banished it, untangling herself and stepping away. Ada cackled; her form turned away from them as she faced the fire again. The ground beneath their feet rumbled, and Doreen turned to face the wall as the carvings across it slowed and stopped. Small Celtic knots and etchings led into a larger drawing of a creature. Not quite a dragon nor a seahorse nor a ram nor a steer.

"The Pictish Beast," Doreen said, moving in to study it more closely. The symbol was carved into hundreds of stones across Scotland and other countries, a beast that did not exist but looked a bit like a kelpie and a dragon and the Loch Ness Monster combined. "How is this a map to *anything*?"

"Not everything reveals itself in the moment," Ambrose said. He brushed a hand over the edge of the creature, and the lines shuddered and reshaped. The rock shook and reformed as a new drawing rose to the surface. It was a tree, with leaves falling from it and a crest in its center.

Ambrose let loose a mournful sigh.

"You know it?" Doreen asked.

"Yes," he said. "It's the marking of my ancestral home."

"Cursed house. Cursed lineage," Ada called, the fire before her growing higher as she poked at it.

Ada's laugh drifted over, and Ambrose waved a hand, actively trying to beat the sound away.

"Wherever we go, we go together," he said, as though he were the one making all the decisions.

"You aren't the boss," Doreen said. She turned to Ada. "Can you point me out of your creepy cave now? Please."

"Since you asked so nicely . . ." Ada said, still poking at the fire.

"Not so fast," Ambrose said, his eyes on Doreen. "Magic, especially old magic, always requires payment. The trials—what do we need to enter them?"

Ada smiled, her set of rotting teeth flashing before the shadows overtook it. "Why don't you reach into my fire and see what's there, Ambrose of MacDonald?"

Ambrose stepped forward and investigated the flames. "I don't think so."

"No?"

Doreen shifted away from the wall and stood beside him. In the flames, she saw an orb, glowing bright red from the heat of the fire. "That's a third-degree burn waiting to happen."

"Into the fire, come what may, if you want it, take it to find the way," Ada sang, her voice soft and strangely sweet. Before the last note receded, she reached out and grabbed Doreen. Smoke swirled around the two of them, the scent of dirt and decay pressing hard into Doreen's nostrils

and mouth. Doreen tasted ash and sputtered as the chain-like grip Ada had on her arm tightened.

"His line can only harm you," Ada whispered, her pearl eyes shifting from white to black, two dark pupil orbs peering deep into Doreen.

Images rushed through Doreen's mind. A flash of cliffs, a carving of stone, purple wisteria vines climbing up stone, the mountains of teeth that haunted her nightmares, and a sea of rock. She gasped, trying to yank away from the Queen of the Order of the Dead. Her grip tightened even more and Ada reached down, thrusting Doreen toward the flame.

"You have to *take* what is yours," Ada said. "Or leave it for another to take it from you. The spell is the truth."

Ambrose had told Doreen she was the most powerful witch of her line. She was from the thirteenth generation of witches, born with natural power. Doreen wasn't afraid of her power; she was a mimic, and if the keeper of secrets, this necromancer of a being, could reach into the flames, then she would too.

"The spell is the truth," Doreen whispered. She began to chant, the words rising up and out. *The spell is the truth, the truth is the spell.* She reached into the fire.

It was ice cold to the touch, and she had to bite down on her lip to keep from jerking her hand back. She closed her eyes and reached further, until she felt a hard, round object. She pulled it out and Ada released her.

Doreen's fingers were closed around the object, and her eyes immediately went to Ambrose's face. It was mere inches from hers, his hands gripped into fists, his brow crumpled. If she didn't know better, she'd think he'd been concerned for her.

Until he opened his mouth, and said, "Well, then, let's see it."

Doreen was tempted to throw it at his head. Instead, she

ignored him completely and turned to Ada. "Thank you," she whispered, a sense of foreboding washing over her as the words left her lips.

The queen bowed her head a fraction before she stepped away and into the fire. It engulfed her, and then Ada was gone.

SIX

It was a room fit for a queen... of the dead. The chamber was lit by candles dripping long tails of wax and filled with jars coated in an inch of dust and soot, browning from age. The contents of which looked like a mad scientist went on a rampage in a graveyard, digging up body parts and canning them for future study. Inside the jars sat milky liquids and bits of matter—dried herbs long since crusted and coagulated, rust-colored goo, and foul-smelling tinctures.

It was the house of the Queen of the Order of the Dead, or as much a house as a spirit could claim. There were several piles of books, stacked halfway to the ceiling, a few ancient chairs that might have been thrones in another life, a scattering of large urns, and a cage of bones that stood in the farthest corner. No fires burned in the room. The candles were the only signs of life—flames flickering and casting shadows on the wall, waiting to be observed, hoping for new movement to tell an undiscovered story.

In the center of the room, on a large slab of obsidian, stood a tall beeswax candle. The flame flickered, hit by a gust of wind from nowhere. The light dimmed and the smoke from its ember grew. Out of the smoke a shadow crept, in the form of a spider. It scuttled and slid, skidding into the cage made of bones. Once ensconced, it curled into a ball before stretching out and then rising, its shape shifting. A tall and slender shadow stood where the smoke spider had once been, before the air crackled and the rest of Ada, the Queen of the Order of the Dead, appeared.

The candle sputtered and Ada eyed the flame, her mouth thinning into a fine line. Her pearl eyes darkened, and she waited, watching until the flickering grew brighter. From behind the stack of books closest to her came a squeak. There, ducked low to the ground, another shadow hid, cowering.

"You may speak," Ada said, her tone indifferent as her gaze flicked over it.

"You lied," the whisper of a voice said, sliding along the floor to reach her.

"I spoke *a* truth," Ada said, crossing to the dilapidated throne and sitting upon it. Her feet levitated over the ground, her being hovering in the air directly above the seat.

The shadow unfurled and followed her, its moves sluggish and confused, as if waking from a long nap. "The trials have never been beaten," it said. "Not since you, and no one has dared attempt them in centuries."

"Did I not mention that?" Ada said, waving a hand over the table of candles and watching the flames grow. Even ghosts of the Order understood blatant sarcasm.

"Would it not be better to simply claim them now?"

"I cannot unless they allow it. They are not mine. Not yet."

"What now, then?"

"We wait," Ada said. "Soon their power and souls will be mine, and I will be one step closer to finding her."

"If *she* isn't lost forever," the shadow said, its voice barely audible.

Ada had been dead for a small forever. Before that she had been a Rose, of the Rose clan, one of three that ruled the Isle of Skye, along with the MacDonalds and the MacKinnons. She was woven into the fiber of both, though only one carried a trace of her blood—from a pact she made long ago with the one she loved.

Ada listened, but she did not speak. She simply reached out and plucked the shade from the ground and fed it to the closest flame. Her smile grew small and terrible as it screamed.

A mbrose awoke tucked beside Doreen in the forest they had stood in before. They were cocooned together and surrounded by the startling emerald green of thriving life. Moss-covered boulders the size of small tables dotted the landscape like large acorns scattered across a wide forest. Oak, birch, ash, native pine, and hazel trees pushed in too close together. It smelled of damp soil, decaying wood, and pine. It smelled like Ambrose's childhood.

Throughout his youth, Ambrose was easygoing and hardy of health. From the age of three, his nursemaids would cuddle him while his other siblings were struck with croup, impetigo, and even coughing sicknesses that were hard to shake. Ambrose, with his dark hair and bright blue-green eyes, with his knowing grin that belonged on a seasoned baron but instead was gifted to a mischievous child, never got the same ailments. The grin grew as did the lad. As autumn winds gave way to winter's chill, Ambrose found himself rewarded for his good temperament, his pretty looks, and his quick mind. At least, by the ladies of his house.

The lady who had tossed them from her cave was nothing like the women of his youth. He did not know how the spirit had done it. One minute they were staring at Ada, the next she disappeared. Smoke filled the room. Then he was waking on the lush green earth, his aching arms entangled in Doreen's soft ones.

Doreen shifted closer to where Ambrose's forearm was wrapped around her waist. He needed to move, to get as far away from the witch as possible. She smelled of rose water and the smoke of the burning fire from the queen's lair. It was strangely intoxicating, and it didn't help that as she lay beside him, with the moonlight cascading across the planes of her face, she looked too much like Lenora. It was the stubborn shape of her chin, the fullness of her top lip, the way she scrunched her nose in sleep as though something displeased her.

He was tempted to lean closer to study her, and that would not do. He couldn't drop his guard with her, not for a moment. He deftly untangled himself and shifted up to sitting. He needed to think, and plan.

Ada was cunning. She'd have the taste for Doreen now, much as she'd had the taste for him once upon a time. He did not believe Ada desired *his* soul. What he was certain of was he needed his revenge. Cursing Lenora's family had been right. He could never regret avenging the woman he loved. That he had made the deal for the curse from a spirit like Ada was, perhaps, where he may have made a small misstep. Ada was made of smoke and lies. He knew she'd beaten the trials, and she clearly wanted Doreen's soul. The soul of a MacKinnon.

He hadn't been lying. Doreen had a special kind of power, being of the thirteenth generation. Her soul would be intoxicating to Ada. Helping her would be a simple way to alter the course of things, and perhaps secure his freedom from Ada for good.

And yet.

Ambrose could not bring himself to allow Ada to take Doreen's soul. To do so would mean sacrificing the last of his humanity. He was, he supposed, not as far gone as he'd thought. Or perhaps, it was knowing he had an option that allowed him to feel benevolent. He could always change his mind.

For now, he wouldn't trap Doreen. Though if it had been her aunt in her stead, he would not have hesitated. Stella was a dragon and had enjoyed the pain she'd inflicted on him with an unbridled ecstasy typically reserved for ministrations in the bedroom under a fully charged love spell.

Doreen *had* freed him. He owed her a chance to be free—much as he owed himself the opportunity to balance the scales. They would set out for the trials, they would lure her family to him, and he would get a chance to transform himself.

For that was the reward for winning the trials: the ability to remake yourself into anything.

Ada had won and she had chosen poorly; if he succeeded, he would not do the same. If he could transform into a god, no one and nothing could ever harm him again. He knew that his immortality existed while the curse held, but if Doreen ever found some other way to break it . . . No, that would be impossible.

There was no doubt in his mind that Ada had held back pertinent information in telling them of the trials. The way to the trials, as the walls had whispered, was going to be a hell of a thing. It would require Ambrose returning somewhere he was desperate and terrified to go.

Doreen shifted, the fabric of her shirt rustling against the fallen leaves. Her hand curled around the object she'd pulled from the fire. He studied her where she lay. It wouldn't take much to shift the object free with how loose her grip had become in sleep. She mumbled something under her breath, and he was struck a second time by how peaceful she appeared, and familiar. Murmuring in her sleep had been something Lenora had done as well.

Ambrose needed distance. He stood and walked away from the slumbering Doreen, doing his best to ignore the pull tempting him to look back. Instead, he climbed up the hill to where he could peer down on the town in the distance. He stood there, remembering the centuries, trying to wrap his mind about the present while worrying over the future.

Soon, the sun started to shift up into the sky and the moon slept. And as it rose, Ambrose remained where he was, steadfastly watching the world, far too aware of the witch behind him.

As the day warmed, a soft groan finally had him turning. Doreen stretched and rolled to her side. She sat up, rubbing her eyes. After a few moments she stood, pulling her long red locks into a messy bun. Ambrose told himself it was the way the wind was blowing the unfastened strands that made him want to tuck it behind her ears. He didn't care to know if it was soft or coarse; he didn't care at all.

"How did we get here?" she asked, her voice a low rumble from just waking. Ambrose rubbed a hand over his sternum, above his heart.

"I have been thinking on that," he said. "Ghost mist is said to be a powerful intoxicant for mortals."

"You're not mortal," Doreen said, with a grunt.

"I can be killed," he said. "It's not easy, but it can be done."

"We were drugged and dumped where we started?"

"Something like that."

"Okay."

His lips twitched at her easy acceptance of the situation. Most witches would be panicking at this stage, yet Doreen simply nodded and started to climb the hill to where he waited.

"What are the trials, Ambrose?" she asked, slightly out of breath when she reached him.

He turned toward her. "What do you know of Avarice?"

"Greed? That it turns wanting into winning and winning into losing."

He lifted a brow. "Apt. Avarice was also a person, a witch, back when the world was full of us. He gave in to his desires for power, discovered the trials have existed as long as the gods have lived with men, and set out to win them."

"And?"

"He entered the gods' challenge for ultimate power. Trials of strength, cunning, bravery, and heart."

She raised her brows. "Seeing as his name is now associated with greed, I presume they didn't go too well."

"He did not pass a single trial. In the end, he tried to destroy the gods and they in turn made an example of him. His name became synonymous with his sin, and his example showed them that mankind was no longer deserving of such magic. They took back most of the power that had flowed freely here, and only a few families were allowed to stay in power. Families they felt were better suited to care for magic; families with, mainly, women."

She smirked. "Womankind does tend to succeed where mankind fails."

He grunted but did not disagree.

"And Ada?"

"She tricked the gods. Desperate to find the one lost to her, Ada undertook the trials when the gods would have prevented her from doing so. Ada's desire to win was as greedy as Avarice's had been, and therefore would have ruled her out as a champion."

"But she won anyway?"

"She won the trials but lost what mattered most."

"Which was?"

"She is a shade. Of her former self and world."

"She doesn't seem to mind." A small shiver ran through her as she remembered Ada's eyes, and she cleared her throat. "If the person's desire to win isn't greedy, how can the trials be won?"

"Only the gods know."

"And the trials are the only way to break the curse?"

He didn't meet her eyes, choosing to look up at the sky as he answered. "So Ada says."

Doreen sighed. "What about the symbols in the cave? Did you understand what they meant and the path from them?"

"Scholars have long thought the Pictish Beast needs a cipher."

"Remind me what a cipher is again?"

"A cipher is a puzzle," he said. Ambrose gazed out over the city before continuing. "The queen loves to complicate things, and if she can mess with us in the process . . . well, Ada would gleefully do so."

"Why does she want to mess with us?"

"Entertainment, perhaps. It's boring being a spirit. They are trapped and waiting and there's only so much people-watching one can do over hundreds of years. But mostly, I think Ada is hopeful we will mess up and need her and be forced to trade something in the end."

Doreen pushed at a mossy patch on the edge of a boulder. "She seemed to want to help."

"She wanted to eat your soul."

Doreen laughed, but the sound faded when she realized he was serious. "She did not."

He shrugged. It was not his duty to convince her of the ways of a world she had too long been shielded from. He owed her a life debt, not an education.

"Be careful trusting the ancient undead," Ambrose said.

"*Now* you tell me." She grinned. "You brought us to her."

"She was the only way."

"And she wants us to go to your home."

"It has not been home for some time."

"Do you miss it?" she asked, swallowing hard. "Your home, your life? What it once was? It must be awful to not be able to go back."

Ambrose was slow to answer, cradling the words before he released them, as though they had the power to break him. "It was not always a happy life. As the third-born son of an earl, in a time when the less important sons went to war and found death as quickly as the seasons brought in the changing of the winds, I never bet on life when I was living it. Funny, I should have bet on death. And how little it wanted to do with me."

"I don't understand."

"Throughout my childhood, I almost never got sick. Germs were as repelled by my charms as ladies were drawn to them," he said, flashing the hint of a smile. It was disarming, and Doreen was thankful it disappeared as fast as it arrived. "I didn't get sick; instead I gained power. Witches ran in the MacDonald line, but they didn't *run* our line. My father did, and his talents were not in controlling weather, or turning earth over with a flick of his hand, or even the sobering skill of reading the lesser minds of his enemies. No, the lord of the estate was cunning in weaponry and planning, and he took down anyone who stood in his way. He would have ruthlessly taken me down, too, and he told me so often. Should I stop being his weapon and start being in his way, he would end me."

"He sounds like a dick."

"He was of a different age," he said, before meeting her eyes. "But yes, he was."

She frowned at how his hand went to the back of his neck. He squeezed it before continuing. "Fortunately, he found a use for his book-obsessed middle child. He had me catalogue the moves of others and, in their sleep, send them nightmares born of the fears I read about. I distracted the daughters of his opponents, catching and releasing them—leaving their hearts banged up but not broken and their reputations in disgrace." He dropped his hand. "For a long time, I hated my father for forcing me to do it, but eventually I began to hate magic."

Doreen's fingers twitched as though she were about to reach out and offer comfort. She stuffed them into her pockets.

"My house never felt like a home, and my life was not one worth living. Not until the night of the harvest moon, when Father welcomed one of our neighboring clans. A céilí, a dance, was to be held in their honor, and it was under the calling moon that I saw her. Lenora." His voice grew quiet, his gaze far off, and Doreen shivered at the longing that flickered in the depths of his eyes. "She of the bright flame-colored hair and deep green eyes, with freckles scattered across the planes of her face like constellations dropped down from the skies to bless her porcelain skin. I never believed in poetry until that night."

A goldcrest sang, its twittering song cutting through the tension spilling out from Ambrose and wrapping itself around Doreen. He took a deep breath and looked over at her. His face was impenetrable. Impossible to read.

"Your family tortured me for three hundred years in three hundred thousand ways. Taking my home away was one of them, but not because of the taking of a place. It was in the taking of Lenora." He held out a hand. "Memories do not fade for me, and so I live with them until I am free from it all. But I have not missed my ancestral home."

He thought of home and there was a flash of a tree in his mind. The deep rust color of bark, the unfurling of curled branches, the opening of autumn's flowers—crimson and gold leaves.

The vision shifted and submerged, dunked into murky water as the leaves tumbled down and down and down.

Ambrose let out a shaky breath as the vision receded. "I don't understand," he said, as the images remained, imprinted, strong and true.

"You . . ." Doreen asked, her head tilted, eyes sharp. "Did you see something?"

He squinted, his brow furrowing, confusion etching across the planes of his face. "I can't have," he said. "It isn't possible. I lost my power when I cast the curse."

"It looked like—"

"It's not possible."

"I think we're proving possible is an exercise in discovery and not futility," she said, capturing his eyes with hers. "Ambrose, what did you see?"

He took a step back from her. He didn't like how he wanted to lean into the sound of his name when summoned in her voice. "I would be wary of anything after being in the company of the Keeper."

"Ada seemed to think I should be wary of you."

His eyes flew to hers, fear and worry flashing before they deadened. "Ada wants to devour you."

"And you don't. You want to use me and then what, dispose of me?" She blinked her wide eyes at him, pursing her lips as though deep in thought, and something swirled low in Ambrose's belly.

"I have no need of your soul," he said, his gaze snagging on her mouth before he turned away.

He did not wait to see whether she would follow or sink once more down into the bowels of Ada's hell. Ambrose did not wait for Doreen MacKinnon, and he did not look back. He simply took a single shaky breath and hurried toward the town of Portree.

Margot dreamed of a castle covered in purple wisteria. Of a woman haunting the towers, sobbing as she ran her nails over stone walls and chipped the sandstone away. Inside, Margot was running after Doreen, trying to save her as ivy sprouted from the floor and wrapped around her, before yanking Doreen down three levels into the hidden pool beneath.

Margot could not reach her, frozen as she stared down into the water, as a woman stood at the edge of a cliff, laughing cruelly before she turned into the shape of a horse and dove in.

When Margot awoke, her phone was ringing. She answered without looking. "Hello, Stella."

"You had the dream too, didn't you?" her mother asked, her throaty voice choked with fear.

"Perhaps," Margot said. Stella dreamt every night. The kind of dream any armchair psychologist would call a nightmare, ones built from her fears and the years of tormenting herself and the Mac-Donald heir. All the MacKinnon witches dreamed. Save for Doreen. The youngest of the thirteenth generation, she'd never had a single dream. "What did you see?"

"I dreamt of Doreen wearing a crown; her eyes were pearls, and her heart was a stone."

"I saw her going into a pool of water, being yanked down by ivy before a kelpie dove in after her," Margot said.

Stella hummed a tune that Margot hated. It was a song sigil, a tune that other witches in their line couldn't refuse. Stella had used it the month before Margot's birthday to call the coven together for an intervention to force Margot to marry her Dean. She had used it when Margot and Doreen had been girls and fallen in tender love, or lust, the first time, to recruit the other aunts and cousins to intervene when needed. It was a bad omen, and it meant Stella was going after Doreen.

"I told you if the signs pointed to it, I would have to do this," Stella said, when Margot did not echo the melody. "We must protect ourselves and the coven."

"Doreen *is* us," Margot said.

"She chose to go with that witch, freed him, helped him open a door to goddess knows where. They could have unleashed all manner of mischief and misdeeds by now."

"You know she would never harm any of us. She loves you, and me. Doreen's run the shop faithfully for years; she's stayed in line while trying to break the curse. It turned out she had to blow up the line. She has only ever wanted one thing. To break the curse that binds us all. You can't be serious going after her like this."

"The curse will not be broken. He will never allow it. She's made a horrible mistake, and he will use her. She is now the partner of my enemy and so is my enemy," Stella said, her voice lowering. "They could end us all, child, *don't you understand?*"

Margot rubbed her temple, trying to soothe the headache building. "You speak of madness."

"You have no idea what we're up against now that he is unleashed," Stella said. "Who he was before he came into power, what he did to get there. The MacDonald males slaughtered hundreds of us, but their power drained as ours rose. He shouldn't have been what he was, and if he hadn't been restrained after the curse, gods know what they would have done to us."

Stella lived in fear of the MacDonalds or any ancient family rising back to power. The gods and the trials, she'd told Margot after she had married Dean, were watching and waiting. Margot thought the gods must be incredibly bored to spend any amount of time caring what the covens did. There were so few of them left, and most of their magic was spent healing. If the gods hadn't screwed the world up, they wouldn't have had to heal it. If there was enough magic, life could be harmonious and balanced. Unfortunately, they lived in the meager balance of power and siphoned what they could to those who needed it, or, if you were Stella, who you deemed deserved it.

After another ten minutes of complaining, Stella hung up, leaving Margot sitting in the dark. As she stared at her latest spread of tarot, she thought of her cousin trapped in the ivy, and hoped she did the right thing by giving Doreen the truth. Or as much of the truth as she could. If anyone could break the chain that bound them, Margot believed with her whole soul it was Doreen.

The only other thing Margot knew for certain was that if her mother discovered her part in what had transpired, Doreen wouldn't be the only one the coven hunted down.

SEVEN

The morning sky was a wicked shade of violet fading into a rosy hue. It reminded Doreen of the color of wisteria. A creeping vine flashed before her. It trailed up and over the side of a castle, wrapping around an arched stone doorway that led into a courtyard filled with decaying trees in bloom, flowering rotten teeth that dripped to the ground, creating pools of a black primordial ooze where they fell. In a blink, the vision was gone.

She shivered in the chill of the sharp breeze, banishing fears as they drifted in. Her mind was simply in overdrive. She studied her feet, ignoring how her gaze kept drifting toward Ambrose. His dark hair and shuttered expression were a magnet, pulling her attention even as she told herself that having curiosity for the witch was akin to having a craving for a poisonous apple. No good would come from being drawn to such a man, and such a man was created by the gods to draw one's attention.

The problem was he simply was not affected by her. The curse was his, and he was the first man in a long time who couldn't have cared less if she existed. To be fair, he'd likely prefer she didn't exist, along with her entire line. He'd certainly have an easier time of it.

Still, he couldn't suffer her thrall. Instead, it was as though he found her an inconvenience and had decided to tolerate her like a grumpy cat abides a curious puppy. She did not know how long their truce could last. Not with his barely concealed disdain and her reluctant but growing interest.

She kicked at the root of a tree as she crossed over it. She promised herself that she would not look at him again unless he spoke to her. It was an asinine thing, to have to make such an agreement with oneself, and yet it was her best defense. Which was to say, not much of one at all.

The countryside of the Isle of Skye was littered with moss-covered and oversized stones, and they'd happened upon a pocket beset with aging trees. And as she climbed over root after root, telling herself not to look at Ambrose, cursing herself when she did, the wind kicked up. A feathery tingle brushed against her cheek. She knew that sensation. *Margot.*

Doreen looked down. There, beneath her feet, overlapping in a wild sort of cursive, were roots spelling out her name. She knelt, and a spray of lavender floated up, the scent engulfing her. It was Margot's signature scent, one she regularly cloaked her spells in. Lavender had natural healing properties and Margot used it to soothe the mind of whoever would be on the receiving end of her magic. She was a conscientious witch if nothing else, and Doreen's stomach squeezed at the relief of Margot seeking her out.

Doreen whispered her cousin's name and ran her fingers over the bramble. Her breath caught as the bark unfurled and rolled into her hand, creating a single sheet of parchment. Here was a nearly forgotten memory, a way that the two had communicated in secret when they were children and wanted to keep something hidden from the prying eyes of Aunt Stella. Doreen unrolled the scroll and blew at the bark, the words rising one by one as if a typewriter were keying out the text.

T h e

s i g i l

i s

r a i s e d.

R U N

Doreen's heart dropped into her stomach as the parchment furled back in on itself and dissolved once more into pieces of bark, crumbling through her fingers. Adrenaline hit her first. Her heart galloped into action, her stomach flipped, and she forgot how to breathe.

Fear slunk along her spine in the next breath. Unwelcome tears tracked down her face before she felt them, drops falling on her fingers, into the palms of her hands, dripping to the earth. If the sigil was raised, if Margot wanted her to run, it could only mean one thing— Doreen was being hunted.

There was no one so formidable as her aunt, and there was no place she could hide should she want to. Doreen had known it was only a matter of time, that her betrayal would strike into the heart of her bond with her aunt, but she had not expected her to raise the sigil. To call forth the surviving members of the family line.

They would come for her, and soon.

She could abandon Ambrose, return home, and beg forgiveness. But the curse would remain unbroken, her life unchanged, and they would force her to help them capture the man standing before her and punish him.

Before they punished her.

Doreen knew in the depths of her soul that she could no more abandon him than she could stop loving Margot. She wasn't the type to run, not even with Margot telling her to, but they needed a plan. A cold certainty settled into her bones. She wiped her face clean of tears and swallowed hard. Her gaze shifted to Ambrose, the man stubbornly marching ahead of her, who was clearly battling demons of his own. The way he had spoken of his home, of his father, left Doreen with an uncomfortable truth. They were not so dissimilar. She thought that, perhaps, he was as unloved as she. And now they were cemented as a team. One she had chosen without thinking the consequences through. It was one of her oldest problems; Doreen acted on impulse. When it felt right, she did what she knew she had to do. She didn't always look down the road farther than the next stop, and now that she was seeing the long and winding road ahead, she realized how twisted it was.

"We have a problem," she called out to him, forcing herself to climb over the rest of the boulders and roots to reach him. He waited, arms crossed, body poised as though prepared to strike. Ambrose was slow to meet her eyes, his expression hooded. She thought if he could, he'd wrap himself in a perimeter with a label that that read *Keep out* to hold her at bay.

"One besides the dead witch wanting to eat your soul and the trials destined to destroy us?"

"You're overreacting about Ada," she said. Men were often so quick to think the worst of powerful and misunderstood women. But, sometimes, they were also right. "My aunt has raised the sigil."

He lifted both brows. "The one that calls your coven back from the circles of hell they inhabit so they can all convene?"

"They're in different parts of the world, not the underworld."

"So you say."

She mimicked his posture and crossed her arms over her chest.

"This isn't a little nuisance I am sharing with you. They're *coming for us*."

"They've always been coming for us," he said, dropping his arms and turning to walk away. "You're only just now realizing it."

She wanted to throw a rock the size of her foot at his back. "You're wrong."

"Am I?" he asked, continuing to climb the hill.

She opened her mouth to argue, because it simply felt good to have a place to put her anger, and immediately shut it. He wasn't wrong. He was right, but she still wanted to slap him for it.

"My cousin got a message to me," she said, her tone defensive, the tears rising once more into the back of her throat.

"Then you have one relative who isn't worthless."

Doreen cleared them on a growl, and the corner of his cheek twitched.

"We need to move, then," he said, glancing back, the almost grin dropping like the upturn of his lips had burned his cheeks. She wondered if he knew how much it changed his face, the near smile, then reminded herself she didn't care about his stupid face.

"They can track us anywhere."

Ambrose shook his head. "No, Doreen. Where we are going, no one can track us."

"We don't know how to enter the trials."

"Not yet." He glanced further up the hill, his brows knitting together. "But we know where we're going."

"To your home," she said, watching as his shoulders rose and fell. Doreen was gripped with an overriding urge to reach for him, to offer comfort. He looked back at her, and the intensity in his eyes had her stepping back instead.

"Yes." He pressed his eyes shut with a sigh, and she wondered what returning to it would cost him. Slowly, they cracked open, and he offered her a cold smile. "I must return home, and lucky you, you're coming with me."

The way to the MacDonald fortress, which was how Doreen had chosen to think of it, led them into town first, where they purchased clothes, ate Brie-and-tomato sandwiches on thick crusty bread, and had their fill of pastries. Doreen learned Ambrose had a sweet tooth and was a vegetarian. Both details surprised her. With his size and hostility, she'd thought him the type who would hunt and kill his own dinner before picking his teeth with its bones.

The café they sat in was quiet, and somehow Ambrose had managed to pay for their food, as he'd done for the clothing. If Doreen hadn't been so hungry, she'd have grilled him about how he, a witch who had spent centuries trapped, had come by the coin. Perhaps he had an unlimited purse like Margot, the container the source of a family mystery, one of many the MacKinnon family lived with, and one of the better ones too. It was a blessing to have such a purse, unlike the MacKinnons' cursed hammer that never hit its mark (and nowhere near as enjoyable). But as it was, she simply ate and tried not to get lost in the false sense of peace the town afforded them.

The town of Portree was like a song you whistled because you couldn't quite remember the lyrics. It was quaint and lovely, and if you blinked, you'd miss it. Any other time Doreen would want to spend days soaking up the atmosphere of the jumbled downtown (that wasn't really a downtown as there was, in fact, no uptown). It offered two galleries—an art gallery and pottery shop—coffee shops, and a pub. Each discovery was lovelier than the next.

A dense fog was rolling in, bringing with it the smell of brine and the sea and a hint of cloves.

Underneath trilled the soft notes of a violin, warning of a coming storm. It started with a single note. A strong plucking of a string, the warble of a lift of song that led into the tripping of notes one after the other, clamoring up like the rise of a sleepy sun. A sweet tickle of a melody. It might be the sort of tune to send a person reaching, stretching for the day. As the notes settled back and dropped off, the final note rubbing too close to the one before it, Doreen gave a whole-body shudder. It was a happy tune with a sour ending, and it was the start of the MacKinnon Sigil. The command had been raised.

Ambrose could not hear the hunt of the minor chords, and he did not know to be afraid. He might not have been regardless, as little seemed to terrify him. She supposed if you could survive centuries of torture at the hands of some of the most powerful witches in existence, you developed thick skin.

"We need to move on," she said, standing and wrapping her arms around her middle, trying to ignore the tapping of the notes. It was as if they were knocking at her shoulder.

Ambrose surprised her by nodding. "It is a short distance by car. The barista is loaning us hers."

Doreen raised her brows. "Oh, really? She volunteered her car, just like that?"

He looked out the window, running a hand through his dark locks. "I can be convincing."

"Putting the whammy on a civilian is a bit icky, so I guess that tracks for you," Doreen said, opening the door.

"Says the woman who has been putting the whammy on people her whole life."

"Thanks to you," she said, waving him out ahead of her.

Ambrose glowered at her. "You're making it easy for me to see how disposing of you when we are done with this will be advantageous."

"Don't be such a baby," she said, a frisson of fear sparking along her spine as she followed him out.

"Don't be such a witch," he said, and flashed a half smile. Doreen nearly stumbled at the sight. The curve of his lips had her shivering. She told herself it was not the stirrings of desire. Her reaction was a flame of irritation, not a spark of lust. He was teasing her, not propositioning her.

Doreen stretched out her fingers, and he tracked the movement with his eyes. Ambrose MacDonald felt like a bad habit she needed to be rid of and yet they were stuck together.

"I once read a spell on how to transform a human into a scarecrow," she told him. "I've always wondered what that would look like." Doreen started the incantation under her breath. She wasn't going to follow through with it, not really; she just needed to shift the power balance back. She refused to feel even the slightest bit out of control around him.

"Stop," Ambrose said, his voice a low rumble. His hand came down over hers, gentle but firm. He pressed his palm to Doreen's. A jolt of wanting lit along the path where his touch lingered. She jerked away and his eyes widened.

Ambrose swallowed and released her. "If we're going to succeed at this and not kill each other," he said, "you're going to need to stop acting like a child." He raised a single eyebrow.

"It's rude to touch people without permission in this century," she said, annoyed her voice came out breathier than intended.

"Noted," he said.

She blew out a flustered breath. "You have to promise to have the car back to the barista, with a fresh tank of gas, and to restore the balance with a payment of sorts."

"What kind of payment?" he said, his long legs eating up the length of the road as she hurried along beside him.

"You're a seer, right? Try to see a way to bring something good into her life. Peace, happiness, prosperity."

Ambrose stopped and stared at Doreen for a long moment. "Is that how you usually operate?"

"Of course," she said. "An ye harm none, do what ye will."

"Not very MacKinnon of you," he said, resuming walking.

"It's very much an honest witch of me."

He ran a hand through his long dark strands. "There's a fine line between harm and help."

"Maybe, but this MacKinnon witch harms none."

After a moment he nodded. "I'll return the car."

"And?"

"And decide on the rest in time." He headed for a black sedan. "Though if you prefer not to ride with me, you could walk the five miles and meet me there after sundown, when the vampires come out."

"Ha, ha," she said, before hurrying down the sidewalk. "Vampires don't exist."

Ambrose unlocked the doors and climbed in. He didn't bother to look at her. "Don't they?"

"You can't drive. You have no license."

"No," he said, shifting in the seat. "I have magic."

"But I do not have a death wish, as we have established," she said. "Trade with me."

As he stared her down, she sighed. "Please."

He opened the door and exited the car, and she slid into the driver's seat. Then she was turning the engine over and rolling the windows down. She could feel his gaze on her, and it sparked something in her spine, making her want to sit up straighter. She pulled out of the parking lot, trying not to give credence to the idea of vampires or any other things that went bump in the night. Ambrose sighed, and she turned her attention to the witch who was directing her onto what she could only think of as a picturesque road to hell.

EIGHT

Ambrose would say of his ancestral home only that "it's a fortified cage, gilded and drafty, and I'm sure you'll fit right in." He was increasingly cranky as they drove closer. The clear blue skies and rolling landscape did nothing to soothe her worry, and she hated that she was worrying about him at all, fearing what Stella and the coven could do if they discovered them. To distract herself, Doreen had discreetly given Ambrose the middle finger while they idled on a narrow country road and he gazed at the sweetly fat roaming sheep who were overtaking the lane in front of them.

Ambrose was, annoyingly, an excellent passenger. Quiet and calm, and in another life, it would have been an enjoyable experience— watching the sun set as they drove through the quiet countryside and exhaustion pressed in. Doreen wished she had headphones so she could tune out the family's sigil and the ceaseless notes that filled the quiet of her mind. The relentless minor chords, bumbling over one another, not quite even, not quite meant to pair.

Eventually Ambrose directed her off the main road onto a smaller pebble-and-dirt one. The sedan bumped along steadily as they climbed a hill and then crested it. Ambrose motioned for her to stop the car and put it in park before he said, "We'll walk over the last bit of hill." He already seemed miles away, his eyes seeing whatever was hidden by the fairy mound before them.

Then he was out and stomping ahead like he could tame the very earth beneath his feet with the determined set of his shoulders and force of his hips. Doreen eyed his swagger for longer than necessary before she unclasped the seat belt and exited the vehicle. He did not stop, but he slowed, and she supposed that was as gentlemanly a response as she could expect from a man who was as tender as a tempest. At least he hadn't tried to club her over her head and drag her by the hair.

The muscles in Doreen's calves and thighs were aching by the time she reached the top of the climb up into the MacDonald estate. She paused, hands on knees, and stared at the vast expanse of land. Brilliantly green cliffs stacked like fists one over the other, reaching out into the ocean before her. In the middle of the bluffs stood a stone castle covered in wisteria and ivy, featuring four turrets and an entire wing that seemed to crawl along the backside of the cliffs like the tail of a dragon. The stone monstrosity reminded her of an ancient creature; it was both beautiful and cumbersome, and as she stared at it, a flash of vision hit her so strongly she staggered beneath it.

She was inside a courtyard with a stone fountain, the roots of a tree sticking through its side. A spray brushed her cheeks, the cold a relief to the heat, flushed through her. Ambrose stepped into the water, his chest bare, and—

She blinked and Ambrose was in front of her. Clothed and with stark irritation marring his nearly flawless annoying face. Stupid stingray.

"What?" Doreen said, the word coming out harsh.

"You've been staring through me for the better part of a minute," he said, his tone curt.

"Oh," she said, and stepped back. "I thought I saw . . ."

"You aren't a seer."

"No."

He blinked, his chest rising and falling. She refused to focus on it. "What did you think you saw?" He ground out the words in an accusation.

She lifted her chin, refusing to be intimidated by his harsh features or tone. "You."

His face remained impassive aside from the irritation. "I've been here the whole time."

She nodded, unable to put into words what she saw, how it felt. How light her heart had been at the sight of him, how thrilled. Doreen had never felt such a thing before, not even with Jack, and she did not trust it. The hope in it *terrified* her.

"I'm tired," she said, instead. "My mind is hazy, and the air is thick with wasted magic. I need to rest."

"Wasted magic?"

She waved a hand around. "The cliffs, the sea, the land that once teemed with it, still carries the echoes. Can't you taste it? Clove and honey in the air. Old magic, not quite in reach, but it remains."

He took a breath. "There are memories, here," he said. "I can't say anything for old magic, but be mindful of the past. That you don't get stuck in any memory for too long." He looked as though he wanted to say more, but instead gave a short nod and walked along her side—though with enough space for three people—until they reached the curved arch of the entrance to the castle.

"This is a little more than a home," Doreen managed, staring up at the trellis.

"It is Bonailie Castle," he said.

"My Scottish is a bit rusty," she said, trying to place the words. "What does that mean?"

"Loosely, it means the Goodbye Castle," Ambrose said, his tone ominous, a hint of a deep brogue shifting into it. "If you darken the halls with ill intent, the castle will spirit you to the motherlands."

"Oh goodie," Doreen said. "A murder castle."

"More than you know," he said, before he walked ahead of her and went inside.

Ambrose's family had several castles. Two were in disrepair, crumbling to the point of being little more than a skeleton of bones. A corpse of history and a reminder that time would waste away anything and anyone. The Goodbye Castle, as it had been called in his youth, had been abandoned, but remained mostly intact. It was one of the most haunted places in all of Scotland, and it was secreted away so well, wrapped in an enchantment cast over the bones that had been ground to dust and blended in with the mortar used to construct the home, that none knew it existed any longer. It was an old spell, one few remembered, and due to its bloody nature—human sacrifice had no better reputation in today's modern world than it had when the castle was constructed—it was not the kind of spell likely to be cast ever again.

Ambrose stood in the main hall, forcing himself not to turn and run. He wasn't afraid of the ghosts or the damp floors and walls. He didn't mind the shadows or the way the air was filled with anise and blew cold no matter where you stood in the entryway. What Ambrose couldn't tolerate were the memories. The reminders of his father, of how Ambrose had failed, and how love could never truly be his.

"It's the price you pay for being born," his father had told him, after sending him sprawling across the cold hard floor for failing to use his sight to see what move for power they needed to make next.

Ambrose had only seen the ocean and the harsh rocks where the sea met the edge of the cliffs. He'd nearly been tossed to meet them, save for Sinclair, his valet, preventing it. "No one will love you, boy," his father had said. "You're hard enough to stomach in small doses. Love is not a creature meant for you." It was not the first time he had been told he was not meant for love, nor the first time he'd been hit by his father. But it was one of the last.

Light beamed through the arched window across from the first set of stairs leading up to the north turret, and Ambrose hissed a breath at the effect. A rainbow of color tripped down the stairs almost like a red carpet rolled out for a visit from the latest dignitary. But instead of it being a welcome sight, Ambrose's mouth ran dry, his heart tripping over itself as he studied the way the refracted light continued its path across the floor and up onto the ornate table that stood in the center of the room.

The hulking slab of marble was empty of flowers or vases or any other modern decoration. To its left stood one oversized fireplace, with its twin standing sentry to the right. As a boy, the dual fireplaces with their sturdy warmth had tricked Ambrose into thinking there was no place he'd rather be than standing before them. Taking off his coat and bringing his hands outside the flames as he cupped the air and attempted to pull the heat inside himself.

He'd suffered the heat of the fire as his father often shoved him nearer, and used to dream it would consume him and put an end to it all. Once, he'd nearly succeeded when he'd used his power to yank a flaming log out toward him. In the end, it had only caught a rug on fire—and earned him two matching black eyes and slew of bruised ribs.

Now they stood cold and empty before flaring to life, the flicker of light from before dancing across the marble table. Dust motes pulsed through the air, creating shapes where none should exist. Ambrose could make out the faint outline of a woman. Slender with ample curves, she shimmered there. Ambrose held his breath, then forced a steady exhale in release.

It wasn't real, he told himself; none of it was anymore. He was the ghost of this castle now.

Doreen was slower to enter, likely caught in the lure of the wisteria and ivy, in the unkempt maze and bushes that greeted those who sought to enter the grounds. He might have been grateful for the moment of pause, if not for the steady old fears trying to seed and bloom inside him. He wished she would hurry.

There was more than his own past to contend with. He did not like the sigil being raised. He knew more of it than even Doreen. He'd been there, after all, when it was used on Lenora.

When the sigil had been raised against Lenora, she had said, "The wind is bringing notes of sorrow. A key plucked and left to trail off, then plucked again. They speed up, like vines tripping up aging stone, racing to find me." Ambrose had tried to look, to see the sound. And what he'd seen in the end was the trailing of dark green jasmine, its leathery leaves climbing up an ash-colored stone wall. The vine shooting upward as he watched clusters of trumpet-shaped white flowers bloom, interwoven with the spreading leaves, each one reaching up higher than the other until they broke off, petals distended, and the last leaf brown and brittle, flaking back down into the earth. It was that last near-blackened leaf that had terrified him. Lenora had been unable to outrun the sigil, in the end.

Ambrose knew Doreen's family better than she, and he understood that as the youngest in the line of the thirteenth generation of witches, Doreen was at the height of the family power. They did not suffer fools, and what Ambrose had observed of Stella (and Kayleen before her) was that they would do whatever was necessary to control that power. Ambrose had been forced to bear witness to many truths of the MacKinnon witches. Secrets they would have preferred to roll up and tuck away like a cigarette behind their ears had landed in his lap while they were torturing him. They were gifts he would put to use later.

He shook his thoughts away. The gossamer outline of a person still shimmered before him, a ghost observing its long-lost master returning home at last. Ambrose breathed a slow, even breath as he stepped forward and through it. He didn't have the luxury of running from the past. Instead, he would go forward and create his future. No matter how bloody or destructive the path he would have to forge.

D oreen did not trust hedges. They were prickly and aggressive, and if you weren't watching where you were going, you could accidentally tumble over one. That was the cause for concern with regular hedges, at least. These bushes, however, were atypical. Laughter rose from the surface of them like mist pouring from a frigid sea. It was a disturbing combination, the high-pitched giggle comingling with the lonely drawn-out note of a guitar out of tune. The sound reminded her of being trapped in a dressing room when she was in elementary school. The door had latched closed and refused to open, and panic built as she listened to the cruel laugh of Stella, who ignored her panic as she shopped and flirted with the saleswoman. Later, Stella would tell her "nerves aren't born of steel, they are made of them. Consider this a free lesson."

Stella gave a lot of lessons.

A surprisingly aggressive patch of sunlight cut through the cold air, heating the tip of her nose and the backs of her hands as she pressed them on top of her head. The laugh continued its ascent from the shrubbery. The tone shifted, the giggle inescapable, familiar, and haunting. And definitely not her aunt's.

It was a sound she had never heard outside of a single recording; one she had worn out as a child. It contained the voice of her mother.

High-pitched and near-maniacal, *this* sound was warped and elongated. A strum of the guitar, light and climbing in melody, paired with the giggle on repeat. The sound drew her closer, an inch, a breath, even as her arms shook and goosebumps prickled across her back. Doreen did not know if this magic was courtesy of Ambrose's family wards, for surely there were many on the grounds of a castle that kept itself hidden, or if it was something else. The taunting giggle getting stuck in the sigil, perhaps. Or a message sent from her coven. A slap across her face before one of them stabbed her in the chest. This sound was vile, twisting a memory and bringing it to life when it should remain dead in the grave.

She forced one foot up and back. She might as well have been trying to raise a monolith for how immovable her limbs were against the onslaught of her mother's laughter. It was not surprising to Doreen that heartbreak was the most powerful of spells. It was matched to the wave of a note stark and warbled when it should have been soft.

The longing slammed into her and drained every ounce of energy from her body, stole her ability to care, to move, to do anything more than collapse into herself like a supernova.

The sun drifted over the leaves, rustling across their coppery surface. A shimmering shape crossed into her line of sight. The laughter ceased, the wind blew cold, and Doreen blinked. A woman hovered before her. Her spirit restless, her sadness pervasive. It was like a mist, brushing over her cheeks, down her neck, across the backs of her hands.

"Who are you?" Doreen whispered, searching her face for a sign that somehow, here was her long-lost mother. But as soon as she opened herself, she knew it was not her. She was struck with a bitter mix of sorrow and relief, soon followed by a wash of calm. It slunk across her shoulders as the appearance of the spirit somehow drove back the laughter.

The woman was a profile of gossamer. She shimmered brighter, and Doreen could almost hear her words, an urgent plea, but as soon as her ear tuned into the octave of spirit, she was gone. It was as though Doreen tapping into her frequency had scrambled the ghost's ability to linger in any corporeal way. A burst of light shot out of the shrubs, and Doreen backed away until she was far from the labyrinth of hedges, gasping for breath and facing the entrance of the castle.

She looked once over her shoulder at the hedge before she took off running for the arch that led to the entrance. Doreen didn't see Ambrose anywhere, but she didn't need to. He was home, whether he wanted to be or not, and there was no other place he could be but inside.

She slowed as she reached the entrance, her gaze catching on the violet wisteria and ivy. Locking onto the immense stonework, and the obscene breadth of the castle walls, she stopped under the arch and looked up to the circle carved into the stone with two trees etched inside it. She reached into her pocket and removed the stone she had pulled from the fire. She ran her thumb across it. The two engravings matched. Only one tree was upside down with a line marked over the top and the other right side up with a line marked under the trunk. Yin and yang.

Doreen cupped the stone in her palm and walked deeper in, through the little courtyard, to the thick wooden doors that were thrown wide open. Inside, she stopped abruptly. Took a shallow breath and stared.

Ambrose stood before her, his shoulders wide, his head dipped. His back was to her, and he had both arms braced on the table before him. Not quite on the surface, but instead curling his fingers under the solid oak that supported a slab of marble on top of it. The view of him was startling. He was like a storybook character waiting to be written. She hated how hard it was to look away from him. Perhaps, Doreen reasoned, because she was in Scotland, on a section of cliffs on the Isle of Skye, and everything about being inside the Goodbye

Castle screamed Gothic mystery. It was natural her mind cast him in a role of doomed knight.

When she pulled her gaze away, her eyes went from one fireplace to the next. They crackled in welcome. Hints of cider and allspice drifted on the air, the scents warm and inviting. It juxtaposed the tension radiating off Ambrose. Such an atmosphere would normally have had Doreen wishing for an oversized wingback chair, a cashmere blanket, and a good book, if not for the disarming man standing before her.

He turned to her, and a cold wind blew down the corridor, sweeping into the room and nearly brushing Doreen aside. The fires flickered out. Her gaze tracked to the walls, which grew damp, then the floor, which shifted from gleaming to grimy.

"Did you see her?" he asked, his voice a pit of gravel and pain.

"Who?" Doreen said, even as her mind toggled back to the image of the ghost hovering near the hedgerow.

"Lenora," he said, the word more breath than sound.

A hard weight plummeted into her stomach. A warbled note rose and slammed into her side, and she shifted away from it. She refused to let the sorrow-filled song move her.

She might have known the spirit who sent the haunting giggles away was Lenora. The woman had been the love of his life. Where else would she go but to the castle that should claim him? Lenora was watching over him; she had been waiting.

Doreen looked over her shoulder, expecting to see her hovering there, and pressed her lips together to bite back the confused irritation pressing against her shoulder blades. It didn't belong there.

Ambrose gave a low snort, and Doreen looked over to him. His eyes seemed lighter, *his* mouth not quite so tight, as he stared at her.

"What?" she asked.

"It's just . . . the wheels in your mind spin so loud even I can hear them."

"Very funny," she said, narrowing her eyes, praying to the gods he couldn't read the truth on her face. "It must be hard as a ghost, to be stuck here."

"Spirits aren't stuck anywhere," he said, his voice thick with pain before his expression shuttered. "Most aren't, at least."

"You don't think she is?"

"No." He shook his head. "I never . . . I didn't see her, when I was stuck in the nightmare curse your coven held me under. I could see into this castle, into all the spaces that are part of my lineage, part of my blood. I saw others but never her. She must move freely enough. He was stuck here, though."

"He?" Doreen asked, stepping closer to Ambrose and looking around him, expecting to see another ghost waiting. The air was clear.

Ambrose inclined his head toward the far north corner of the room. "The viscount." He cleared his throat, and when he spoke, the emptiness in his tone left Doreen cold. "Bloody bastard married a lass his brother fell in love with and then sent her back to her family naked on a horse in shame. They tossed her out and left her to her death. The viscount's brother threw him into the dungeon after she died. Tortured him."

"That's horrible." Doreen's eyes widened as she downloaded the information. "He died in the dungeon?"

"Yes, after he killed his brother."

"How did the viscount kill him if he was being tortured by him?"

"He got one arm free and choked him with the last of his strength. Then starved the rest of his days, still half attached to the wall by a manacle."

Doreen shuddered, looking for the viscount. "He's not showing himself to me."

"Small mercy," Ambrose said. "Give him time."

"Something to look forward to, then," Doreen said, flashing him her brightest smile.

He rolled his eyes, appearing far too normal for her comfort.

"Was this your family dining table?" she asked, looking to the giant slab of marble. It could seat at least sixteen people.

"No one has ever eaten off this table," Ambrose said, a thread of sorrow returning to his tone.

"It's a bit large for an entry table," Doreen mused.

"It's where we would honor the dead," he said, brushing his fingers over the wooden side once, before moving away.

"Honor?"

"They would rest here on the marble while we sat vigil with them before we returned them to the earth," he said.

Doreen couldn't repress the shockwave as it worked its way up her spine, even as she thought there was something lovely about a vigil to honor those you lost. A final goodbye.

"No wonder the ghosts don't leave," she whispered.

Ambrose gave a shake of his head but didn't reply. He led her down a wide hall, dank and dark aside from a flicker of light coming in through thin slats every seven feet. "Why are there holes in your castle?"

"Artillery," he said. "Need a place to shoot arrows, catapult the silver, that sort of thing."

"Catapult? I can't tell if you're joking."

"I never joke," he said.

They turned down one hall, then another. Doreen peeked in rooms as best she could, feeling as though they were scurrying like mice down the passages. As they passed the ornate sconces, their centers lit up with flames, though no torches remained. Fire drew itself to Ambrose, much as the wind seemed to be chasing after Doreen's footsteps here in the castle. Each room Doreen spied into was tiny. High ceilings lifted them up, but they contained no space in which to spread out. They were the opposite of the halls, which felt wide and cavernous.

"Can you slow down?" she asked, struggling to keep up with Ambrose and his uncommonly long legs.

"I prefer not to."

"Can you at least tell me where we're going?"

"No."

"Why not?"

"Because I don't know where we're going."

"That makes no sense."

"Sure it does," he said. He hesitated, then added, "Maybe it doesn't. If I tell you what I'm doing, you might not like it."

"Why don't you try me?"

"I'm following a ghost trail."

"You're what?"

Ambrose paused, looking over his shoulder. "I should have guessed. You don't know what a ghost trail is?"

Doreen looked down at the ground and along the walls. "I don't see any trail."

"Close your eyes," he said. "Open to the space between here and hereafter."

"I tried that in the garden of attacking hedgerows," she said. "Lenora was there, and when I tried to open myself, she disappeared."

Ambrose's brows drew together.

A trilling of notes, like fingers tapping one after the other, danced through the air. Doreen swallowed and forced her wince into something resembling consternation. Or so she hoped. "Is this the viscount?"

He shook his head. "It's Sinclair."

"Who?"

"My valet."

"From when you were a child?"

"Yes."

"Is Sinclair also into murder?"

"Not usually."

"Terrific," she said brightly. "So, is following a witch trail like following a phosphorous night-light of a trail? Because that is what it sounds like."

"No, it's an 'I'm a trained witch, and your family purposefully kept you in the dark so you are modestly inept' sort of thing."

"Ouch," Doreen said, rubbing her sternum as the jab found and hit its mark.

He sighed, and scrubbed a hand over his face before turning from her. Doreen wondered if the sight of her made him physically ill; if he couldn't help but be reminded of those who had tortured him. Her throat constricted at the idea.

"I have a connection to Sinclair," he said after a long silence.

She studied the back of his neck, how the dark hair curled there and found a freckle hiding beneath the curl. She scolded her eyes and looked down the long corridor instead. "What kind of connection?"

"He saved my life."

"Your life?"

"Yes."

"How?"

"The usual way. Stopped someone from killing me."

"Wouldn't that have bound you to him?"

"I may have also saved his."

"I don't understand," she said, her eyes winning the war she waged and returning to him.

Ambrose rubbed a hand over his head, his long fingers brushing the curl when it got to his neck. Doreen swallowed as he turned to her, and she studied his face. "I was colicky as a child. It was . . . hard on my mother. Sinclair was close to her, and he stepped in at night, walking me up and down the halls so she could sleep. They said the movement soothed me."

"How did that save your life?"

"My father didn't care for my crying; he'd planned to smother me in my sleep, but Sinclair intervened by caring for me and giving my mother the rest she needed so she didn't come apart. Sinclair was outspoken and often caught my father's ire as well. His calming me, and in so doing calming my mother's nerves, saved us both. He was always there, to step in."

"Bloody hell."

"It could have been."

"Have you noticed all the males in your line were bloodthirsty assholes?"

Ambrose's nostrils flared.

"Just asking."

"It was a different time."

"It always is." She wanted to ask what else his dad had done, and how he'd survived, but she didn't think now was the time to pry. She wished she didn't feel compelled to pry at all. She waved an arm ahead of them instead. "Lead on?"

He inclined his head before turning down another hallway. They walked a short way, stopping in front of a dark stairwell. Doreen made herself look at his back instead of the diverting freckle on his neck.

Ambrose lifted a hand, and a torch rose from its holder, floating into his outstretched hand. He curled his fingers around the handle, muttering something under his breath.

"Is fire your element?" she asked, as the heat of the flames licked alongside her neck and cheek. "Along with being a seer?"

"No," he said, turning his face from hers.

"And yet all the lights flicker alive in your presence here."

"Fire is the castle's element. I am the spark."

"Does that mean the castle sat in darkness for the past three hundred years?"

"While your family tortured me? Yes, likely it does."

"Oh."

"Worrying the ghosts might turn on you?"

"Maybe."

Ambrose's lip might have twitched, or it could have been a frown trying to pull it down. "Mind the steps," he said, and then he was moving up and away. So went the light, leaving Doreen to scramble after him into the narrow stairwell.

The stairwell was a slim tube. Doreen thought, as she climbed the small angled steps, that it was like being stuck inside a straw as it was shrinking. The light in the stairwell was a concerning shade of yellow, her vision changing as panic set in. The fading light shined against the cracks in the stone. Doreen put one hand against the nearest shrinking wall and tried to draw in a breath. Each inhale seemed to bring the walls closer to her. "Why is it so fucking tiny in here?" she managed to gasp out.

"To conserve heat," Ambrose said, "and to give the advantage to those upstairs."

Doreen tried to draw in a deep breath and failed. "How?"

"The person coming downstairs has a wider expanse of stair, since they are cut on the diagonal. When coming down with a sword drawn, it makes it easier to stab the target, kill them, and keep moving."

"Of course. Silly of me not to realize," Doreen said, before her knees gave out. She slumped into the wall, her heart beating in her ears, the stairwell beginning to close in on her completely.

Ambrose stopped, bent, and pulled her up and in front of him. He didn't say a word, just held the light above his head and wrapped a solid arm around her waist. The feel of him had her breathing in, and then he was shifting so he could guide her up the next step. He walked them one step after another, his chest and heart against her back, urging her own to keep beating.

"Did you know my great-grandmother dreamed of lining the interior of the stairwell with fabric the color of moss and flowers the size of her head?" Ambrose said. "She was fixated on it. Used to draw them in her sleep. There is a room on the uppermost level where all the walls are covered in the remnants of her charcoal creations." Ambrose spoke in a low, velvety tone, chatting on about his grandmother and her peculiarities as he guided her up. The patter didn't make a lot of sense, but it distracted Doreen enough to keep her moving until she reached an opening and could stumble out of it onto a solid floor with walls the typical distance apart.

Doreen's breath continued to evade her, and she gasped tiny sips in, one after the other, while thinking perhaps she would need to be airlifted from the castle. She was never going back in that stairwell again, could hardly see how she would make it another step, and so there was no way she'd get down ever again.

"You're not breathing," Ambrose said, his voice deep and low, the words coming out in a discernable puff across her neck.

She failed to draw in a deeper breath. "Hard to breathe when you're having a panic attack."

Ambrose kept the hand on her waist steady. He placed her shaking hand on his chest and took a deep breath in. She watched her hand rise and fall. "Now you," he said. Doreen followed the rhythm of his heart and found she could draw a deeper intake of air, and then another.

As her breath grew more balanced, her thoughts spiraled.

There was little standing in the way of Doreen having a complete breakdown, outside of the man before her. The stingray who studied and steadied her. That he was anchoring her was troubling for so many reasons. She followed the sound of Ambrose's breath, letting her chest rise and fall to the rhythm. In the back of her mind, she heard a violin sing. A warble of one string, the tug of it being pulled back and rubbed too closely to another. The room shifted, spinning upward, as her heart sped up and then plummeted.

When she was a kid, Doreen had lost control of her magic, and with it, her breath. But Margot had steadied her, saying, "It's not a matter of mind over emotions. It's a matter of not trying to control the uncontrollable. Be here now. Be. Here. Now."

"You are," Ambrose said, his voice cutting in through the static of her mind.

Doreen found her footing back in reality like a baby finds the ground with its first steps. "Ambrose?"

The room drifted back into focus. Doreen took in the light cutting across the slate-gray floor, making the cracks in the stone sparkle. Her eyes tracked to Ambrose's shoes, the faded patches on the scuffed dark boots. She wondered how old the boots were. Had her aunts allowed him to change them over the years? Were they three sizes too small and meant to torture him further? Or did he acquire them after she freed him? She didn't remember him having shoes of any kind when she'd found him inside the Dead House, but also didn't recall him buying these in Portree. Doreen looked up, and her gaze snagged on the thickness of his thighs, the tautness of his forearms, and finally the pinched consternation of his determined mouth.

"I am?" she asked, her words scratchy and unsure.

"You said, 'Be here now,'" Ambrose said. "I thought it might help to know you are. You didn't go anywhere."

"I had a panic attack."

"It's hard to exist inside the Goodbye Castle," he said.

"I used to suffer from them," she said. "When I was learning how to use my magic, we didn't get a lot of formal instruction because Stella was busy and prickly. I messed up a lot. Margot thought that was why my breath got stuck inside me." She swallowed around a knot in the back of her throat. "Margot was the only one who ever helped. She didn't judge the episodes, or me."

"Why would someone judge you over something you can't help?" Ambrose asked, the hand on her waist squeezing gently.

"I thought you had been eavesdropping on the modern world," Doreen said, trying to keep her tone light, to keep the hurt tucked away. "We judge first, provide compassion last. If at all."

"Then I am sorry."

Doreen looked up at him, shocked. "What?"

"It is unfair to be judged for things out of your control." His eyes were less turquoise in the castle here; she saw a grayish blue circled in a thick ring of black. "But what you experienced in the stairwell wasn't a panic attack."

"Yes, it was." Her fingers twitched under his hand, where he held it to his chest. "The room shrank, and I thought I was losing my mind. My heart morphed into a Clydesdale, and I knew I would die if I had to spend one more second in that tiny mouse's closet of a stairwell." She shuddered. "Imagining Sinclair and Magnus the Third in a swordfight to the death did little to help my undiluted fear."

Ambrose's eyes softened. "It was not a panic attack," he repeated. "Truly. That was a battle waged by the spirits of the Goodbye Castle."

He squeezed her hand and released where he held it. She did not move hers from his chest, though. She studied the dark blue of his eyes, how there was a band of silver before the black. "Ghosts of your freaky fortress caused me to nearly lose my mind?"

"Not exactly," he said, staring back intently. "There is a line drawn here, and the veil between what was and what is blurs on this not-so-hallowed ground. It grows so thin, anything can happen. The truth of what was blends into the possibility of what can be, and it changes the coloring of the landscape around us and under us."

"Oh, wow." Doreen stepped away, breaking contact with his body.

Touching Ambrose was too confusing. She ran her hands over her face, pinching her cheeks, trying to return the circulation back to her limbs. "I don't know if I feel better or worse knowing that."

Ambrose reached out, his fingers gently tapping against the inside of her arm. "That is your proof."

She looked down at her arm. Directly beneath the bend in her elbow was a patch of white, a series of large dots that connected.

"It's a birthmark," she said. "A constellation to nowhere."

"It's more than that," he mused.

Doreen brushed her thumb across it. "All the women in my family have them," she said. "Witches' blood, witches' marks. King James VI would have loved us."

"He would have loved trying to drown you after his cronies forced a week of sleep deprivation on you." Ambrose removed his hand, the touch lingering long after his fingers left. "Ada showed me something I don't think she meant to," he said. "On the walls. Or something, perhaps, she didn't realize I would understand."

"Your vision? I thought it showed you to come here?"

"It did, but I saw something else too. I didn't understand it until now. Lenora once told me a story. About thin places and the markings witches left for them. How the mark she carried was from fragments of something not of this world. She gave me the knowledge of how to recognize the thin places should I ever need to cross between the worlds. So many of them are guarded by stones carved and crafted, built from sacrifice and power. Like the Goodbye Castle. It has the same fractals in the walls as the ones in Ada's cave, the same as on your arm. That is why Sinclair led us here."

Doreen looked to the wall where Ambrose was looking. It seemed perfectly ordinary. "I still don't see anything. No fractals or phosphorous anything. Not a drop."

He glanced at her. "What did you take from Ada's fire?"

"This?" She took it from her pocket, rubbing her thumb over it as she looked down.

He held his hand out.

"The tree of life," he said as she placed the stone there, "inside a circle. Ada meant for this to guide you."

"I don't know how to use it."

He stared, tracing the stone with the pad of his finger. "Lenora had a favorite spell, one she used often. She would tap on the face of skipping stones and whisper to them: *The awakened power in me sees all.*"

He handed the stone back to her. "Perhaps start there?"

Doreen tapped three times on the surface of the stone, speaking the words he'd shared. She was glad to have his help, and yet . . . she barely resisted wrinkling her nose. Lenora was her ancestor, but gods, it grated hearing him talk about her like she was the first coming of a deity. As Doreen whispered the last of the words, the center of the stone shifted from solid to transparent. From a solid rock to . . .

"*Oh,*" she said, the realization sinking in. "Lenora taught you how to make hag stones."

"Aye," he said, his smile small but beautiful. Then he blinked and stared so deep into her eyes, she had to force her feet to root so she didn't wobble. "I wonder, though, why no one taught you."

She swallowed, hating the reminder of what had been kept from her, as much as she hated the reminder that those who had shielded her from that knowledge were coming to stop her.

Panic and fear be damned, she and Ambrose needed to move faster. Doreen lifted the stone and looked through the center of it to the wall. The same lines she had seen at Ada's were scattered across the surface. Pictish Beasts and fractals interwoven together. She narrowed her eyes when she realized Ambrose had been correct; the spot on her arm looked a lot like broken parts of the fractals on the wall. "I see what you mean."

"As I said, we are in a thin place," Ambrose said.

"What do we do?"

"We cross."

"How? Draw a circle, create a door?"

Ambrose shook his head. "It's a bit less complex than that."

She furrowed her eyebrows, waiting, hoping she looked menacing. When his lip twitched again, she had her doubts, but his head gave a tilt to the archway on the other end of the room, and then he nodded to her stone.

Doreen lifted it again and saw the tree of life and the Pictish fractals repeating in a pattern around the edge of the doorway. "Oh."

She blew out a breath, grateful the shakiness had departed from her limbs. She walked toward the doorway. Ambrose followed close behind. "Where *is* your Sinclair, by the way?"

"Ah. He's trying to block the door."

She looked over her shoulder. "Are you joking?"

"No."

"Why is he trying to block the door he showed us?" she asked, squinting but not seeing him anywhere, through the stone or without it.

"He likely feels compelled to give me the answers, while trying to protect me."

"Protect you from what?"

"What do you know about thin places?"

Doreen swallowed, thinking that if a *ghost* was afraid of something, it did not bode well for them. "Margot and I found a book about them once in a box at the apothecary shop," she said. "The author said thin places were the spaces where the world was loosely knit together, and you couldn't experience them with any of the five senses."

"I don't know that I believe in coincidence and magic. The book was likely meant to find you, and what the author wrote is true," Ambrose said, his steps as slow and measured as Doreen's as they inched toward the arch. "However, there is an *asterisk* to it. Those who are open to the truth can find their way to thin places at any time."

"And what do we find in the thin places?"

"A door to a world beyond this one. The start of an adventure."

"You mean the trials?"

"Sinclair led us here, and it may well have cost him to do so. We're in the gloaming now, the twilight between worlds."

"It's another spell."

"It is the spell."

"The spell is the truth," Doreen whispered. *The truth was the spell.*

Was Doreen ready?

She reached the arch and stared up at how it shimmered. Twinkling light as soft as gossamer filled its opening. Here was the door to the trials. There was no going back, and there was no guarantee that if she stepped through, she would succeed.

But there had never been any guarantees for Doreen, and if she was willing to bet on anyone, it would be herself.

Though she wasn't alone.

Going on instinct, she held out a hand. Ambrose took it, threading his fingers with hers. For a moment, Doreen was back in the fountain, Ambrose bare before her, and she was flooded with hope.

It didn't matter if she was ready; it hardly mattered what they would find on the other side. They had to keep going, and they needed to outrun her family. She gave him a gentle tug. Together they stepped through the doorway and out.

And onto the thin lip of a very old, crumbling, precarious ledge.

The skies were ashen. Slate-gray clouds bordered by darkness, and just beyond them it faded into a white mist that blanketed the edge of the world. The wind whipped against their faces, as cold and severe as the warning had been in Ada's eyes when she'd made the deal with Ambrose so many years ago. The rain lashed for long minutes, and Ambrose dared not move a single inch. Thunder cracked across the moors, the sounds not unlike a cackling queen, calling for the games to begin.

Ambrose's palm was sweating, and the rain didn't help. After many, many years of torture, if there was one thing left that he feared, it was heights. He blamed his family. So many had succumbed to dastardly ends by way of elevation. They were pushed, dropped, felled. Off cliffs, ledges, and roofs.

He could not let Doreen see this, not when she had nearly crumbled to dust in front of his eyes not so long ago. Not when his heart had stuttered at her fall in the stairwell. A current of possessiveness ran through him now, and he might hate it, but he had yet to dislodge it.

And dislodge it he must. There was little more dangerous than the way his heart had squeezed over seeing her in distress.

Ambrose focused on what the first test for the trials would be. Thin places steal time, but they expose what is true. Ambrose knew what was necessary, what this journey required. To reach the other side of this one, they would need to take a leap of faith. It's why they were on the bloody ledge.

He swallowed and looked down at the determined witch beside him.

"Don't say it," she said, her voice coming out a squeak.

"Okay."

"We have to jump, don't we?"

"You asked me not to say it."

"Fuck."

"Pretty much."

She let out a hysterical laugh, then looked up at him. "Together?"

Ambrose took in a breath, but it only reached the shallow places of his lungs. He stared deep into her honey eyes and thought how much she looked like herself in this moment. Not Lenora, not her mother, not anyone other than Doreen, the forgotten witch of the MacKinnon line. Fierce, even though terrified.

"Together," he said, knowing that he was agreeing to follow her into hell, and that after this there would be no turning back. He could only hope the outcome would be worth the fall. They would enter the trials, he could trap her family, and he would gain his redemption.

Doreen smiled, tilted her head up, and pressed her lips to his cheek. Ambrose started, his mouth parting in shock. His heart gave another thump of warning and he thought of what he could never tell her.

The trials would be a success for him, but it was a lost cause for her. Because the darkest secret Ambrose kept was this: a MacKinnon witch claiming his heart was the only way the curse would be broken.

And he would find a way to die before he ever fell in love with another MacKinnon.

He swallowed and started to untangle their hands—the proximity, the way her eyes were steady on his, it was too much. Doreen's grip loosened and dropped. For a moment, his fingers strained for what had been there moments before, anchoring him.

Then she reached up, wrapped her hand in his shirt, and yanked, sending them both tumbling over the edge.

NINE

Dust doesn't bother ghosts. Dust, dirt, grime, cracked floors, scattered glass, damaged hearts, dried blood, cracked toenails. These were things to be used. To blend into paste and press to the wind as they merged and formed something new. Something petrifying.

Ada liked decay. She liked mess and disorder, the way the world was more broken than whole. It was a reflection, she thought, of what waited for her in the mirror. In her caves, she moved in and out of the shadows, taking a pinch of shade here, a nibble of essence there. Her hands roamed, and if one looked close enough, they might see the way they pulled a hint of light from the darkness.

Shadows were echoes of souls, so the bits didn't fill her up the way the real thing did, but she found it satisfying in the way icing complements a cake. They were fuel and they were power.

Ada stopped in the crypt hidden inside the tunnels under the canals. Here was a forgotten graveyard, one that once housed the bodies of former queens and kings, of witches meant to rule and reign. Superstitious, that's what the living were, and why they forgot about these witches and their lineage. If they had remembered, they'd have to be terrified of them. Creatures who had held the true magic of the world, before it was plucked away by the gods.

She crossed to one of the crumbling holes in the far wall and reached inside. She pulled out a small box with a set of symbols carved across its surface. She scratched in new lines, the symbols solving the lock, and then opened the box, revealing a smaller box made of pewter.

She scratched the same symbols into its surface and the top sprung open, revealing a small wooden doll, with a gaping mouth and tattered dress.

Ada removed the doll, brushing a hand down the few strands of human hair clinging to its head. She pressed a finger to one brow and then the other, before singing softly to it. She cradled it in her arms, circling the room, the haunting lullaby bouncing off the floors and walls, filling the air.

"Wake for me,
  Light the day,
  Bring me truth,
  Show me the way."

As Ada sang, the doll's eyes filled with light, blinking up at her. Impossibly, its mouth stretched wider, a cavernous yawn, emitting a brilliant glow. Light sparked and glittered, and Ada lowered her face to the doll's, pursing her lips as though she were preparing to kiss the screaming mouth.

She leaned in, hovering an inch away, and sang louder. The light lifted from the doll like breath on an exhale and flowed from its mouth into Ada's until her form flickered. Ada's eyes shifted from pearls to an iridescent violet, and back again. She drew in a long lilting sound, like a deep bell being rung, before she burst into a firework of dazzling light and ether: particles and starlight. The remaining dust in the room flew into the air and sprinkled down, raining ashes and history. The doll rolled onto the floor, rocking from side to side, its mouth open, the eyes blackened out.

Ada was more, but someone, somewhere, was less.

D oreen fell for a very long handful of seconds before hitting the water hard. It slapped against her side, bubbles coming up and tickling her nose as she tried to pinwheel her arms. She couldn't feel Ambrose's hand anymore. He had let go, or she had let go, and now she was going to drown in a murky body of water beneath the castle.

Doreen thought of what a tour guide had once told her, about how the people who lived in castles had thrown their bodily fluids out the upper windows and into the moats that surrounded them. She was swimming in pee water . . . or worse. Of course, there could be fish and other creatures in the water, so they likely peed in it as well. Really, she was swimming in a petri dish, that might also have a Loch Ness Monster, which would have a lot of byproduct, and . . . she forced her mouth to stay closed as the scream built and the pressure to breathe crushed against her lungs. She swam up, and up, and up, and as she reached for the surface, her breath fighting to get free, she remembered.

The Goodbye Castle didn't have a moat. Or a body of water surrounding it, outside of the sea beyond the cliffs.

Where the hell was she?

Doreen broke through the surface, gasping and panicking. She looked over to see Ambrose swimming toward her. Strong arms slicing through the dark water. Relief cut through her, until she took in the terror on his face.

"Go!"

"What?"

"Now," he shouted.

Doreen saw beyond Ambrose's broad shoulders to where the water splashed behind him. There was foam floating on top of the navy waves, ripples spiraling out. But her mind struggled to compute the rest of the image. What she was seeing was *impossible.* Rising out of the water were two large nostrils attached to an elongated snout. Wide eyes tinged with crimson flashed as it surfaced above the water for a moment. Sharp, pointed ears peeked out, twitching back. As it dove, its jaws snapped into the water, as though it were practicing how it would eat them, and that's when she understood.

She was seeing not a horse, but a myth. A kelpie.

The breath froze in her lungs, and she tried to think. There was no physical way they could ever outrun a kelpie. They moved at an impossible speed on water and land.

She knew enough about the creatures from Stella's library and the mythology tucked away there. There were few approved books Doreen and Margot hadn't perused during the hot and endless summers of their youth. But she had no idea how to get rid of a kelpie.

The not-quite-a-horse gave a cry that was part whinny and part roar, and Doreen wished for Margot. She would know what to do. Margot had handled their last water threat: one spring they had gone swimming in No Man's Lake on the edge of town and faced a pack of abused dogs that had gotten loose. They had been in the center of the lake when they heard the dogs prowling on the shore. Doreen had panicked, screaming as she saw them slinking into the water. Margot had asked Doreen to swim closer to her. Then when Doreen tried to rush her to shore, Margot had quietly told her to wait. She'd been calm, controlled.

Once the feral dogs were close enough, Margot had started to cast. A spell she later confessed she'd made up in the bathtub years prior while playing with her Barbies. Without missing a beat, Margot spelled the water to form an underwater cyclone. It pulled the dogs under until the girls were up on the shoreline and far enough away before she released them.

It was Margot's spell, and it would have to do.

The words returned to Doreen in a rush the way all key memories find their way home. She spoke them quickly and clearly:

"Into the water
  You will go
   To lose your strength
   And save our souls."

A child's spell, pulled from one of her cousin's favorite poems, it had the potency of rarely being used and hardly ever spoken. The water swooshed away from Doreen, careening out and into the racing kelpie. It let out an anguished cry before being sucked under.

Doreen didn't wait. She shifted from treading water to freestyle and swam as fast as her arms could pull her. She reached the water's edge and clambered up, and then Ambrose was beside her, dripping wet and looping an arm around her waist once more. Together, they ran up the embankment and straight into the waiting entrance of what looked exactly like, and yet could not be, the Goodbye Castle.

The fires lit as soon as they crossed the entryway, and the doors slammed shut behind them. Doreen stumbled forward and dropped into the seat of a tall wingback chair. She fought to catch her breath as her eyes took in the room. It looked almost exactly as it had the last time she had been in it. Two oversized fireplaces, and a looming hallway and stairwell. Only now, there was no marble table, no scent of cedar and clove. The air was perfumed instead with the aroma of decaying roses. The addition of the two deep-green wingback chairs weren't the only changes either.

Directly above Doreen and Ambrose floated a chandelier. At least, that's what Doreen thought it was. It hovered overhead, a series of hooked pieces of ivory tethered together with enough space for candles to be wedged inside.

"That's new," Doreen said, looking up, and as she spoke, the candles flickered to life. Black flames licked up into the dusty rafters.

Ambrose squinted overhead. "That's a statement not even my family would make."

"What do you mean?"

"There are a lot of uses for bones, but a candelabra is not one the MacDonalds typically chose for austere décor."

"Those are bones?" Doreen asked, her toes curling in her wet shoes at the idea. "Those poor deer."

"I doubt those are from Bambi."

"No?"

He shrugged.

"If you're implying those are human bones, I just . . . I can't." She stared up, the boat shape of the centerpiece shifting from an intricate vessel to a basic structure of connected bones. Understanding clicked in Doreen's mind and she let out a squeak. It was a rib cage, and spreading out from it were longer bones attached to a series of smaller ones. "It's a torso, with arms and hands. Dear gods."

Ambrose shifted closer to stand beside her at the edge of the chair. "The original castle was built with the bones of those who wronged my family. Why should this be any different?"

"I am trying to avoid the reality that we are not where we should be, thanks," Doreen said, swallowing.

The moat, the chairs, the bone chandelier. That fucking kelpie. They weren't in their version of Scotland anymore. They couldn't be.

"Where did we go when we went through that door and over the ledge?"

"Where do you think?"

"I think part of me is scared of the answer."

"Let me know when you get over your avoidant tendencies," Ambrose said, closing his eyes and resting a hand on the back of her chair. "Or if you hear that hound of hell coming."

"Hounds are dogs."

"Hound means to pursue," he said. "We have pursuers here in the—"

She shook her head. "Don't finish that sentence."

"—motherworld."

"Shit."

Doreen pulled her knees up into her chest. She wrapped her arms around them and tucked her forehead into the crook of her knees. She turned her head to the side, needing the reassurance of seeing him. "The trials are in the motherworld? As in the underworld?" As in purgatory, the stopover between the living and the dead. The gateway to hell.

"Where else would they be?"

"Somewhere sunny and nice."

"Sure. What did you do before?" he asked, one eye peeking open. "To the kelpie?"

"I used one of Margot's spells she created when we were kids to torture her dolls. She used it to save us from a pack of angry dogs when we were in the middle of a lake once."

Ambrose was silent for a loaded moment. Doreen wasn't sure how she felt about being able to read his silences. It was too intimate, especially when she considered how prominent his cheekbones were against the dark slips of hair that clung along the ridge of his brow. She wanted to brush the strands back, know how his skin felt to the touch. Gods, being in the motherworld was scrambling her brain.

"Your cousin, the one who warned you, that's Margot?"

"Yes, she's my best friend. Or she was. Before she married her Dean."

His mouth twitched. "I didn't realize a name could sound like a curse."

"You've never met a Dean."

"You are telling me she can create new spells?"

"Um."

"Which means, since you used her original creation, you can mimic."

"None of that is what I said."

"It was implied. You're a mimic."

"I am extraordinary," she said, feeling exposed, and yet, caring less. They were in an underworld, attempting trials, and they were a team, just the two of them. Truly. No going back now.

"It's not done," he said, both eyes open and on hers. Warming her in ways the fire was failing to.

"What isn't?"

"New spells and mimicking them. New spells require a counsel, or at least a coven. Solitary witches can't create them, or they didn't used to be able to. Solitary witches can't copy and re-create without knowing the intricacies."

"You've clearly never met Margot."

"It's not only her, but also you. The thirteenth generation." He let out a huff that may have been a sigh. "The rules do not apply to you as they do your ancestors, do they? Be careful of the magic you use, Doreen. When you create a spell in a place, the place keeps the memory of the spell. The truth of it."

He closed his eyes again with a sigh, and she turned hers back to the fire, relieved and a little annoyed Ambrose wasn't more intimidated. The logs crackled and snapped, and beneath the fire she heard it. A whisper of a melody. Not longing, not like the sigil. This melody was broken. It felt like a pause in the air, the kind where you reveal a secret only to have it used against you. Sorrowful. Distant sounds, a dissonant chord, one plucked too long before it was played again, this time with the ringing of a bell echoing at the end, close and then far off.

"Do you hear that?"

He shook his head.

Doreen stood and shifted closer. She gazed into the flames, watching as they transformed from gold to black. Inside them she saw a room, an antechamber, and a small wooden doll. As she stared, the doll rolled onto its side, its eyes finding hers and its mouth gaping. Doreen shivered, and the song whispered from its gaping mouth, the bells chiming, and the guitar plucking a mournful string. Doreen leaned closer, an inch, two, a breath further toward the flames and . . .

She was yanked back, one of Ambrose's arms around her waist, her heart in her throat.

"Are you trying to kill us both?" he asked, his voice low and thick with something she would call fear if she knew him any less.

"I . . ."

"Nearly dove *into the fire*."

"There was a doll," she said, her heart racing, the song still wrapped around her tighter than his arm. "A room and a song."

"It's a trap. The whole place will be a trap. We can't trust it or anything in it." He released her and took a step away. "We can't linger here any longer; we need to find the next step in the trials, complete it, and get the hell out."

"It's ridiculous the trials are held in this shadow of a world," she said, anger slipping out with her confusion and fear. "There is no otherworld, or there shouldn't be."

"The trials could never be in our world, Doreen," Ambrose said, rubbing at his brow. "They clearly require a leap of faith, which we took. I didn't consider where we'd leap to, but I should have."

A *click-click-clack*, long and startling taps, echoed down and around them, and drew their attention from the fire.

Doreen looked around, before she realized where the sound was coming from. *Up.* Her eyes were slow to travel to the ceiling and to the chandelier looming there. A single bone twitched, and then another. A slender finger, ivory and spiderish, lifted. One hand tapped out against the rib cage, a haunting melody that sounded like a person dancing into the room. The notes were familiar, and she tried to place them.

"He's right. You really shouldn't linger too long," a voice said, causing Doreen to jump back into Ambrose. A form materialized from the shadows flickering against the far wall. It drifted forward, the shape of a woman taking form. She was of medium height, with wide hips and long dark hair.

"Master of the lords and ladies," she said to Ambrose, before bowing. Ambrose blinked at the ghost. Sinclair had greeted him like that whenever he returned to the castle in the evening, teasing him that he was the little master of all the lords and ladies around him. Could this be his valet?

"Sinclair?" Ambrose said, as he stared, blinking, at the ghostly form.

"In one realm, yes, you did call me that," the ghost said.

"What do I call you here?" he asked, the disbelief still heavy in his voice.

"I am the creature of the castle," Sinclair said. "I haunt this realm, and you are not where you belong."

"Is that why we shouldn't linger?" Doreen asked, her hand automatically shifting to rest on Ambrose's shoulder. He relaxed into her palm at the contact.

"No," the ghost said, turning to face her. "You should not linger, Lady MacKinnon, for the rules of the upper world do not apply here.

There is nothing that will not hunt you here, nothing that will come without cost."

"We're here for the trials, Sinclair," Ambrose said. "We are aware there will be a cost."

Sinclair's mouth opened and shut. Once. Twice. She tilted her head, as though listening, before replying. "The trials are more than you imagine. So may the cost be. You must prove strength. Then courage. Then cunning. They are not easy."

"We are aware the tasks require all of our focus and will," Ambrose said.

"You consent?"

"We are here, aren't we?" Ambrose said. When Sinclair turned to Doreen, she gave a slight wave and nod. It was odd to converse with ghosts, especially in a place as cold and strange as this.

"Then you must seek the place where voices rise, where what should stay buried cannot, and where only the clever prevail. Find the cave of echoes, and do it fast before you lose your way."

"A creepy ghost *would* know where to go," Doreen muttered, her eyes drifting upward once more. "I hope it didn't bait us into a trap."

When she looked back, she found Sinclair bowing so low her hair brushed the floor. She shifted to go, before turning to them one last time, her form flickering. The ground rumbled and Sinclair's face grew clear.

"You are not safe," she said, her eyes on Doreen. In them, she read a warning, and worse—fear. For Ambrose? For her? "You cannot be here. Do not dare to trust."

Before she could ask more, the ghost was gone.

"What the hell was that?" Doreen asked.

"I have no idea."

"She seemed scared."

"And angry."

"I didn't think sprits had emotions," Doreen said.

"They don't," he said. "Not in the human way. At least not outside of Ada, but I think being a psychopath and a shade is less emotion and more personality type."

Doreen huffed out a sigh. "Your valet just warned us of imminent danger. Can you not take this a little seriously?"

Ambrose stared at her. "What part of jumping off the ledge of a castle, nearly being eaten by a kelpie, and then saving you from destroying yourself in a fire is me not taking this seriously?"

"The part where you focus on the wrong thing."

He shook her hand off. "I know what matters here, and it's not the chandelier or the fireplace."

"No kidding," she said, bringing her palms together, hating how his rejection cut.

"Sinclair told us what we face with the trials, and the location of the first one. I know where the cave of echoes is, any good Scotsman does. I can take my family ghost's warning at face, or spirit-face, value, because I do trust Sinclair."

"Fine, oh wise one," she said. "If we end up dead, it's your fault."

"Today is not the day for our death. Let's move," he called over his shoulder before walking down the hall, away from Doreen and toward the front door.

"Smart-ass ancient idiot," Doreen muttered.

"I heard that," he yelled.

Shaking her head, she followed him out.

The ghost in the wall, unseen by them both, watched and waited.

TEN

The sorrowful melody followed Doreen out of the castle into the grounds beyond. The sky overhead was wool gray with wisps of clouds speckled throughout, like smoke stuck in the atmosphere, unable to shift or move. A chill cut across the earth, sharp and biting. It brought hints of clove and rose, and something muskier, earthy and old, beneath it. The notes of a violin rose, quivering like a breaking heart. The drawn-out tones were piercing, and they were not alone.

A whisper rushed beneath the sound. *The woods are lovely, dark and deep. The woods are lovely, dark and deep. The woods are lovely, dark and deep.* The words sifted through the air, a poem Doreen had memorized as a teen, when she'd found that only the escape into poetry could mend the cracks inside her at being a girl who needed a mother and having a Stella instead. These near-forgotten words rained down on her, the cadence soaking into her bones as it blended with the rise of the violin's bright notes.

"Do you hear that?" she whispered to Ambrose. The patter of the rhyme brushing across her skin, a melancholic whisper at the edge of her ear.

"Oh, I hear something," Ambrose said, his expression tight.

All doubt Doreen might have had about where they were had evaporated as soon as they exited the castle. The moat awaited them, its water choppy, and beyond it the sky still the color of an oyster starting to oxidize. A shade beyond healthy. The horizon was tinged with indigo stars and a moon three sizes too big. The night smelled ripe with rain that didn't fall.

Together they walked down a pebbled road, the rocks beneath them a bright aquamarine. The stones they trod were rounded and looked vaguely like sea glass. Their beauty, especially against the near-sepia world, was unnerving.

"Are you going to tell me where we're going?" Doreen asked, peering down the path to where it shifted into a dirt track and eventually an overgrowth of weeds.

"Fingal's Cave," Ambrose said, wiping perspiration from his brow. It was ridiculously warm out, particularly for Scotland. Or Not Scotland, as Doreen supposed she should think of it.

"Isn't that a bit far from your castle?"

"I suppose it would be, but I don't think it will be."

"That makes no sense."

"No, but neither does anything here. We dove through the sky into a moat filled with a deranged kelpie and got a tip from my former male valet who is now a soft-spoken female ghost."

"Are kelpies anything other than deranged, historically speaking?"

He spared her a glance. "We're walking on a path that appears to be leading to Cill Chriosd, which it very much should not be. We wouldn't be able to get to the start of the trials and Fingal's Cave if they were where they should be, seeing as this is technically seventy kilometers away from where we're going, but as Cill Chriosd isn't where it should be, I suspect nothing else is either." Ambrose waved an arm to his left, and Doreen looked over to see a ruined stone structure in the distance, tucked beneath a ridge of mountains.

Mountains that looked like teeth.

She wrapped her arms around her waist as she stared at them looming on the horizon. "Those shouldn't be there either," she managed.

"I agree. It's worrisome that here there are no Black Cuillin ranges," Ambrose said. "Only red, and they are far larger than they should be."

"A red range, a midnight sky, and a supersized moon. We are in the land of death."

"Death is not loss, life is not winning," Ambrose said, looking around them, seeming to mark each misplaced landmark laid out before them. "Each to the other is a friend."

"Not the sort of friendship I've spent my life dreaming of," she said.

"You've spent your life dreaming of breaking the curse."

"Sure, because I want to find love. I want more, though. It would be nice to have friends."

"I suppose it would."

"Didn't you have friends?" she asked. "Before?"

"I had servants and expectations. Then, I had Lenora."

"Ah."

"What else do you want?" he asked, glancing at her for a split second before turning his face back to the road. "Besides breaking the curse."

"I would like to win," she said. "And not end up dead in the process."

"We are here to try to win," Ambrose said, before he flashed a quirk of a lip, making her stomach clench. "And I've been nearly dead for some time."

"*I'm* here to try," Doreen said, wishing he didn't affect her so much.

Wishing she didn't want him to tell her he'd like to be her friend, before he grabbed her hand and maybe threw her off the path to kiss the stars down from the violet sky.

This place was really messing with her.

"I have no idea what you're doing," she said, both to him and her mind.

He cut her a hard glance. "I am here, at your side. Isn't it obvious?"

"Nothing about you is obvious," she said, her voice coming out rough. "Other than how cranky you are."

"I'm not cranky," he said. "I am determined. I would like to win the transformation. You want to break the curse; I want to make sure nothing ever curses me again."

"Different but the same," she managed.

The wind blew a hard, angry gust that sent another round of whispers down on Doreen's shoulders, brushing against her cheeks and dripping down her forearms. She tried to wipe them away. This time they were in Margot's voice, the violin no longer heart-piercing and enchanting, but a shriek ripping into tin and tearing: *The woods are lovely, dark and deep . . . and miles to go before I sleep.*

"Shut. Up," Doreen whispered through gritted teeth.

"And you called me cranky," Ambrose said, taking a step away from her.

"It's the voices, and that bloody violin."

"Try humming."

"What?"

"Think of a different, soothing melody and hum it. In your head or out loud." He unleashed a growl that any demon would envy. Rubbed at his ear, yanking it, then pressing his palm to it. "We need to move faster."

Doreen wanted to argue. They had already been trudging for miles. They must have. She was drenched with sweat. Her shoulders pulled as tight as an overworked seam. Every muscle in her body strained at the effort of continuing down the never-ending path.

A bird bawled in the distance, a cry too human for comfort. She looked down and realized they had walked past the same cluster of stones at least twice. She looked up and there were the same mountains. They had been walking for at least an hour, possibly two, in a circle. Going nowhere and not terribly fast either.

She cursed under her breath, and looked over to see the stone structure in the distance. She struggled to make out the detail around the small foothold shapes set in front of it. Her vision blurred as she stared, unblinking. The whole of it reminded her of a helpful device. The dots and curve of the land, the green against the white.

"It's a map," she said. That was why they kept looping to this spot. Because they had missed what they needed to see. "I wonder . . ."

She took a single step to her left.

One step.

Two.

She stepped off the path.

The sky shifted from gray merged with midnight to dusk, the land under her feet fading from deserted earth to soft-shorn grass cushioning her aching soles.

Behind her, a pasture waited, hills rolling up and out into the horizon.

Before her stood the remains of the building, and surrounding it were a hundred graves placed along its edges.

She turned to Ambrose, to ask him what had happened.

But the path was gone, the castle erased.

Doreen was alone.

Doreen ran up and down the path, jumped on and over it, trying to return to Ambrose. She shouted his name, the wind whipping her voice with each call. Nothing brought her to him or him to her. Panic pressed against her throat and down into her belly. She looked up at the hill before her and hurried forward to climb it, hoping it would provide her a better view of the land so she could find Ambrose.

Instead, she found a cottage on the other side of it. It was a forgettable sight, the stone covered in soot and grime, the chimney too narrow for a strong fire, and the windows warped from age. And yet, as Doreen stood before it, her shoulders relaxed, her neck stopped cramping, and her jaw unclenched.

The door swung open, and the scent of sugar cookies drifted out.

Doreen didn't think. She didn't hesitate, not even a little. She walked inside.

The girl waiting couldn't have been older than ten. She was dressed in a fencer's outfit, white pants, shirt, gloves, and a strange wire mask that sat on top of her head, as though she had just pushed it up. Her feet were bare, and instead of a saber, she held a rolled-up piece of parchment.

"You're late," the girl cried as Doreen joined her inside.

Doreen's mouth dropped. The girl was familiar, as were her dark eyes and fiery hair. She couldn't determine how she knew her, but she did. "I know you," she said.

"You should. You don't," the girl said as she walked into a side room and shut the door.

Doreen stood inside the cottage, waiting, suddenly quite unsure of what drove her to enter. She would never march into a house she didn't know, in a place that shouldn't exist. But she had been compelled.

She studied the well-furnished room, with its faded hardwood floors covered by a large rug that reminded her of the sun setting into an ocean set ablaze. Angry waves of red and soothing yellows curved together into a series of intricate knots that left her stomach flipping. Doreen gave herself a shake—she needed to find Ambrose, not stand here staring at décor.

The door to the side room opened again, and out walked a woman in her twenties. She had the same dark eyes as the girl, though her hair was a bit less coppery and a lot looser. She wore a dress the color of freshly mowed grass.

"Hi," Doreen said, peering past her to what appeared to be a tiny bedroom.

"That's better," the woman said, her voice carrying the same cadence as the girl's. "I never know who I am until I'm faced with myself."

"What?" Doreen asked, shocked at the voice and how close it sounded to the child's.

"The mirror," the woman said. "I've only one, you see, and it's in there."

"And the little girl?" Doreen asked. She looked deeper into the room and saw that it was not full of a bed, side table, dresser, or reading spot as she'd expected to find in a bedroom, but instead it held a wall of mirrors. Not one, as the woman had implied. As Doreen took them in, a face moved inside one, looking back at her. It was the face of the girl.

Doreen automatically took a step back.

"You've never seen a self-wall?" the woman said.

"Is that what that is?" Doreen kept inching toward the door, the waiting faces in the other room as blank as a mannequin's.

"It's where I keep myself, so I don't get too full. It's hard having so many lives inside, you see. This helps me stay clear. Not that there's been a reason to. You're my first visitor since I was banished."

"Who are you?" Doreen managed, as she bumped into a rocking chair.

"I'm never really sure," she said. "But I call myself Eleanor."

"And you live here, by yourself?"

"I have tried to leave. I don't get far."

"I am truly in the underworld," Doreen said, more to herself, as she tried to get away from the eyes of those stuck in the mirrors.

"*I* am in this under of a world, and you're mostly here," Eleanor said, her eyes raking over Doreen. "You glow too bright to be truly well and stuck. Lively and luminous." Her voice dropped into a conspiratorial whisper as she leaned closer. "Those of us who are stuck lose our shine."

"Why are you stuck?" Doreen whispered back, drawn into the wide gaze of her eyes, how childlike she seemed.

"Death, taxes, the usual," Eleanor said.

"Are you stuck because of the trial?"

"No, but these trials are not mine to take," Eleanor said.

"I'm sorry."

"Me too."

"How long have you been stuck?" Doreen asked.

"I don't really know. There have been two others before you, those sent on trials who found their way off their path and ended up at this door. Though I wasn't there then, I inherited this house."

"Like Hansel and Gretel."

"Oh, do you know them too?"

Doreen swallowed a squeak and the woman laughed. "Kidding," Eleanor said, with a bat of her lashes. "You should see your face. Only don't look in my mirrors or it will get lost."

"I have never felt so unsettled in my life," Doreen said, before she paused. "It is the opposite of how I felt looking in at your home, though. Then I found I wasn't quite so worried anymore."

"Did you?" Eleanor asked.

"Yes."

Eleanor nodded. "So you *are* a MacKinnon. You're safe here if you're of my line. The house recognized you, and you recognized our song of longing. It's the only gift I can give." She smiled, then added, "I'm a MacKinnon too."

Doreen studied her closely. The tiny mole beneath the corner of her mouth, the arching eyebrows that looked like boomerangs when she frowned. There were similarities there, to be sure. But—

"Why are you here if you're my family? How?"

"That's the right question," Eleanor said, before plopping down in the rocking chair at Doreen's elbow. "I am here because of the curse; I am bound to a creature more demonic than any devil. I assume I'm not the only MacKinnon to suffer this fate; we are all tied together, little lights and strands of DNA bound to the one who wants us. You are the key to breaking the curse, should you win the trials. If you want to succeed, you will have to succeed at freeing us all. Complete the trials and win. The fate of your entire line, what will be and what has been, is in your hands now."

TEN AND A HALF

Ambrose could not find Doreen. He walked on the path, off the path, around the path, and yet he did not disappear into no-where as she had. Behind him the Not Quite Goodbye Castle rose in the distance. Ahead of him was an endless walk—to where, he did not know—on a glistening aquamarine road. Whispers of his past kept raining down on him, backed by the steady beat of a drum that matched his heartbeat. The rhythm and chant were driving him to the edge of madness.

Nonetheless, he kept walking and stepping off the path and back on it, looking for a way to find Doreen as panic curled and unfurled like a clenched fist. The winds blew colder as he went deeper into the motherlands. He wished he could remember the stories Sinclair had told him of this world in his youth. Of a place out of time, before it or beyond it, but it was as much a bedtime story to him as Ada and the Order had been to Doreen.

Ambrose cursed Ada as he walked, railing at the sky. He had been a fool to trust the queen of the dead, for she served only herself. He'd learned that years ago, when he set the curse, and should have heeded the truth.

Ambrose couldn't tell Doreen that in order to break the curse he would have to fall in love with a MacKinnon witch. It wasn't simply that he refused to give up his heart. There was more to the curse than he could ever admit.

"You really want to bargain your love away?" Ada had asked him three hundred years before, the first time he came to see her.

"I no longer have a heart," he'd said, meaning it. Every part of him was in tatters, desecrated. "I would be done with love once and for all, and I would make sure the MacKinnon witches can never fell another as long as their line exists."

"It is a long line," Ada said, her eyes a milky white, a flash of violet here and gone in the depths. "An impossible-to-control one. There is a cost for this curse. Love for love. Should you break it, you will break and end yourself."

"I am already ended," he had said, before he sliced into his flesh, giving his blood in an oath and the only vow he would ever make.

Should he end the curse, he would die, and he was not ready to leave this world yet.

Now he cursed the MacKinnon witches for locking him into this position, for taking Lenora and wasting so many years torturing him. He wanted his hands on the necks of those who had tried to kill him, and he wanted control. His heart pounded in tandem to the stalwart beating drum he heard in the air.

Ambrose cursed and walked, marched and swore, until his soles were sore and his muscles ached.

Until the road rose to meet him, and the whispers grew into fevered proclamations.

Until the drum was no longer distinguishable, but a series of thumps strummed together in an angry crescendo.

Until the rocks in the road formed a familiar slope of angles and arches.

Until he was so distracted by trying to locate Doreen—looking off to the side for a new path or clue, cursing her name as he worried for her—that he never thought to look ahead.

And walked straight into an unmarked pit.

Margot was worried. She had gone outside to wait for the aunts to return to Macabre Manor (as Stella liked to call their home) and discovered wisteria blooming. *Everywhere.* Tendrils of the flowers spanned twenty feet in every direction. Soft and vibrant lavender-colored wisteria snaked under and over trellises and pillars. It overtook the dark roses, smothering them and devouring them whole. The devouring of the MacKinnon roses was a bad omen, a sign the world beyond dreams was crossing over into this one.

It meant one thing to Margot. Doreen had crossed over too.

If Margot knew, so did the rest of the coven. While there were many secrets among the MacKinnon witches, the boundary of the worlds was not one of them.

Margot had left Dean behind when she went to the manor, curled up in his reading chair, his thick-rimmed glasses perched on his forehead, not yet falling down his face but precariously suspended. He had such a kissable face, and she had lied to it, telling him she was going on a work trip to buy new herbs for the shop they were planning to open. Their shop, the Inkblot, was to be a mystic tattoo store two towns over, stocked with all her remedies and featuring Dean's talent as a tattoo artist. Being a healer was the one job she was good at, and she thought the very least she could do was give Dean a good life after hoodwinking him out of the one he deserved. He should be married to a woman who he'd legitimately fallen in love with, one who didn't control his emotions by way of hers and supported making all his dreams come true. Whether it was intended or not. Dean deserved free will. If she couldn't give him that, she would try and give him what she could.

She brushed at the goosebumps rising over her arms to stave off the shame churning in her gut. Margot *hated* the curse, and she hated how weak she was compared to Doreen. She'd never had the courage to go against the family. Or, rather, she had refused to find her courage until it meant doing whatever it took to help her cousin.

Dust kicked up along the long, thin dirt driveway that led up to the manor. A familiar and ancient station wagon came barreling down the drive. The burgundy 1984 Chevrolet Caprice classic station wagon shined in its freshly waxed glory, complete with faux-wood paneling and a rooftop luggage rack. Through the dust cloud, and over the furry, purple-lined steering wheel, Margot could make out the dark curls of her aunt Kayleen's deep auburn hair, next to the twisted braid of her mom, Stella.

They exited the car, Stella in a pair of joggers and a white tank top that popped against her brown skin and showed off her toned arms, courtesy of the hours spent in her greenhouse, as well as her affinity for Pilates. Her aunt Kayleen wore a flowing pale-yellow gown that likely came from the pages of an autumn Anthropologie catalogue. Kayleen was only a few years younger than Stella, and while their faces bore a resemblance courtesy of their green eyes and sharp cheekbones, their style and manner couldn't be more opposite. Kayleen had flowing reddish chestnut hair and olive skin, wore sharp heels, and had polished nails shaded her signature delicate rose. Margot didn't think Stella owned a single bottle of polish. If she had, it would never have been the soft pinks that Kayleen favored. It would be a bright green or blue, something vibrant and demanding.

That was who they were. Both strong as steel and as powerful as the tide of a changing sea.

Margot wore a faded Clash T-shirt and ripped jeans paired with ancient Doc Martens, the scuffed combat boots having seen better days. But they were her favorite pair—Doreen had given them to her for her birthday twelve years prior. Her black nail polish was chipped, and her curls were in need of attention. But that's who Margot was. She'd always had a hard time letting go of the things she truly loved.

"Margot, darling," Kayleen called as she exited, waving a crystal wand to clear the dust and energy away. Margot pitied any lone speck that dared try and damage her aunt's ethereal dress. "Are you meditating on a grapefruit seed or just counting the clovers?"

"Neither," Margot said, not bothering to raise her voice. While her aunt and mother were in their fifties and sixties respectively, neither had an issue with hearing. In fact, neither looked a day over thirty-five. It could be the MacKinnon blood, or it could be that they were witches who were vain. Which was what Doreen used to joke Stella and Kayleen could have named their rock band if they'd ever formed one: Vain Witches. "I'm simply blooming slow like a dandelion and waiting on you."

"Excited to convene?" her mother asked, lifting a single imposing brow.

"Doesn't smell that way," Kayleen added.

"No, I smell . . ." Stella sniffed at the air, big guffawing inhales. "Trouble."

"Ha, ha," Margot said.

The two of them had always been like this, finishing each other's sentences, imparting unwanted wisdom, and talking like they always knew best. When Margot had been a child, she'd believed them. That it was wrong to be kind to the townie who ran from the sight of her, that people were fools and they deserved the addition of an affluence spell (for the MacKinnon family, of course) attached to their healing-heartache or grief-be-gone spells (that the family sold to them at cost and a half). But then Margot grew up, and all the adults in her life toppled off their pedestals as she realized she was kept fully under their thumbs. Now, she had done what they'd wanted and married Dean. She had been a "good witch," only to see how twisted their methods truly were—especially when it came to Doreen.

"I'm here to help," she said with a smile as fake as her recently whitened teeth, hoping it distracted from the lies choking her throat. Another cloud of dust cropped up and she blew it back as a new BMW, a vintage Volvo, a Ford Model T, and a handful of Ducatis rambled up the drive.

Margot wrapped her arms around her waist, trying to keep her expression relaxed. There were pops and cracks as the two giant maple trees in the yard filled with one witch after another. They appeared seated on branches, or hugging the limbs or trunks of the trees, before dismounting easily to the earth.

Stories of witches always regaled listeners with how they used brooms to fly. What a silly myth. As though any coven *needed* a broom.

Witches sat on branches, not brooms. The roots of certain trees were planted and formed connections to the soil and the hands that turned it. The MacKinnon witches traveled by maple and oak, from one township to the next. Designated homes stayed in their family lines for centuries, the land protected, the saplings and their parents serving as passages to and from continents and states and countries. It was much cheaper and faster, Stella always said (and less obnoxious), than flying by plane.

Soon the grounds of her childhood home were swarming with jam-packed picnic baskets, checkered blankets, and women over-dressed to the nines. All of their voices fought to be heard, one trip-ping over the other with jubilant exclamation, and, underneath it all, the constant call and terrifying truth, the single, repeating, rebellious chord of the piano striking an elongated echo of the G minor key.

Margot understood its meaning. No one liked being double-crossed, and none of the MacKinnon coven looked forward to doing the double-crossing either. In this scenario, the family stood together as betrayed victims. Margot saw the truth they did not wish to acknowledge—the hypocrisy amongst these witches.

"You're going to help her," Margot said, going up to her mother. "Doreen. You *will* help her, won't you?"

"Stubborn child," Stella said, pulling out a purse the size of a large pot. It doubled as one, bespelled to be a traveling cauldron. "She never could do things the easy way."

"Mom."

"What?" Stella said, setting the purse on a table. "It's the truth—every chance Doreen has had, she's stomped into smithereens."

"You can't be talking about Jack right now."

"Worthless boy. He was so clueless spells wouldn't stick," Stella scoffed.

"He was never for her."

"So we learned."

"No, so she proved to you. You shouldn't have tried to force it."

"She didn't," Kayleen said, entering the conversation with a thump as she dropped a bag of anise on the table. "I was the one who bound them."

Margot closed her eyes, fighting for calm. "No kidding," she said, opening her eyes. "How do you think Dore figured it out?"

The summer Doreen turned twenty-five, Jack Morgan moved to Pines. He was a journalist. Tall, tempting, and funny. He pursued Doreen with the single-minded focus one usually exhibited with winning a chess match. Doreen did not like Jack, but she was drawn to him.

"It's the oddest thing," she said to Margot on her six-month anniversary with Jack. "I think about breaking up with him but end up craving pancakes and am back in his bed. Every single time."

Only two witches in their coven used maple syrup to bind their spells. Stella and Kayleen. On their one-year anniversary, Doreen tasted Better Elms Maple Syrup on Jack's lips when he kissed her good morning—straight from brushing his teeth. She knew then that the aunts had spelled him, and her.

"We didn't want her to die," Kayleen said to Margot now. "Gave them the right sort of push is all. He was a catch, and she was clueless."

"He was never for her, and she broke his heart."

Kayleen frowned. "It was an unfortunate side effect."

"He tried to kill himself."

"He failed," Stella said. "And we made sure he wouldn't be able to harm himself again over her."

"It did little to heal the pain you caused Dore."

"Magic comes with a cost," Stella said, and Margot threw up her hands in frustration.

"You two should come with a warning."

Stella tutted at her daughter and went back to setting up the table for the blessing ritual to celebrate the reuniting of the family. Margot returned to her own circle, frustrated that her mother and aunt never saw reason.

It wasn't until she took a sip of her moon wine that she tasted it. Better Elms Maple Syrup, somehow lining her cup.

Then, Margot grew worried.

Eventually, Stella walked to the stone slabs that served as steps outside the wide black double doors of the family house. Kayleen sat at her feet, off to the side, stringing together clovers and daisies. She looked like a hairspray model (not a touch askew because it would wreck the view!) as she formed long chains that extended from one group of the coven's witches to the next. It created a circle that wrapped around the entire group, blocking out the world and binding them to one another. Chained together.

Margot ignored the wine and worked on her own chain, her fingers moving quickly as she waited, fearing what could come next.

"Sisters," Stella began, her voice loud and clear, though she swayed just enough for Margot to wonder how deep her mother and aunt had been dipping into the moon wine. "We know why we are gathered. One of our own has gone astray and freed the witch who cursed us." Hushed exclamations broke out, and Stella raised a finger, pointing in the air. The wind whooshed through, quieting the crowd. "I know, we're all inconsolable at this turn of events, this *betrayal*, but I need you to listen. We've seen the portents of coming doom. The wisteria of warning blooms unchecked across this property. It's found its way inside the house, creeping up the wall in what used to be Doreen's room. Nothing will stop its spread, outside of her return. The attic is thick with the smell of rose, clove, and cedar, and there are a growing number of thin places in the world."

"Not to mention the dreams," Kayleen added, looping another small daisy to the chain before she gave a dainty hiccup.

"Yes." Stella nodded. "As the line between us and the veil thins, our dreams show us what may come to be."

"The Order will be involved," Kayleen said.

"I fear that may be so," Stella said.

Margot spoke at this. "I thought you said the Order was a myth."

"Most myths are built in fact, child," Stella said. "Most facts are born from myth."

"Thanks for being so vague," Margot grumbled, scooping up another clover. It was a decidedly Stella answer, where Margot was in the dusk, if not the dark.

"What do we do?" one of the cousins from New England spoke up. "Can we reach Doreen, bring her back?"

"We should imprison her *and* him," one of the Florida cousins suggested, earning a hiss from Margot.

"Why not?" the New England cousin, Elspeth, asked. She had short pink hair and a crooked front tooth. Likely, Margot assumed, from someone punching her extremely smug face. "It's fair play. She set him free and wants to break the curse."

"She's not the only person who wishes the curse didn't exist," Margot said, rolling her eyes.

"I mean, maybe before I realized how strong I am without the worry of my heart being broken," Elspeth said, giving a loud snort.

"Or dying of a broken heart," said Stella.

"Or living in fear of losing a person you've decided is more valuable than yourself," said Kayleen.

"Never being in control of your emotions," the Florida cousin added, shuddering.

"It's such power," Elspeth said, nodding. "We don't have to settle. We can choose who we want and have them, for as long as we need them."

"What do we do with the other twenty-three-and-a-half hours of the day?" Stella cackled.

Margot sat back, disgusted at how easy it was for her family to see their curse as something they could use, to not recognize they were controlling others' free will. She thought of Dean and swallowed hard.

"None of us have suffered like our ancestors," said Kayleen. "And none of us want Doreen to suffer at the hands of Ambrose MacDonald."

Margot's fingers stilled on her band of strung flowers.

"No," Stella agreed, reaching down and plucking two clovers from where they grew by her feet. She ran her finger up and down the green stem of one before softly brushing the tuft of seeds that came together to form the flower. "Fool of a child that she is, she is ours." Stella knotted the flower in one move, effectively binding a knot around its neck before tossing it to Kayleen. "And we don't want to lose you either, Margot," Stella said, lifting her eyes to her daughter. She took the other clover and held it up, then she knotted it at the bottom. "You tied my hands when you decided to help Doreen."

"I'm not—"

"Sneaky? No, you aren't. Left a trail a mile wide to see; all I had to do was scry to find it. *You* led her to the Dead House, and him." She sniffed. "We are all chained to the fate of what comes from Ambrose MacDonald's freedom. His line has been in league with the Order for near a thousand years. This is not the first time the MacDonald line has attempted to destroy ours, and each time they try, they have failed. It's time to take advantage of the board."

Cold fear bloomed in Margot's stomach. "Life is not a game of chess, Mom," she said, doing everything she could to keep her voice calm. Her eyes tracked the small clover in her mother's hands.

"If you think that, dear, you shouldn't have started playing the game," Stella said, before she tossed the flower to Kayleen.

"What do you mean, his line has been trying to end ours for a thousand years?" Margot asked.

"There was more than one reason we bound that man, more than one reason we helped Lenora escape."

"Escape?" Margot asked, her mother's words no longer making sense. "Our ancestors sent her away, they didn't rescue her."

"Of course they rescued her," Stella said, with a scoff. "They trusted her and she them. Which, sadly, is more than I can say for you, daughter of mine."

"We tried to keep you out of this," Kayleen said to Margot, her green eyes searching. "But it's a family problem, and you are now one of the snags. You should have stayed with your Dean, and left Doreen to us."

"What kind of person would I be if I sat back and did nothing?" Margot asked, as she slid her hands into her pockets and shifted onto her heels. She wrapped a hand around the protective stone in the left one and the sprig of rosemary in the right. Margot never did anything without a measure of preparation, and this meeting was no different.

She simply never dreamed she might actually have to use the charms she carried.

"You wouldn't be a MacKinnon," Stella said, without smiling. "That's for sure."

Margot tasted syrup on her lips and thought, for a moment, that she glimpsed an apology in her mother's eyes. Thought that maybe she would tell Margot how to help Doreen, advise the coven to support and help one of their own.

Then Stella raised her hands, and the members of her family, her cousins—every single damned one—lifted the symbol of their coven into the air, raising the daisy chain of clovers and daffodils, of weeds and flowers. Kayleen held the two knotted clovers—Margot realized the two must represent herself and Doreen—that she had woven into the circle. She tied them together, much in the way Stella had taught Margot and Doreen to tie their shoes when they had been girls.

"Criss-cross, over and under, that's the way the bunny goes. One ear and two, loop and swoop, and now the way the bunny knows."

Once the two clovers were tied together, Kayleen bowed her head. The rest of the circle followed suit. Eyes open, chins tucked.

"Don't do this," Margot whispered, knowing what was coming. Not wanting to believe it.

There was no initiation into the family MacKinnon. The coven had reclaimed themselves when they came to America, and in reinventing themselves, they'd recovered who they were. As a witch of their line, you were born to be diligent. To work for the greater good. To be great.

There was a single spell to break a bond as strong as theirs. One Margot knew had never before been used. A spell for separation. A spell that enabled you to know a person existed, but removed them from your sight, from your circle.

A spell to expel a body from the coven.

"We knock on the door," Kayleen said, and with the hand not holding the chain, she reached up and knocked against the air.

A loud thump sounded, booming through the forest surrounding them.

"We ask you open," the voices of the rest of the coven called before they too raised a hand and struck.

A succession of rapid-fire booms rang through the air.

"Let her in," Stella said, her voice low and rough. She kept her eyes off her daughter as she nodded to her sister, who, with one fluid motion, ripped the two clovers from the chain and tossed them to Margot. She let them fall into her lap. She could not stop this; she could only try to soften her own fall.

Kayleen reknit the circle in one swift motion, casting out Doreen and Margot with the ease one tosses dust from the bin.

In unison, the coven finished chanting their curse: "The circle is closed, the witches are cast out, henceforth we see them no more."

The women stood, lifting the chain again as they went. The air surrounding Margot grew thick. She struggled to draw breath, and light—bright and blinding—cut across the grounds. The coven chanted the words to their spell, over and over, and Margot swayed on her feet. They threw the clovers into the air, and Margot thought she heard her mother say, before the clovers and life as Margot knew it came tumbling down, *"The spell is the truth, the truth is the spell."*

Margot could glean a door creaking open. A warm wind filled with gripping fingers brushed against her. She threw up her arms in protection, raising the tokens in each hand and whispering a single name: *Doreen.*

A maelstrom of wind and laughter poured out from the not-yet-visible door to nowhere, wrapping itself around her, and yanking Margot into the darkness beyond.

ELEVEN

Doreen stood facing a cliff. The earth beneath her feet was bright and green, the air filled with the salty sweetness of the water below. The sky overhead shifted from a somber gray into a faint, friendly shade of violet. There was a mist below blanketing the ocean, and behind sat the stone cottage with its chimney diligently pumping smoke.

It was not an unwelcoming picture, what surrounded her, and yet, as Doreen stood at the edge of the cliff, she could not feel her hands or her feet.

Eleanor had rushed her outside when Doreen swayed into the door.

"Fresh air, or as fresh as dead air can be," Eleanor said, guiding them both down to the cliffs.

She wasn't wrong. It did seem to help Doreen put her feet on the soil and focus her gaze on the distant horizon. Eleanor's proclamation had knocked Doreen into a new plane of fear. Their whole family was cursed, true, but there was *more* to the curse. What Eleanor had told her—that the curse went beyond the grave, that the very *souls* of Mac-Kinnon witches were trapped in the underworld—had shaken her to her core. Doreen was the one, and the *only* one, who could break this curse.

It was impossible.

"I really don't understand," she said, taking in a breath that didn't really fill her lungs. Deep breaths in Not Scotland were like eating cotton candy. They were tasty but you didn't get full, and after a while you ended up lightheaded with a stomachache. "Ambrose cursed our family from finding love because we sent Lenora away and she died. How could that affect our souls in the afterlife?"

Eleanor blinked. "Whoever told you your history, it is sorely dotted with holes."

"No one told me anything," Doreen said, her voice rising. "No one tells *anyone* anything, which is why Margot and I had to discover practically everything on our own, and even then, it was clearly not enough."

"Secrets have a way of ruining everything," Eleanor said, slipping a hand into Doreen's. As she did, the panic that had been building in her like a fragmented song shifted. It went from a crushing melody into a coda resonating in a single focused chord for long seconds before her terror finally faded into silence. Doreen realized, as it settled, that the aggressive melody of the sigil had stopped following her. No more raining words or song, no more fear peppering her back.

"I can't hear the sigil here," she told Eleanor.

"You can only hear yourself on my land," she said.

"Why?"

"Because I was loved."

"Love," she said. "It all comes back to that. Is it Ambrose's curse affecting me like this, damning us to this purgatory?"

"No, it isn't," Eleanor said. She squeezed Doreen's hand, released it, and reached into one of the deep pockets on her dress skirt. She pulled out a small pouch and passed it to Doreen. "Sit, please, you're making the skies nervous. Reach in and pull out a handful. Toss them as you sit down—not too far, mind, just in front of us so I may see."

Doreen took the bag and undid the burlap strings. She didn't even think to object. She was overwhelmed and operating on the rise and fall of adrenaline. Sitting sounded ridiculously nice.

She reached in and her fingers brushed over coarse wood. She pulled out a handful of what appeared to be tiny branches and tossed them at their feet. Then she sat and stared at the symbols presented back to her. Three wee branches with their surface bark scraped free, with five carvings soldered into them.

"Excellent work," Eleanor said. "The 'Ambrose' curse is a nuisance. It is a curse within a curse. It is not what led you here, not precisely. You were always on your way here." She looked up at Doreen, meeting her eyes. "Did you never wonder of your past?"

"We moved to the Americas to escape from King James VI and his minions of horrific kill-mongers," Doreen said, resting her head on the curve of her arm. "You think I was always doomed for the underworld?"

Eleanor grunted but continued studying the spread before her. "It is not doom, and that isn't quite right. We had not moved yet when Ambrose met Lenora. When a young man and a thrill-seeking young woman had a whirlwind love affair that was not approved of by their families. When the woman betrayed the man and changed the course of his life."

"Yes, it's very Romeo and Juliet, isn't it? Wait, she *betrayed* him?"

"That wasn't the story you were sold, was it?"

"No," Doreen said. "I was told Lenora died because of a broken heart. Ambrose lost his mind and cursed us in his grief."

"Did she die of a broken heart? Or did she die before her heart could love?"

"What are you talking about?"

"There is more to their story than you, than even your Ambrose, knows."

"He is not mine, and you're wrong," Doreen said. "She haunts him. At his castle. It's a love that stands still to this day."

"I very much doubt that," Eleanor said, finally looking up from the spread. "It's not love that leads a ghost to haunting. It's debt. Either way, that's not the origin of the curse."

Doreen's head spun. "Then what is?"

"It started with love, true enough, but it was unrequited love, which is the origin of your true curse, and it began long before Ambrose and Lenora. It ended in death, as curses so often do. The MacKinnons and MacDonalds are bound to one another in tragedy. You will have to come full circle to do what you need to free us all, and especially if you wish to free yourself."

"Free us all." Doreen closed her eyes. "Ada said the trials will break the curse."

"The queen of the dead is an amoeba of a spirit. She is at fault for the original curse."

Her eyes fluttered open. "What is the original curse?"

"It is her story, and I cannot tell it on this land."

"How can I break a curse I don't know?"

"The true trials give you an opportunity to transform."

"The true trials?" Doreen's head spun as she stared at Eleanor. "What are *these*, then?"

"You are a pawn in a game that was started long ago. This world is not the world of the gods, but of a creature who wishes she were one. It is a prison world."

Doreen shook her head and realized her whole body was shaking too. "I don't understand."

Eleanor's mouth shifted, her lips moving, but the words didn't come free. She looked up at the sky and then back to Doreen; this time when she opened her mouth, the words followed. "I have said more than I thought I could, and it is all I can say." She tapped the earth, flicking a finger out to point at the pieces of adorned wood. "Here is the truth, for the ogham does not hide it, not even in the motherlands."

"You want to read runes now?" Doreen asked, wrapping her arms around her trembling body.

"Saints, no—runes keep their secrets; they are made of mystery. We're trying to clear that away, and that is why we have the ogham."

"These will tell me the truth of the trials?"

"What they can."

"You can't just tell me?"

"I can only say so much."

"Oh, for goddesses' sake," she muttered.

"Ogham are connected to the earth, from which we come and return. They are also tied to spirit, of which we are made. They *reveal*."

"In threes?" Doreen asked, eyeing the three twigs in front of her.

"You chose three. It could have been six or nine, but as you are a witch who walks with purpose, it makes a certain sense you would choose three. You aim to harm none and you practice knowing a curse can come back on you three-fold. Three times the curse. Once from Ada. Once from your Ambrose, and now there is you—you will be the curse of now or the freedom from it."

"Terrific."

"You are shaking."

"You are observant."

"And you're angry."

"Of course I am," Doreen said, gritting her teeth. "I'm *trapped* here and you're telling me there aren't trials, that the curse isn't the same one I need to break."

"There are still trials, they are simply not the ones you expected.

The rules of the trials are Ada's, and as she completed the original trials, hers are the same. You will complete them and free us."

"Fantastic. Ada made a prison world, we're in it, and I still have to do the trials."

"It is good you are angry. You will need that fire."

"I'm nothing but fire," Doreen said, and looked down. "What do these three not-runes say?"

"They speak clearly," Eleanor said. "One is *beith* of the birch, one is *fearn* of the alder, and lastly, *nion* of the ash. Love magic is at work. Wise counsel must be heeded—that's where I come in—and finally, the strength of women will succeed to conquer all."

"You do realize readings are always vague enough to be applied to anything."

"Not when you're open." Eleanor pushed the runes toward Doreen. "Your quest is not an easy one. You must keep your heart and head open. Seek wise counsel and refuse that of those wishing to sway you onto the wrong path. Your ancestors have the answers you seek and when the time comes, you will have the opportunity to join them and transform that which needs to be changed. *If* you don't screw it up."

"Of course," Doreen said, unable to keep the sarcasm out of her tone. "Thanks for the vote of confidence."

"There is also the problem of Ambrose."

"Seeing as how I have lost him, how big of one can he be?"

"That depends on you," Eleanor said. "On your kind and caring heart and integrity."

"What does my heart have to do with it?"

"You wandered off the path, but into where you were meant to be. You found me, the wise counsel."

"That's what you are?"

Eleanor shot her a look. She reached into the bag and pulled out a single ogham. "*Tinne* of the holly. The holly king is your Ambrose. It is uncertain if he is working for or against you; he perhaps has yet to make up his own mind. A warrior, but a bullish fool too. Still." She tilted her head from side to side, as though deciding something. "Ambrose did not let you go. He kept looking for you, and he did not find his way to where he could have been aided by his own wise counsel. He found his way down into a pocket of time, and time is not kind here. Not when it holds an echo of the past. It is a torturous existence to step into, and he has fallen inside. You can help him, or you can continue on your own."

"He fell, as in literally?"

"Yes." She leveled her gaze at the horizon. "He found a cave that is not a cave and it trapped him."

Doreen shifted her weight, unthinking, preparing to stand. "The cave of echoes?"

Eleanor nodded.

"Then I have to go."

"Says who?"

"His valet. We met her in the castle, and she said we needed to go there for the trials. That's where he is, and where I should be."

Eleanor raised a brow. "This valet is a ghost of his line?"

"No, but a ghost he knew."

"Or perhaps a spirit seeking mischief."

"Or seeking redemption? Why is there a cave of echoes if these aren't the true trials?"

"These *are* trials, only not the ones you were promised. These trials are for your freedom. And for mine, and the rest of us trapped here. Trapped like Ambrose is now."

There was a brief flash and Eleanor shifted from black-and-white into Technicolor. Once, and then again, so fast Doreen almost thought she imagined it.

If not for the pained expression on Eleanor's face.

"Are you okay?" Doreen asked.

"The queen of the dead keeps her shades close, and you are now in her personal hell. None of us are okay."

"Why would Ada want to trap us?"

"You know what the Order is?" Eleanor asked.

"The queen and her shadow army."

"Yes." Eleanor flickered again. She leaned closer. "They are the souls that do the queen's bidding and keep her going, give her the long life that sustains her over the centuries. She can control them in death, and she wants to control you in life. She needs you, and she has trapped you so she can take your soul."

"No," Doreen said, swallowing past the panic. It couldn't be true, and yet. . . . Ambrose had tried to tell her. He'd said that Ada had wanted to eat her soul in the cave, and if he was telling the truth . . .

"I have nothing to gain and everything to lose by telling you this," Eleanor said. "Yours is a difficult path to tread. You have the choice now: to save Ambrose and to fight, or perhaps you prefer to take the easier path. One where you forget and live like us? It's painless, the crossing over."

"Ada sent us here," Doreen said. "You're telling me she orchestrated it all."

"She couldn't take you straight out, so she found a workaround. Her army is her captives. You would make a great addition. She could eat on you for centuries."

Doreen shuddered. She ran her hands through her hair, grasping for sense in the senseless. What if it was true? What if it wasn't? Should she trust Eleanor, this strange creature she'd only just met? What if she was lying to her about everything?

She turned back and stared at Eleanor. "What would you say if you were wearing another face?"

Eleanor smiled. "I would say the same, as I am always truthful to my own. You are mine and I am yours."

A shimmer of light shifted from Eleanor and into Doreen. The truth of her, of the woman before her, wafted around her. There were no lies in her soul.

"Shit."

"I am sorry to be the bearer of this news."

"I can't leave Ambrose," Doreen said, rubbing at the chill settling into her skin. "I won't abandon him in some—what did you call it? Cave that time forgot—the cave of echoes. I can't allow him to be tortured again. That is not who I am." There was more to her decision, an undeniable truth blooming under Doreen's feet that she didn't want to examine too closely yet. The punch to her stomach at the idea of anything happening to Ambrose. "And I sure as anything don't want to become whatever you are." She swallowed. "If this is all a trap, if Ada is trying to lock us away, then I have to break out. To break us *all* out."

"I hoped that is what you would say," Eleanor said. She took the ogham bag and dropped the pieces back into it. She passed them to Doreen. "These are yours now. Keep them close."

Doreen accepted the bag. They stood on the edge of the cliffs, facing one another. She was uncertain what move to make next. Eleanor reached out and pulled her close, holding her tight. That same sense of peace descended over Doreen, and she squeezed back.

"We all wear many faces, but it's the truth inside us that reveals what we need most. Look to yourself when you are lost and stay open. Remember, true love is tricky but worth the leap, wise counsel does not judge or ask for payment, and your sisterhood will never desert you."

Then she was gone, walking back into her stone cottage, and Doreen was stepping onto a path that led her to an uncertain future. Her lost Ambrose awaited.

TWELVE

Ambrose stood facing a series of tall pine trees. Their bark was a swirl of brown and gray, layers of each color one over the other like strips of dyed paper blended. Up high in the trees were three squirrels. They were chasing each other, running in circles as they scurried up high and then low. They chattered as they went, a quiet chitter that was strangely melodious. There were familiar markings in the trees, pressed in amongst the peel-worthy bark.

He tried to reach for a marking and found he could not move. His arm was pinned to his side, his body a weighted and heavy entity. He felt as though he had been frozen with his eyes open.

He needed to find her.

A shadow moved forward from behind the furthest tree. It was coming closer and closer.

He remembered this. He had been here before.

And there was no escaping what was coming.

The Queen of the Order of the Dead shifted across the land like a storm wind scuttering across choppy water.

For Ambrose, watching her movements was terrifying. The mismatched bones left her skittering in disjointed bursts, like a disorganized spider. Her face was calm, but her shadow self was something else. Angry, violent, desperate; its rage knew no bounds.

As the shadow slipped closer, a memory of the past returned to life inside him. Ambrose felt the despair he'd suffered when he stood in this forest three hundred years before, and his teeth chattered at the weight of such misery.

"You're brave to come to the Forest of Forgetting," the queen said, her voice slipping from the shadows, wrapping its way around Ambrose and slithering inside him.

"It's said to make a bargain with the queen, one must bring her an offering she cannot refuse in the place that refuses to forget her," he said, and though his lips did not move, his words arose, slow and sluggish. "They must gift her a trinket from the man who started it all and set her curse in motion. Hastings MacDonald was my ancestor."

Beyond the copse of trees that Ambrose was tucked in was a determined set of cliffs. They were haunted, it was said, by the dying wails of those who drew too close and plummeted to their deaths. The spirits there were greedy, trying to claw their way back to life, and they would drag any soul they could down with them.

Ambrose knew the words he would give next to Ada, even though he didn't wish to ever relive them.

"If I can't have love, neither can they," he said. "If they want to tear out my heart, then I will bind theirs. Tell me what to do."

He'd pricked both his thumbs, and filled a small pitted cup. He set it down before her and reached into the air behind his back. He was reaching for a bag he did not carry in this world but had before—on the day he'd originally come here to this forest. He pulled from it a muslin cloth, wrapped around a heavy object. "This is more than a trinket, and I hope it will do," he said, tossing it down. The object rolled forward as it hit the ground, and Ambrose's stomach turned a quick spiral once, twice, before he pressed a palm there to steady the rising nausea.

He saw it play out before him, like a film running across reality, a dinged yellow jawbone poking out as the bone rolled. Ambrose told himself not to think of who it belonged to.

A flash of a graveyard, of mountains shaped like teeth, and a name that would not be denied. Not in life, not in death.

Hastings MacDonald's head—or what remained—rolled to a stop at the feet of the queen of the dead.

D oreen walked down the hill, replaying what Eleanor had told her. She was stuck in a prison world, made by Ada, who wanted to feast on Doreen's soul. Ambrose had been right, and she was exceedingly irritated at him over it, and that he was stuck in the cave, far from her. With an abundance of sighing, she found her way back to the main path. This time there was only one direction to go.

As she walked, she thought of Margot, of Stella, even her mother, and, of course, the curse. Her entire life had been one curse after another, and it should have been terrifying, but she only found herself more determined. Eleanor said she could break it, and while Eleanor was clearly a trapped spirit of some sort, she had felt like home. Like Margot, and that told her more than any words could.

It left her hoping, which was a dangerous thing. That maybe, if she freed the people here, she would find her mother too.

Her entire life had been spent searching for love and being denied. Searching for her mother and being unable to find her. No matter how improbably, Doreen had never stopped looking for either. She didn't know how.

So Doreen would complete the first trial of strength. That must be what the cave of echoes was. She would be strong enough to defeat whatever Ambrose faced. None of this was going how she thought it would. She hadn't battled a legion of kelpies or other obvious monster with her strength or outfoxed it with her cleverness. She was barely surviving in this world, and she was on edge.

She continued down the scenic path, its rolling green hills seeming to mock her, until she came to what could only be an entrance to a cavern. It was three feet by three feet, a gaping hole in the road that resembled a mouth mid-scream. Rocks were formed around it, an outline that *should* have warned travelers what was in front of them. There was a break in the circle of rocks surrounding the entrance, and this was most likely how Ambrose had tumbled down like Alice in the rabbit hole.

As she stared into it, the solitary, mournful note of a violin rose, and whispers chased after it. Steadily they grew louder and louder.

The woods are lovely, dark and deep.

Yes, here was the cave of echoes, echoing up to meet her. Doreen muttered the words from the poem over and over, the strings sinking into her skin, and she tried to work out how to get Ambrose out without going in. She peered down, waved a hand into the hole, called his name, and her thoughts drifted to a different Robert Frost poem than the one raining onto her.

She sighed and announced, "The only way out is through."

Then, with as much grace as she could muster, Doreen sat on the edge of the hole, and slowly lowered herself in before dropping deep into the darkness.

She landed with a thump, the force knocking her onto her back. Up she could see the sky, and when she looked toward her feet, she saw light flickering in the distance. After checking everything was intact, or as undamaged as could be after falling into nowhere, Doreen brushed her hands over the ground. Grassy and firm. She stood and started forward. Heading toward the beckoning light.

As she walked, her surroundings grew clearer. She was in a forest, and it looked quite a lot like where she and Ambrose began their journey when they'd first arrived in Scotland. Tall trees, thick roots, large boulders, and a running stream along one side. The skies here, however, were not the baby blue of the horizon outside of Portree. Instead, they were rose pink and filled with thick lilac clouds.

Everything was in shades of sepia overcast with pink and purple. The haunting sounds of the violin chased after her feet, playing a melody so similar to the one her coven used to raise the sigil that Doreen kept looking over her shoulder, expecting to find Stella lurking behind a tree. This sound, however, was sadder, lonelier. The notes trailed off, then were plucked again, rising in a steady crescendo that had her rising on her toes as though she could reach the sound.

To her great relief, whispers of poetry no longer fell from the skies. And the trees on the edge of the periphery, which had been curved and out of sight, straightened and shifted into view. She had the thought that perhaps she was in a snow globe, walking along its curved edges.

Finally, she came to a clearing in the center of the forest. There stood a large block of stone. It was perched precariously, listing to the side, and at its base was a swath of muslin. The entrance to a cave rose up across from it, and beyond came the roar of a sea just out of sight. Doreen found her thoughts slowing as she stood there. A glinting stone met her gaze at the base of the trees up ahead. She walked to them and realized each tree had a section of stone circling it. She bent down and ran her fingers over the blue stone there. She reached in and pulled a hunk out. Azurite. A memory crystal.

Doreen slipped it into her shirt, closer to her heart and her spirit. As soon as the stone touched her chest, the haze cleared, the crystal doing its job.

She knew this place. Magic hid from the world here; humans were not meant to linger. This was the Forest of Forgetting. Another myth come to life. She looked at the tree in front of her, at the stones.

It was said the Forest of Forgetting claimed its victims by slowing their minds and eventually consuming them. Not exactly the sort of strength she'd imagined she would need to exhibit.

A low moan sounded. She paused, cocking her head as she listened. It came again, and her heart stuttered. *Ambrose.* Beneath the painful exhalation, she knew without a doubt it was the timbre of his voice. She hurried over, running her fingers over the bark of a tree that seemed to have released it. The moan rose again, and she realized it did not come from the tree, but the stone behind it, the one in the middle of the forest. She ran to it and walked in a circle around it. There did not seem to be a way to break it open. Her eyes drifted to the base, and she saw a grouping of symbols carved there.

IARRTAS. (Gaelic for *request*.)

The Pictish Beast symbol. (Because it was clearly stalking her.)

And, finally, A'TABHANN. (She was mostly certain it meant *offering*.)

A request, a beast, and an offering.

Another moan reverberated through the forest, and Doreen's heart knocked against her chest. How much air could Ambrose have, if he was stuck inside? She remembered reading stories of souls trapped in trees, how if the trees were cut down their spirits would be lost forever. How long before a person's soul became the tree? Or in this case, the stone?

Thinking fast, she gathered the rose quartz surrounding the holly tree. She talked to Ambrose as she worked. "I know it's you in there," she said. "Only you would end up trapped in a damn stone." She laid the crystals in a circle around the large stone, ignoring how her hands shook.

The moan came again, softer this time. Sweat dotted her back, her arms began to tremble, and still Doreen kept her focus on setting the circle. She refused to think about Ambrose dying. About being stuck with his soul in a stone, in a prison world, with Doreen unable to yell at him again.

She needed to get the words for her spell right. The pressure mounted as she flipped through her mental grimoire, looking for the right one. After a few moments, she noticed a hush had fallen over the forest.

No sounds aside from her own erratic breaths were stirring. Panic bloomed, a bright and terror-filled bubble in her chest. Doreen threw out the search for the right spell and went with a protection one Margot had created, modifying it. She reversed it, and cast the spell low and true—her voice shaking as the words rose up and out.

"Guard him, free him, keep him safe. The only way out is through. Guard me, free me, keep me safe. The only way out is through."

Around and around her words went, stringing into a melody that matched the rise and fall of the violin still weaving its way through the forest. It was the first time she'd altered a spell like that, and she was terrified she wasn't strong enough to succeed. The large stone shook before her. The trees groaned as chips of rock tumbled from it, and the earth quaked beneath her feet. Suddenly, a crack splintered the stone, zigzagging up and over, before the stone snapped apart. As two solid slabs gave way, a form slid out, tumbling free, and collapsed at her feet.

Doreen shook, her mind and heart racing. Ambrose was covered in a chalky substance and barely breathing. She jumped into the circle, keeping the magic there centered, and went to work. She did not rely on magic this time, but science.

She tipped his chin back, pinched his nose, and brought her lips to his. Twice she blew her air into his lungs, twice she watched her lifeforce fill him. Then she pressed her hands to his chest, over his heart, prepared to pump, when he coughed, wheezed, and dragged in a shuddering breath.

"Less dead?" she asked, barely able to contain her joyous relief as he stared, blinking up at the sky.

"Barely alive," he said, his breath jagged, before turning his eyes to hers. They met and held for one charged second. He pressed a hand to his stomach and rolled to his side. She waited, not taking her gaze from him, and slowly he was able to progress into a seated position.

When he'd stopped gasping and coughing, she spoke again, the words a giddy rush. "How'd you like being a stone?"

"About as much as I'd guess you like being cursed to die or having to marry a bespelled mortal."

She let loose a half-hysterical laugh. "You admit your little curse sucks, do you?" she said, with a lightness her limbs did not feel. Finding him in the stone, not breathing, had short-circuited Doreen's nervous system. She was sure that was why her heart was still racing and she wanted to laugh and cry at the same time. She reached out and punched him in the shoulder. "Don't *do that* again."

"Ouch," he said, rubbing the shoulder. "Have a care, I was about dead."

"I am all too aware," she said, rubbing a hand over her cheek. "What happened?"

Ambrose shook his head. "I need to get the hell out of this forest first."

When Doreen only gave him a hard stare, he sighed. "I don't trust the trees."

She glanced up and over to them. The limbs were arching forward, closer to the center, as though leaning in. *Listening.* "Oh, wow."

He lifted his brows in a *See?* movement and she bit back a smile. It was such a relief to see Ambrose being so . . . Ambrose.

"How do you propose we get out of here?"

He shrugged. "The only way out is through."

"What did you say?" Doreen asked, a chill rushing through her.

"I . . ." He gave his head a shake. "The only way out is through. I don't know why I said that."

"I do," she said.

Stella used to tell her and Margot, "You must be careful. Magic is as unpredictable as a summer storm. It can change its mind like a mediocre man or stick in the cracks and cause trouble later. Use your heads, never your heart."

The words of her spell had left his mouth. Doreen had saved him. She had, since meeting Ambrose, been using her heart and not her head.

"Funny thing happened to me," she said, shifting forward, grabbing more stones to set a circle. A perimeter to ward them free from harm. "I met my ancestor. Learned we are stuck in this prison of a world thanks to Ada. We must complete her trials to get out of here and save the souls trapped here because the queen of the dead has trapped us all."

Ambrose gave a slow blink. "I told you we need to get out of here."

"You aren't in any condition to run, and I am guarding us with the circle, warding us here."

He grumbled but cleared his throat. "Ada trapped us?"

"Yes. In a world where Ada gets to keep us and eventually eat us."

"I will not point out how I already told you she wanted your soul." Ambrose ran a hand down his face.

"Telling me you aren't going to point it out is, in fact, pointing it out." Damn stingray.

"Gods, that was not what I was hoping to hear."

"I would say it could be worse," she said, "but then it would get worse. So . . . it could be better."

"Right."

"On the upside, I did it," she said. "The first trial. I had to choose to follow you here and face the forest or leave you behind. I chose to save you. It was no stroll through the tulips. I was brave and strong. We have one down out of four. Now, do you know how to get through wherever we are and get to the second trial, because I am pretty sure it's your turn."

"You did wonderful," he said, his voice velvet soft. "Thank you for helping me, Doreen."

She couldn't stop the blush his words triggered. She looked away, clearing her throat. "Of course."

His eyes focused beyond them, to where the sound of the waves of an unseen sea overlapping drifted inward. "As for what comes next, I may have a bad idea."

Doreen rose and offered him a hand. "Let's have it."

No sooner did he stand, both feet firmly planted, when the ground rumbled. He stepped closer to Doreen, and the earth shook. He stumbled to sitting again, his legs shaky, and a cold breeze blew in as the skies darkened.

Lightning crackled across the sky, and the cave bellowed an angry roar as a whirling dervish of particles rose in front of it. Bits of matter, bone, and atmosphere blended, swirling around and around. Faster and faster, the wind pooling in leaves, twigs, dirt, and dust from the ground. Doreen reached for Ambrose, his arm coming around her as she fell into him.

A scream built in the back of Doreen's throat, and she tamped it down, fear a breathing entity, exhaling down her back and trying to clamor into her skin.

Suddenly, when Doreen was certain she and Ambrose would be lifted into the air and sucked into the vortex spiraling before them—protective circle or no—the cyclone stopped. The particles came to an abrupt stop, hovering in the air for moments before they dropped to the ground.

Revealing the figure of a woman with her hands raised, her eyes focused, and her powers pooling in the palms of her hands.

Margot.

THIRTEEN

Ada unrolled a piece of parchment and lifted it from a wooden chest in the cave on the northern side of the island. She thought of the many truths she kept tucked away, and of the lies littered throughout history. The parchment she currently held contained a drawing of a man who had not been much of a human.

King James VI of Scotland, also known as King James I of England, had been a sorry sack of bones. More scared of his own sexuality than the witches he'd hunted, he'd found a way to come after women stronger than him and prove his machismo to men weaker than him. The truth was, he had been a fearful, broken human.

It had been a joy for Ada to ransack his grave.

King James was never canonized, and he wasn't saintly, not in his behavior. He thought witchery meant women were servants to a creature of the night. He had no idea it was all about connection with the world. With a source of energy. The man credited for transcribing the Bible had, in truth, done nothing more than order its translation.

It's funny how history remembered mediocre men for doing the hard work of others, for owning the world. When really, the world belonged to people like Ada.

Ada had known the wind as a child. She used to hide flowers and wait for the wind to find them, sending their petals and stems twirling back to her. Daffodils and clovers dancing in the air like ballerinas commanding the stage.

She didn't have other children to play with, living as she did in a castle at the edge of the cliffs. She had the earth instead. She would lie on the ground, meet it back-to-back, and draw its energy up, up, up into her toes. Sip it into her shins, inhale it into her stomach, and drink it along her arms, until finally it filled her mouth and flowed through the rest of her. Ada'd wait until she was filled to the brim with the earth's energy, before sending it plunging back down. Over and over, she and the earth. Each time sending a larger vibration, a cresting wave, until she was spent and slumbering, the rhythm of the world her lullaby. The hum of the earth was the highest vibration, a series of suspended chords as ethereal as the mist rising off the water and hovering in the air. That sound was deep in her soul.

Ada was protected in the arms of the earth. Safe. Loved. It looked after her, and she, it . . .

Until it didn't, and then it was too late. Everything that mattered, the one person who truly mattered, was gone. So Ada did what no other witch before her had dared to do. She stole the song of her sorrow from the hum of the earth. Called it forth and took it without permission or remorse.

Then she set out to do what needed to be done.

In the low light of the cave, where flame flickered and shadows danced to an unhappy tune, Ada returned the parchment to the box and pulled a second from it. This one was newer. The ink on it was still tinged red from the blood pen she'd used to mark it. The face drawn here was young and clever. It was in the eyes, how unflinching the gaze was even in an illustration. She didn't like how it felt in her hand, this scroll, but she needed it.

Ada drifted toward the flame burning in the center of the room. The flame did not flicker or fade, and she barely glanced its way until she was standing in front of it. Then she held the paper over the flame, wincing as it sparkled and lit. She stepped back right as it went up in a shooting blaze. Smoke billowed and poured out into the room. It soaked into the floor and then oozed back out, a slow drip of a haze coming from the stalactites hanging overhead. As the smoke spread out into the room, it took a shape that was very nearly human.

Like a photograph developing in a dark room, it came into the light slowly as the silhouette found focus and form.

"Hello, Eleanor," Ada said, her smile a bulb turned up too bright.

Eleanor dusted herself off, looking down at the dress she wore. It was white and flowy, and nothing at all like anything she ever would have chosen for herself. "We both know that isn't my name and this isn't my dress."

"No, but it could have been, if you had stayed put."

"You found me regardless."

"I always find you. All of you. You're mine, after all."

"We are all our own. You are a thief."

"I would think you'd be grateful to be summoned."

"Oh, yes, it's such a silver lining in my eternity to be called by my own blood and bones that you stole and hid."

"I told you," Ada said, sounding bored. "You are mine. Bound by promise and blood."

"What do you want from me, Queen of Bones?"

"Respect would be nice. But since you're incapable, I want you to distract the new arrivals. Shouldn't be too hard."

Eleanor blinked. "You're worried about them."

"I worry about nothing."

"Yes, you are, if you are sending me and not one of your shadows. You need the real deal instead of an echo of a spirit. Hmm. Why? Ah, I know. You think they'll figure out the false trials. Return here and take your bones from you and command you to do their bidding. Oh, wouldn't that be something."

"It is a waste of the blood and bones I ground and use to call you if you're just going to mouth off to me, child."

"Don't be so hasty." Eleanor gave a slow curtsy. "As you will it, I will go. What else can I do?"

Ada waved a hand, and Eleanor stepped back to the stone wall. "It's been hundreds of years, Queen of Bones. If you haven't found her yet, perhaps you should stop looking."

"And perhaps you should join the shadows," Ada replied, not bothering to look at the spirit standing behind her.

"That's the funny thing about how you've cursed us all," Eleanor said as she faded into the cracks in the room. "We're all part of the shadows now."

Then she was gone, and Ada was alone once more, with only a box of fading parchments and broken memories for company.

Doreen stared at Margot, not believing her eyes. Her cousin was a mess, her hair blown back and her clothes dusty and smudged. Yet there she stood, blinking and coughing, before them.

"Dore?" Margot managed, as the air cleared.

That single word, with an inflection on the o, sent Doreen propelling herself out of the circle and throwing herself into the arms of her cousin. Margot was slow to respond, gasping for a moment, until finally she raised her arms and squeezed Doreen so hard she could barely breathe. "Is it really you?"

"If you mean am I really in a creepy underworld and you're here too, then yes, it's really me," Doreen managed to say while being constricted by Margot as if she were a boa.

Margot released her enough to lean back and search her face. "Underworld?"

"I met Ada, the Queen of the Order of the Dead. She's real and in desperate need of a facial and a boycott on chemical peels. The Order exists, Margs. Along with a slew of other terrifying things."

"The Order exists," Margot said, looking around for the first time. "But this isn't the underworld. It can't be."

"How could you tell?" Ambrose asked, and Margot gave a start, spinning to face him.

"Holy gods," she whispered. "Who chiseled him from stone?"

"Don't let him hear you," Doreen said under her breath.

"Is he going to try to attack?"

"No, he just has an ego the size of Manhattan."

"Funny," Ambrose said. "How did you know this isn't the underworld?"

"Because it looks like Scotland. Not the fire of hells and desolate land," Margot said. "I can hear running water."

"It's the sea," Doreen said. "Beyond the trees are the cliffs."

"We're in the Forest of Forgetting," Ambrose said. "Or a memory of it. It's where I came the first time. For the first deal I made with Ada. I came here."

"You made a deal before?" Doreen asked, swiveling on him.

He nodded. "Yes."

"And you failed to mention this?"

"I was working up to it when you disappeared on me, and then I was stuck in a boulder suffocating, so forgive me for the delay."

"What was the deal?"

"I think you know."

"The curse," she breathed the words.

Ambrose swallowed, looked beyond her. Doreen glowered at him.

"It's the first of her trials," he said. "The cave of echoes, voices of the past. She re-created them for us. Here."

"I'm *not* in the underworld, right?" Margot said, her voice rising.

"No, it's a bit worse than that," Doreen said, not taking her eyes from Ambrose. "Think of it as Alternate Scotland. But with angry demon horses and our ancestors. What it really is, is a trap for us by the queen of the dead."

"She wants to eat your souls," Ambrose added.

"Our souls?" Margot whispered, her voice still shaky.

"It could be worse," Ambrose said.

"How?"

"I don't know, it seemed a nice thing to say."

"Something nice coming from the fool who cursed us," Doreen said, unsure what to do with him next. "I can't believe you took me to her. Did you *plan* for her to trap me here?"

Ambrose stared at the two witches who faced him. Doreen, with skin as white as a porcelain doll and just as smooth. Her eyes honey brown and her hair a coppery red shade only an artist could dream up. Margot, with her chestnut curls and brown skin, her sapphire eyes, and lashes so long they mesmerized. They didn't look like sisters, but they spoke and moved like them. Doreen had said they were cousins, but here stood a bond stronger than any he'd had with a single family member. It was in how they shifted closer together, their bodies responding without them ever making eye contact.

Both were prepared to move at him, to take him down. It was time to tell the truth before Ada's forest told it for him. He couldn't risk it replaying what had happened, using him as a puppet.

"I came to Ada after Lenora was sent from me, after I received word she had died. I was desperate and heartbroken."

"And?" Doreen asked, her hands curled into fists at her side.

"And I made a deal."

"With a ghost," Doreen said.

"With the queen of the dead."

"Who is *the* ghost," Margot added.

"I made a deal," Ambrose repeated. "And she gave me the spell for the curse."

"The one you cast against us," Doreen said.

"Against your family. You didn't exist."

"We barely get to now," Margot said.

"You knew Ada," Doreen said. "And you brought me to her, after she cursed my family."

"She's the only one who knew the way to the trials."

"These aren't those trials."

"I didn't know that!"

"Ah."

"Ah?" Ambrose said.

"You *wanted* to do the trials, to transform. You never cared about helping me."

"Why would he help you?" Margot asked.

"Doreen, you saved my life, you freed me," Ambrose said. "I am bound to serve you, and I vow to be honest with you."

"You're her bodyguard?"

"He's a pain in my ass," Doreen said. "Did you already know about the trials when I let you out of the Dead House?"

"Yes."

"What *are* the trials?" Margot asked.

"They're a way to transform," Doreen said. "Magically, I presume. And the way to break the curse."

"The curse Ada gave him?" Margot asked.

"Apparently."

"No, they are the way to make sure no one ever hurts me like your family did again," Ambrose said. "That is what the transformation means."

Doreen's mouth dropped. "So the original trials don't even *break my curse?*"

"I'm the only one who can break your curse," he said, raising his voice to match hers.

"What?" Doreen lifted her hands, and a violent wind blew cold as it crossed through the forest, bringing with it darkening clouds and the smell of ashes and roses in bloom.

"Dore?" Margot asked, holding a hand overhead.

"That's not me," she said, dropping her arms as the winds swept through, building as they blew, strong and harsh.

"It is a forgetting storm," Ambrose said, and swayed on his feet. "We need to get into the cave."

Margot raised a brow. "You want me to go into a cave with you, when you cursed my whole family and my Dean?"

"What's a Dean?" Ambrose asked, putting one hand out as he slumped.

"It's her husband," Doreen said, glaring daggers at him. "The one enthralled to her. Thanks to your curse."

"It's not a thrall," Margot said. "It's real."

"You can't know for certain."

"Are you two always like this?" Ambrose asked, running a hand over his brow, his color dropping from pale to practically see-through.

"You're not looking good," Doreen said, studying him.

"The storm is bad," he said, before he swayed a second time and stumbled forward.

"Shit," Doreen said, stepping into the circle and weaving an arm across the back of him. "Lean. Don't you dare die on me before I have a chance to kick your ass."

Margot stared, mouth wide open.

"Are you going to gawk at me or help?"

"I'm going to ask what the hell is going on."

"We're in an underworld prison, Ambrose was nearly dead for some time, and I am saving him now and maybe throttling him later. You showed up, and so did the storm, so unless we want to wait for it to start raining rabid cats or demonic horses—"

"Don't you mean dogs?"

"Not after swimming in the moat. Unless you want to risk what will come next, we might want to get out of its way, and going into the cave is the only option I see."

Margot sighed, dusted herself off, and walked over to where Doreen stood inside the circle. "How many times have you saved him, Dore?"

"A few."

"Gonna be tough for him to balance the scales."

"As long as he doesn't hex anyone, we're good." She winced. "Bad joke." She poked him in the side. "*Do not* hex us again."

Ambrose didn't respond, having fully fainted, but a loud crack shook across the sky, and the temperature dropped another ten degrees.

"Okay, we really need to get him into the cave *now*."

Margot stood on the other side of the circle, and Doreen steered him closer. Margot took hold of Ambrose's other side, and they exited the circle, hurrying toward the cave as fast as they could whilst dragging a large man. Once they had him inside the entrance, they paused under the overhang to catch their breath. Ambrose was deadweight, unconscious and unmoving.

"He said he could break the curse. He's known this whole time," Doreen said. "I'm an idiot."

"No, you're not," Margot replied. "You don't know what it might cost if he does." She paused. "I can't believe I'm defending him."

"Ha. Well, I'm going to find out the cost." She looked up at the dark sky, shifting as she held Ambrose up. "He must really want the transformation."

"What's the transformation?"

"Ada used it to turn herself into the ghoul she is now."

"She beat the trials to become a queen?"

"No." Doreen rubbed her shoulder with her free hand. "She didn't want to be whatever she is. She said she chose wrong."

"Maybe he thinks he knows how to choose right."

"Maybe he is full of shit."

"He's certainly full of something; gods, is he heavy," Margot said as rain sleeted down and she staggered under his weight. "The storm is moving closer, and I don't want to get hit by acid rain or whatever that might be. We need to go in deeper."

Together they dragged him inside. A light flickered on, and Doreen and Margot shared a look.

"Is there electrical wiring in the caves of the underworld?" Margot asked.

"I'd like to say yes, but I am thinking no."

"So what do we do?"

A shape shifted out of the shadows and stepped forward. "I think you may be running out of time," Eleanor said, giving Doreen a small smile. "I had hoped things might be easier for you, but things so rarely are easy here."

Doreen's shoulders relaxed and she shifted her weight to better support Ambrose. "I was worried you were a kelpie who learned how to run."

"Little is worse than the guardians of the waterways," Eleanor said, wrinkling her nose. "Come inside, before the skies open and the forgetting begins."

"The forgetting?" Margot asked. She looked from Doreen to Eleanor.

"Margot, this is Eleanor. One of our ancestors, the one who helped me when I was lost and explained what this place is and how we are all screwed, and how Ada is a queenly asshole."

"The rain brings with it the ability to steal your memories; it will make sure you have forgotten what you must remember," Eleanor said, sniffing the air. She nodded to Margot. "You are one of ours as well, though I do not think you were meant to be here."

"My mom bound me out of the family line, and I was able to call myself to Doreen, though who knew I would be entering hell."

"They did what?" Doreen said, shock skittering over her features and leaving her paler than Ambrose. "They've never unbound family before."

"They unbound us both."

Doreen blinked, her face pale and eyes bright.

"I'm sorry," Eleanor said. "Come in, kin of mine, and bring that miserable bag of bones. We don't want a single memory of yours to wash away; you can't spare to lose any on this night."

Eleanor shifted back into the cave, Margot and Doreen slowly hauling themselves and Ambrose in after her.

FOURTEEN

The wind whooshed past Doreen as she and Margot moved deeper inside. Slowly its whistle gave way to a low hiss. The cave was dry and warm, and not as dank as she'd assumed it might be. The floors were sand, and the walls had carved notches in them for torches and lanterns. As they walked, one lantern lit, and then another. It looked as though someone walked up and down these pathways often. Doreen did not linger over the modern features. She walked straight through after Eleanor, turning left and then right. Huffing as they shuffled Ambrose with them.

"You're sure we should trust her?" Margot asked, straining for breath as she tried to whisper.

"I do," Doreen managed, thinking back to the shimmer of Eleanor's soul, how pure it had been. "But even if I didn't, we don't have a lot of options."

Eleanor led them to the wide mouth of a doorway where they could look out and see the ocean. No rain fell on this side of the cavern. A fire was burning by the ingress; it was the third one they'd encountered in the caves. This one competed with the light outside and it was doused with a wave of Eleanor's hand.

"So magic works in hell?" Margot asked, grunting and shifting her weight yet again under Ambrose's heavy form.

"Yours does," Eleanor said, looking over her shoulder. She had changed out of her green dress. No longer looking ready for battle, Eleanor was now in a white dress, her hair woven into an intricate set of knots. She was also a good handful of years older than when Doreen last saw her.

"You're looking pretty fancy for a cave," Doreen said, once she and Margot had laid Ambrose on his side.

His breathing was good, and his color was slowly seeping back into the surface of his skin. She both wanted to sigh in relief and kick him hard in the side.

"I was not expecting this outing," Eleanor said. She let out a loud sigh that echoed the wind. "I should have tried harder to sway you to take the other route."

"If I had done that, I wouldn't have gotten to explore yet another dank cave with zero chance of spelunking," Doreen said, unable to quench the urge to joke. She was overwhelmed, angry, and scared.

"What was the other route?" Margot asked, giving Doreen a gentle rebuke with her eyes.

"The easy way," Eleanor said, before flashing Doreen a hint of a smile. "She chose the hard way."

"I chose saving him," Doreen said. "I could have left him here and gone on."

"Not if this is part of the trials," Margot said.

Doreen turned to Eleanor and raised a brow. "Good point."

"A variant of this would still have presented itself, only you would have gone through it alone."

"So the trials aren't set?"

Eleanor shook her head. "They are set within the rules of this world. If you, a MacKinnon witch, forsake one of your companions, the trial will alter itself to be just for you. If you have a companion, it will be for you both. You saved him, with your strength of character and will. If you had left him, you would have had to save yourself with your strength in another way."

"I saved him," Doreen said, her eyes returning to Ambrose.

"Yet again," Eleanor murmured.

"So it's not just me focused on that point," Margot said.

"I didn't know he had tricked me into being here," Doreen said.

"He didn't trick you," Eleanor said. "He can't break the curse unless he chooses to die."

Doreen's eyes widened as she stared at Eleanor. "Wait, what? He has to choose to die?"

"A heart for a heart," Eleanor said. "If he breaks it, he will break himself."

"How can you be sure?" Margot asked.

"Because I am."

"And if these were the real trials," Doreen said, "and he was able to transform?"

"He could save himself from death and still break the curse. Or he could kill you and your family. Who knows which he might choose."

"Good goddess," Doreen said, falling to a crouch and dropping her head into her hands. "This curse gets more and more fun."

Eleanor nodded, and her form flickered. She shifted in and out, from black-and-white to Technicolor. Once, twice, three times.

"What was that?" Margot asked.

"Are you okay?" Doreen asked Eleanor, who blinked, as though trying to clear her vision. "You did that before, at your house."

And Sinclair, in the castle—she had frozen and shuddered in a similar way.

Eleanor flickered again, and this time her outfit flickered as well. Technicolor Eleanor wore a deep-green dress with her hair down, and black-and-white Eleanor the white dress. Her face shifted from serene to fearful and back again.

"Did she do that before too?" Margot asked.

"No," Eleanor managed once she stopped in Technicolor, wheezing in a breath, her eyes flashing. "Listen. She's not going to stop, and you're in danger. You will never get out unless you find the truth kept in the apprentice's chapel. Use it to get out and stop her. You must, or we're all doomed. Please, *go* before—"

She flickered again and was back in the white dress, her gaze on Ambrose, who had awakened and muffled an involuntary gasp. He stared; his face transformed into a look of devastation.

"You never were very comfortable with the truth," Eleanor said to him, her face shifting into an overwide serene smile. "The truth won't hurt you, Ambrose MacDonald. Not when you've experienced so many lifetimes of pain." Her smile shifted then, into a soulful upturn of the lips. She focused on Doreen, fluttering into Technicolor once more. "Now is the time for you to change your fate. Find the truth. *Go.*"

Then she was flickering like a faulty light switch, moving away into the shadows as Ambrose staggered to his feet and cried out.

"*Lenora,*" he shouted, his voice cracking on the word. "No, Lenora, I'm sorry. Please, *please* don't leave me again."

Then he was stumbling after her, smacking into the wall as she faded into it. He scratched the surface with hurried fingers as his body trembled, until he collapsed into heaving sobs.

Ambrose didn't speak after he fell apart. It had been, Margot thought, like watching hope die. He'd gone from stupefied to desperate in the beat of a heart, and then splintered into broken chambers. Margot didn't know what that sort of heartbreak felt like, and as she watched him, she realized she'd been fooling herself to think she ever could.

Dean would never leave her. Never shatter any part of her soul. He was safe, and while she loved him, she could never touch the emotion that Ambrose was drowning under.

He sat against the side of the cave, saying the name *Lenora* over and over as if in prayer. Doreen sat beside him, her eyes shuttered.

She was not speaking, though Margot knew her mind was busy—she wore the same expression she'd had the summer Margot discovered there were spell books in the attic of her mother's house, ones kept under magical lock and key. Doreen had plotted, and once she had a plan, she and Margot had worked together with Margot creating the spell that would enable Doreen to get into the attic and steal the books.

It was a spell they would use many times while researching how to break the curse and grow their powers. Doreen the mimic, able to duplicate any spell, and Margot the creator, capable of crafting any charm from thought.

"Dore?" Margot finally whispered, when she could no longer tolerate the silence—save the occasional whimper from Ambrose.

"I'm here," Doreen said.

"Eleanor . . . she's Lenora?"

"It would appear so."

"His dead girlfriend."

"Yes."

"And she is trapped in this prison world."

"Seems so."

"And has been helping you."

"Yes."

"And told you to leave him."

Doreen blinked up at her. "You are asking questions you already know the answer to."

"Villainous."

"Perhaps."

"Do you know what the apprentice's chapel is?" Margot asked.

"We passed a chapel on the road from the castle," Doreen said, frowning. "I'm not sure how we get there, considering we're in a cave in a cave, or if we should go there."

"Do we have other options?"

"Not especially."

"Is this chapel a part of the trials?"

"Everything might be a part of them."

"Hmm," Margot said. She tilted her head. "And what precisely do you mean a cave in a cave?"

"I had to jump down a well to get here. Now we're inside another cave. I'm getting far too familiar with them, and I don't have a clue how we go up when all I want to do is go home."

"Ah," Margot said. "Remember how the aunts bespelled you and Jack and you almost married him?"

Doreen narrowed her eyes. "Hard to forget."

"At times like this, when we're trapped in hell with a grumpy witch and untrustworthy ghosts, and we've been excommunicated, do you ever wonder if you might have grown to not hate him for leaving every cabinet door open in the kitchen when he got a glass of milk."

Doreen let out a short laugh, and it seemed to jump-start something in her. She checked on Ambrose before scrambling up and starting to pace. "Even now I could never tolerate Jack and his randomly opened cabinets."

"Didn't he clip his toenails at the dinner table too?"

"He pooped once with the door open."

"No!"

"He also told me that my orgasm was my problem."

"We should have known then that the aunts cursed you."

A weak smile flitted across Doreen's face. "I never told you because I was so embarrassed, but I knew a few months before I told you."

"You did?"

Doreen nodded. "It was easy, being with Jack, even when it didn't feel right. It sounded harder to not be with him, and craving him was fun—though I didn't know then that it was fake. I liked that he craved me—I've always liked it when anyone I want craves me—and being able to give in to it was a relief in so many ways."

"I understand that," Margot said, her voice soft.

"Dean?"

"Yes." Margot wanted to say more, but her heart hurt too much to think about it any longer. She gave Doreen's shoulder a squeeze before she walked to the entrance of the cave and looked out. "We could walk until we find a way?"

"Sure."

Margot glanced at Ambrose's folded-up form. "I don't know if he's capable of moving."

Doreen's eyes narrowed in response. "I'm not leaving him."

Margot bit back a smile. "Okay."

"Jack . . . it didn't ever hurt to lose him or think of losing him. Though I was terrified that I hurt him as much as I did. That I could."

Margot nodded.

"Ambrose. His heart is really hurt."

"Doreen," she said gently. "He's the reason we're cursed."

"And the one who can save us."

"With a mighty cost."

"I know." Doreen paused. "I won't hurt him either."

"Did I ask you to?" Margot said.

"No, but you were thinking it."

Margot snorted. "I was thinking how jealous I was of him." She stared at Ambrose, how he curled in on himself. "It's like you said— it's real, what he feels. I didn't understand the extent of how false what I have is until this, seeing him get turned inside out."

Doreen looked down at Ambrose. "Though this may be too real."

"Do you still want it? That feeling now that you see it in action?"

"I do."

It was Margot's turn to nod, but she was nodding because she thought, perhaps, Doreen no longer had a choice in the matter. Not that she would say so out loud.

Doreen scooted closer to Ambrose, crouching to whisper something to him. He sighed, his body shifting closer to hers.

"You think he can walk?" Margot asked.

"Yes," Doreen said. "He just needs a bit more healing."

"I don't suppose you have any herbs on you."

"No, but it's sorted."

"How do you mean—" Margot stopped. Doreen pulled out a small athame and cut into her palm. Margot stared in horror at the blood dripping from Doreen's hand to the earth.

She pressed her palm to the dirt and smeared a line of brown and red, drawing a circle around herself and Ambrose. Margot's mouth dropped. Doreen was using *her own* blood. She was giving her energy to fill him up.

"You're exchanging your health for his?" Margot couldn't keep the horror out of her voice.

"I'm doing what needs to be done," Doreen said. "I know how to fill myself up when I'm drained now and he's too weak to do it for himself."

"You know how to refill your power?"

Doreen's response was a shallow smile. "He taught me. One more thing the aunts kept hidden."

Margot rubbed at the ache in her neck. "Yes, I think it's fair to say they only trust themselves."

"Clearly."

"Dore. Do you trust him?"

"I spent too many years being in the shadows, Margs. Watching, observing, hoping. The first time I met Ambrose, he looked through me. His aqua eyes, ringed in black, and his stubborn brow. I thought he hated me." Doreen didn't hesitate. "He's never tried to hurt me, though. He might seem pissed about it, but he's only ever helped. I don't think he can or will hurt me."

Margot stared at the circle, at the determined set of her cousin's mouth. "I trust you."

Doreen's eyes sharpened. "Even though I won't leave him behind?"

"I always trust you, Dore."

Doreen smiled, and Margot felt every bunched muscle in her back relax at the sight. They were still themselves—hell, even with a curse—and whatever it was between Doreen and Ambrose tethering a new binding in place.

"What are we going to do about Eleanor/Lenora?" Margot asked.

Doreen hesitated. "Eleanor has more than one face, so I think we have to be careful."

"Did she flicker when you first met her? Donna Reed to Jessica Jones?"

Doreen shook her head. "No, she was pure Jessica Jones. Though to be fair, she gave off more Veronica-Mars-meets-Arya-Stark vibes."

"I can see that."

"What aren't you saying, Margs?"

"The flickering . . . It was like she was being forced between two minds, two people."

"Two faces. When I was at her cottage, she had a room of mirrors.

She said it was where she kept her faces. How she couldn't be all the pieces of herself at once. I didn't know she meant it literally."

"It's odd," Margot said. "She warned us about Ada, and the Order is known to have dominion over the living whom Ada possesses and their souls when they die. Maybe Eleanor is one of those souls."

"That's terrifying," Doreen said. "Poor Eleanor."

"Her name was Lenora," Ambrose said, shifting upright, his gaze heavy, the intensity in his eyes causing Margot to lean forward, prepared to save Doreen if the MacDonald witch turned cruel. "That's what she called herself. Your ancestors named her Eleanor, but she said it was never the right name for a woman like her. She was right. She was loved when others were not."

Doreen reached into her pocket and pulled out a satchel. Ambrose's gaze went to it, and he swallowed hard.

"She gave this to me," she told him.

He stared, unblinking. "Her ogham." He looked at Doreen, and his features shifted. The harshness of his gaze softened, and his fingers twitched at his side as the hair tucked behind her ear came loose and brushed against her cheek. "Did you throw them?"

"I did. I threw three. *Beith* of the birch, *fearn* of the alder, and *nion* of the ash. Eleanor said it showed love magic, wise counsel, and strong women."

Margot cleared her throat. "Well, as a strong woman, I can say we need to get moving. Can he walk on his own yet, or do you need to drain yourself some more?"

He looked to the circle drawn around them, as though only now seeing it. "Damn it, Doreen."

"Hush," she said, standing. "I'm still livid with you." She toed the line, then used her hand to rub it clean, erasing the circle. Brushed her palm over her skirt when she was done. "Not a fancy cleanup, but it works all the same."

Then she walked toward the mouth of the cave, facing the sea. They had been in a forest, and now the ocean awaited. The world they were in was changing around them with every breath. One couldn't expect to walk through one door and out the same door into the same place. The trials were setting them on the course it chose.

Ambrose lumbered up and staggered forward. Margot waited, watching. Ambrose and Doreen stood side by side, looking out. Margot thought of Dean once more, and of what it might mean if they succeeded at breaking the family curse.

She was scared to lose him, but she would not fall apart. Not like she would if anything happened to Doreen. She sighed and walked to join them.

"Shall we?" she asked, stepping between them and looping arms with Doreen and Ambrose.

She stepped forward, placing one foot on the beach, then the other. The two others followed. She lifted her chin and started to ask if they had any inclination of which way the wind might blow, when the sand shifted.

The beach sank beneath her feet, the sand falling down faster than an hourglass, and all three were sucked in and under.

FIFTEEN

Doreen sputtered as she was spit out of the sand, landing with a thump on a plot of soft green earth. As she coughed and dragged in breath, two more thumps sounded beside her. Margot and Ambrose tumbled close by, each gasping to breathe.

Doreen gave them a once-over, checking that they were okay, before dragging herself to a standing position. She leaned forward and yanked off her shoes, digging her toes into the earth, desperate to believe she was standing on the ground. She was befuddled and disoriented from traveling upside down through a hole in the earth, and she'd given too much of her energy to Ambrose.

Her depletion was fighting to take her under, and she shook it off, refusing. She dug into the matter of the land, the ether and all the elements, and did what Ambrose had shown her on that hillside in the Isle of Skye.

As she channeled the rhythmic buzzing hum of the earth into her, a great whoosh of power shot up her ankles and clamored along her calves, sinking into her thighs. A bright sound burst out of the soil, a dizzying accompaniment of chords that should not have worked together. A strange progression of major to minor, a mixing of modes. Tonally, it should have sounded like a nightmare, but instead it was like being inside a memory of the first time she discovered magic. The dizzying sense that accompanied realizing you were a tiny being in a giant world.

Doreen sighed in relief, her vision going from fuzzy to clear as she took in the world around them. The music softened and the tension shifted, the vibrations of the strings overlapping until they were in unison, vibrating at the same speed, bleeding into an exhale of a resolution.

Doreen didn't try to shake it off. She inhaled the notes, pocketing them into her marrow, and rolled the tension from her body. She looked around for the first time, beyond the patch of land where they had been deposited.

She stood in the center of a cemetery.

Aged stones dotted the landscape like teeth in a yawning mouth. Doreen shuddered at the sight. Ahead of them stood what appeared to be the pink ruins of a former church. Multiple arches were carved into a sandstone structure that stood four stories high. The sides of the building tapered off, each level of carving and cutouts more impressive than the last.

"A peregrinate spell," Margot said, shaking out her shirt, her voice thick with alarm. "And not a well-crafted one. Who the hell puts a traveling hex in the middle of sand?"

"Best guess is Eleanor," Doreen said, her voice gruff, her throat aching. "Perhaps trying to help us get where we needed to go? I think we've found our chapel."

"You haven't asked me," Ambrose said, shaking the sand out of his hair. He lifted his aqua eyes to Doreen. "About her."

"I'm more interested in a conversation about you being able to break the curse, but to be honest, you don't strike me as the able-to-talk-while-dead type," she said, her voice low.

"What a good type that is," Margot said with a wistful sigh.

Ambrose shot Doreen a look. "She's odd."

"She's a MacKinnon."

His lips twitched. "So was Lenora."

"You can break it, but if you do, you die," Doreen said. "That's what she told us about the curse."

"That's the crux of it," he said. "I don't have a choice in the breaking. That's the other part."

"How can you not have a choice?"

"That's the way of curses, Doreen. If I am able to break it—which I don't know for certain—and I succeed, I die."

"Unless you beat the trials. The real ones."

"Yes, then I could transform and not die."

"But we aren't in the real trials," Doreen said.

"No, but Ada is the one who cast the original curse, so there is still a chance for you to be able to find love."

"Eleanor mentioned an original curse."

"You can defeat it and Ada."

"And you?"

He swallowed. "I think I am out of chances."

Margot squirmed from where she stood by a trio of gravestones. "Not to interrupt what I am sure will eventually be a touching moment of weird, but there's something seriously wrong with the graves."

"When it comes to asking you about Eleanor," Doreen said, slow to move her eyes from Ambrose's, "I don't need to know who she was to you. It's clear for anyone to see. She died, and then you cursed us." She thought about what Eleanor had told her in the stone cottage by the cliffs. "You loved her."

She felt him fold in on himself, his body shifting as though prepared to take a blow. He was bracing himself too late. "I never got to say goodbye to her."

Doreen reached out for him but dropped her hand at the last moment. "I think now, you may get the chance."

"It isn't her," he said, his voice cracking. "It can't be."

Doreen tilted her head, thinking. "She told me she wore many faces. So it's a version of what remains of her, perhaps."

Margot cleared her throat. "Really think you might need to see this, Doreen."

"Her being here has to be involved with the trials," Ambrose said.

"Or it's simply because she's bound here, and to Ada," Margot said, her voice as shrill as a poorly plucked string on a violin. "Please look at the *damn graves*."

"Fine," Doreen said, stomping over to Margot. "You could have just told us instead of . . ." Her voice trailed off, her hand going to her mouth.

"What is it?" Ambrose asked, crossing to where they stood.

Three graves stood side by side. With three names carved into them.

Margot Early MacKinnon
Ambrose Porter MacDonald
Doreen Antoinette MacKinnon

The earth beneath them was fresher than the others, and as Doreen stared at her name, her skin crawled with revulsion . . . and a lick of fear.

"What in the hell is this?"

"A warning?" Margot asked. "Or a promise."

Ambrose cursed, leaving them to walk among the other graves, pausing to read name after name. He circled where they stood and returned, his face drawn. "I know every name in this graveyard," he said. "I was tortured by most of them. They are the names of your kin."

Ambrose's jaw was clenched so hard it was a wonder it didn't shatter. Doreen didn't apologize again for the sins of those buried and gone, though she wanted to. She couldn't undo what had been done to him.

Doreen closed her eyes for a solitary moment before she turned, crossed to the graves behind them, and began to read. There she saw her grandmother's name . . . and her mother's. It nearly felled her, the sight of the letters that made up the name of a person she had never gotten to know. Doreen rested a hand on the grave as her legs trembled. She took slow breaths, praying her mother was not one of the souls Ada controlled, while also desperately wishing she could find her. Talk with her.

Doreen looked beyond her mother's marker to the rest of the MacKinnon line. She walked the ground, pausing at each grave as they led one after the other to Lenora, and then those who came before her. Each name was also carved into a brick in the wall that led up to the doorway of the crumbling church. Not quite a yellow brick road, but a pathway of named loss, nevertheless.

There was a single marker carved at the foot of the door. No grave, no dates, just a lone name.

Margaret Meghan MacKinnon
~Lost but Never Forgotten~

"Margaret?" Doreen asked, looking at the name. She'd never heard this name before, which was a surprise because their grimoire had a list of every last one of them scratched across three pages. She and Margot knew them all.

"Margaret MacKinnon?" Ambrose asked, jogging up.

"Yes."

He looked alarmed that she didn't know the name. "She's who was meant to tie our families together, the MacKinnons and the MacDonalds. The betrothal of Hastings. The one who broke his heart and started the original feud between our line."

"What does she have to do with the trials?" Doreen asked.

"Never heard of her," Margot said, peering at the marker.

"She is the original cursed MacKinnon," Ambrose said. "She is the reason Ada became the queen of the dead."

The original curse. Eleanor's whispered warning. Ambrose's words settled in a cold wash and flooded Doreen's system.

"Ada was clever and wicked," Ambrose said.

"She'd have to be," Doreen said. She was, after all, a vengeful spirit. Who happened to command an army of the dead.

"Ada won the trials, but she asked the gods for something they could not give. She wanted dominion over a soul, the ability to find it in death. She became a keeper of the dead instead," Ambrose said. "She has a need, a want for MacKinnon souls, in particular."

"And now we're in her own personal version of hell," Doreen said. "Trapped in it."

"I did not know this would happen," he said, his gaze sharp.

"We are haunted here," Margot said. She nodded at the chapel. "Don't you hear it?"

"The sigil?" Doreen asked, turning to her cousin. "Or something else?"

"Not our sigil," Margot said. "It's too eerie, too sad. Our sigil is chaotic; it's longing and need. This is something else." She rubbed at her sternum, right above where it housed her most precious organ. "It's sorrow."

Doreen forced herself to breathe. She nodded and let her eyes flutter closed, listening. "Sweeter, lonelier. The kind of notes that move like memory and seep down into your sorrow. Mold to your bones." It sounded like the pain she kept in the box inside her heart, where she'd stuffed the loss of her mother.

It sounded like grief.

"If Ada's grief is here, then perhaps she is too," Ambrose said, and he walked up to the front door of the chapel and slammed it open. Darkness lurked behind the doorway, and he strode in to greet it. Margot gave a little shout.

"He's a bit mad," she said, one hand resting at the base of her throat.

"Clearly," Doreen said, her gaze on the space beyond the door, a tug at the corner of her lips.

She waved for Margot to follow, and as Doreen entered, she brushed her hand over the doorframe and whispered a spell of protection. For whatever they found inside.

Finally, she disappeared into the dark where the grief sigil originated, and no other sound dared to follow.

It was so dark Doreen could hear her thoughts pinging in her brain and the sound of her heart pounding in her chest. She reached out as she moved, grasping air instead of wall. "Does anyone have a light?" she asked, hoping to find a footing in the void.

No sooner had the words left her mouth than flames flickered in all four corners of the room.

She gulped and turned in a circle. Doreen stood in a room filled with books. Stone pews were stacked with them, arranged as though they were in a library. Doreen counted ten rows of three. Thirty long pews filled with books. There was no altar, no stage for a pulpit. Only row after row of books, and then, along the wall, more books piled floor to ceiling.

In each corner of the room, including the farthest corner—which had crumbled into a gaping hole in the exterior leading to another interior room—were torches lit by unseen hands.

The floors were painted black. Doreen rubbed her shoe across, and the color smeared. Ambrose leaned down and brushed his hand along the books, his fingers coming away with gray powder.

"What is this?" she asked.

"Ashes," he said. "Soot."

"It's raining ashes in a chapel in the underworld, and the churches are filled with soot," Margot sang as she came up behind them, the words matching the strange melody following them.

They spread out, Ambrose and Margot heading to the pews in the middle of the chapel, Doreen shifting to those along the wall. The books started by the door, their covers faded and fragile, near to crumbling. Doreen didn't touch them for fear they might disintegrate. In this hallowed place she was scared to touch anything for fear it, or she, might fragment into nothing.

As she moved from one wall to the next, the books changed. They had a luster. None were titled, but they aged in reverse like Benjamin Button—from falling apart to well-loved to pristine. When she finally reached the farthest wall, the covers were gleaming and the pages appeared crisp. She gave in and picked up the last one, and nearly dropped it as she read the title page.

The Uncommon Life of Doreen MacKinnon
By Doreen MacKinnon

Fingers trembling, she turned from the title page to the first paragraphs of the opening chapter. The words were handwritten, and it was *almost* in Doreen's slanted script. If not for the angry loops attached to her *g*'s and *y*'s.

The words on the pages were familiar, echoes of her thoughts about being lonely, wishing she had a boyfriend, wanting to be known and loved. Yet Doreen knew she had not written these words. They were an amalgamation of her feelings. Like someone had gotten a glimpse of what they thought she was feeling and ran with it.

This did not stop the leaded weight from thudding heavily in the pit of her stomach. She flipped ahead to the last chapter, halfway through the book, and saw a single name.

Ambrose MacDonald

Beneath it was the entry:

The first time I met Ambrose, he looked through me. His aqua eyes with their black ring, and his stubborn brow. I thought he hated me.

It did not matter that he never saw me how I wished he would see me.

It did not matter how long the wait, or if he saw me at all. He so often never did. The singular study on my end was enough to sustain me.

I whispered to him on the cliffs. With my eyes closed and my bare feet planted in the earth. As I rolled forward, my toes gripping the ground, my weight shifting forward, I would imagine him behind me.

This morning, I stood there, thinking of him yet again.

The wind rustled my dress against my calves. Invisible fingers brushed against loose strands of my hair, grazing my cheeks. I pretended it was his fingertips and rocked back onto my heels, to imagine for a moment he was there to catch me should I fall. I inched closer to the edge of the cliff; of danger, of possibility.

Beneath me, waves crashed, the sound an answer to the unseen storm brewing beneath the surface. I knew that call; it was building in me.

I leaned forward once more, my breath filling deep into my belly, expanding my chest until I thought I might float up and away like a leaf into a breeze. I am performing for myself; on my own, as I drift forward again onto my toes. The skies overhead turn the shade of a faded bruise. My heart on display, battered for only me to witness.

As my dress billows up around me, it tries to pull me away from the edge of this daydream. Of impossible things. Of a moment I live only in my head. Of this all-consuming desire.

The sun breaks through the clouds. It crests across my face and heats the cold running through my bones. I am always wanting him. I am always cold. I hold these fragile dreams close. They are a whisper, thinner than a single strand of hair, more fragile than the loosest thread along my hem.

I feel beautiful.

I am thankful there is not a looking glass to inform me. For surely it would prove me wrong, and I would see myself through his eyes. In them, I am never as pretty as I might or could or should be. In them, I will never measure up.

The wind grows colder, and I shift forward. Aware,

knowing none of it is real. It is all a story in my mind, and I am alone.

Standing at the edge of a cliff:

I take a step back. One. Two.

When I turn, the dream will be gone, the spell broken. I back away another step. Afraid to turn. And when I do, at last, he is there. Waiting. Only, even as I am standing before him, it is me that he does not see.

Below us, the gurgle and gush of the water is constant and free. I blink, and he is gone. Once more I am alone in my thoughts. In my desire. My wants and my daydreams.

It only takes a moment for me to realize he was never there at all. It was always, and ever, only this edge of the cliff and me.

Doreen did not read on.

Her hands trembled as she set the book down. She stepped away.

The words were not hers, aside from the first ones—which were ones she had spoken to Margot before. The rest, though . . . she had not written them, but as she read them, they felt true. It was as though someone was watching her, taking note of what she could not, would not, voice. Pulling out the tender and tentative truth of what she did not wish to admit. Of how she was feeling for Ambrose.

Doreen swallowed, and turned to step away again. To put space, distance, between the book and herself.

But as she did, a shape formed in the empty space beside her book. It filled in, and a new book with a sparkly purple cover appeared.

Her whole hand vibrating, Doreen picked the book up and turned to the title page.

Margot MacKinnon

She looked over to her cousin, who was perusing the books stacked in the pews. While she stared at Margot, trying to work out what the books could possibly mean, the chapel shifted.

It happened much in the same way Eleanor had flashed from black-and-white to Technicolor. How Sinclair had stopped and struggled to speak at the castle. One moment the chapel surrounding her was a makeshift library; the next, it was an aged and barren space, typical for a forgotten country chapel.

There stood an altar, with five rows of unlit candles and a dais. In the center, a tall black candle sat by itself.

In another flash, Doreen saw the old chapel imposed over the chapel-slash-library as it was now. They existed simultaneously, which was impossible.

"Do you see that?" she asked, keeping her voice low, as though the very presence of the books demanded a whisper.

Ambrose looked over to her, and he blinked. He put the book in his hand back into its slot on the pew and looked down at the row of books before them. He saw, Doreen supposed, what she did. That they were in two realities. He took a step back and she realized he should have been standing over a gaping hole. He started when the tall candle in the middle of the room wasn't there for him to bump into.

"Doubles," he said.

Margot stared at Doreen before shifting her gaze to Ambrose. Her eyes moved to the book in Doreen's hand, and Doreen followed her gaze. The book shifted as they watched. From a journal bearing her cousin's name to a large bone.

Doreen's arm shook. She looked at the shelf, and realized it was still a stone shelf, but it was filled with various bones and jars and liquids that looked like they belonged in a devil's laboratory.

"Put that back, Dore," Margot said, her voice quiet but firm.

Doreen set the bone down, her breath catching in her throat. "What *is* this place?"

"It's a graveyard, the real one," Ambrose said. He nodded to the hole in the floor. "I think whatever we're meant to find is in there."

"You think Ada is in that hole?" Margot asked.

"I have no idea what is tucked down there."

Doreen tiptoed back toward them, dusting her palms off on her pants. "The books on the far wall are journals. I . . . I found one meant to be mine, and Margot's appeared while I was standing there. Before the library turned into a decayed house of bones."

"Those are the same," Margot said, nodding toward her row of pews full of books. "They present as journals written by our ancestors. I think . . . this is their dust, ashes, and bones. A collection of our family line. I don't know why ours would be here, besides the fact that we are here."

Doreen gulped and shuddered. "So, it could be Ada's cave, somehow?" They looked down in the hole together, staring into the darkness. "I've really had enough of caves for a while," Doreen said.

"How do we retrieve what we don't know to ask for?" Margot said, looking down.

"I used the Secretum Veritas to find the Dead House."

Margot turned to her. "Really?"

"The Dead House?" Ambrose asked.

"Where my aunts kept you," Doreen said, wincing as she explained.

"Apt name," he said, before wandering over to the door to look out.

"What do you need to do it?" Margot asked. "You can do it again, yes?"

"I used the bark of my wand and a bloodstone, herbs from my

garden and a bit of Stella's hair from her hairbrush. I had an idea of what I was calling, though."

"What was the cost?" Margot asked.

Doreen squirmed.

"You haven't paid it yet?"

"No."

"You're in a hellscape."

"And?"

"It didn't occur to you that this was the cost?" Margot said wryly.

"Which part? Getting hoodwinked by the queen of the dead, tossed into the underworld, or facing the horrors of this place?"

"Maybe all?"

"Huh."

"Was it worth it?"

"What?"

Margot's brows shot up. "Finding him."

"Yes," Doreen said, without hesitation, not meeting Margot's eyes.

Margot thought about it. "Love, I think, is worth it."

"I've always hoped that would be true." She met Margot's eyes. "But that's not what this is about."

"You might end up surprised," Margot mused.

"Is it worth it to offer up some of my blood and call it a day?" Ambrose asked, rejoining them.

"Not in this world," Doreen said. "We don't know what we would bind you to—Ada, the rest of the dead kept here . . . Who knows?"

"If it breaks this world, isn't it worth trying?" Ambrose asked.

"No," Doreen said.

"I'm offering."

"You're a moron."

Ambrose leaned down so they were face to face. "I'm not afraid."

"Maybe you should be."

"Maybe *you* should look around. We're in a prison we can't escape, and I am being haunted by my dead ex-girlfriend. What do you have to lose?"

Doreen paused. Her eyes narrowed. "Oh my goddess, do you *want* to be tied here? *Stuck* here? With her?" She threw up her hands. "Of course you do. Fine, give me a rusty nail and I'll slice you open. Lean over so I can stab your aorta."

"What?" Ambrose took a step back. "That's not what I am saying. I don't want to be stuck here."

"I think you do."

He gave his head a slow shake. "No." He stepped closer to her. "Doreen. Whoever that is, even if it's Lenora, she isn't *my* Lenora."

"*Your* Lenora," Doreen said. "Says the man who was sobbing over her in a cave, prepared to turn into a stone and never move a pinkie toe again after seeing her." She crossed her arms tight over her chest, and the muscle in his jaw bulged again.

"It's fine, Ada could pop up and eat us at any moment, but go ahead, choose now to argue," Margot said, and inched away from them, slowly making her way to the other side of the room, where she picked a book off the stacks and started flipping through it.

"It's normal. I was in shock," Ambrose said to Doreen in a loud whisper. "How did you expect me to act? I was *shaken*."

"Heartbroken."

"Of course I am," Ambrose said, his voice rising. "I bloody loved her and *lost her*."

"And now you want to *stay with her*," Doreen said, slamming her pointer finger into his chest. "Admit it."

"There isn't anything to admit."

"You want to stay."

"I don't."

"Do so."

"No, I don't."

"Liar."

"I do not—" He stopped talking, reached up, and grabbed her finger.

"What?"

"You're jealous."

"I . . ." She tried to yank her finger away. "No, I am not. Give that back."

"You *are*."

"She really is," Margot called from where her nose was stuck in a book.

"It's called self-preservation," Doreen said, trying to tug her hand free and failing.

"Doreen," Ambrose said, tugging her to him. "Who is the liar now?"

"I don't want to get stuck here, and without you I can't break the curse. You said it yourself. That's all."

"You sure that's the story you're sticking with?"

"Speaking of story," Margot called when it was clear Ambrose and Doreen had reached a stalemate and were locked in a staring contest, neither moving nor admitting the truth of what they were feeling. "You two might want to read a few more of these creepy bone histories before we make any rash decisions. Unless one of you is about to confess your undying love."

Ambrose dropped Doreen's hand, and she took a step back. He looked away. She hurried over to where Margot waited.

"Are they all journals?" Doreen said.

"Did you look through this one?" She held one up. "It's your mother's."

Doreen sat down hard on the pew and snatched the book from Margot. She yanked it open, fear and hope flooding her.

Frances S. MacKinnon

The name was there, but the words were not. Instead, it simply read:

Soul Not Willing

"What the hell does this mean?"

"I don't know." Margot shook her head. "Do any others say the same?"

Margot walked around, flipping through the journals while Doreen held the book as though if by clinging to it she were holding on to a tangible piece of her mother.

"Why would Ada take these?" Ambrose said.

"What do you mean?" Margot asked.

"Ada needs souls. She siphons their life force and power."

"Maybe the *souls not willing* are the souls she couldn't take," Margot said.

"You think so?" Doreen said, her heart a painful vise in her chest.

"Yes," Ambrose said, giving her shoulder a gentle squeeze. Doreen exhaled, hope and relief flooding through her. "It makes a kind of sense. These could be a record."

"Hey," Margot said, pausing. "Hear that?"

Doreen looked up. Cocked her head.

"It's another ripple in the room, but instead of showing two places," Margot said, "it's like there are two sounds fighting to be heard. One of them won't hold."

A book tumbled from the shelf, coming to a stop at Ambrose's feet. He picked up the book.

Eleanor Lenora MacKinnon

Ambrose let out a mournful huff. He flipped through the pages, looked up, and swallowed hard. "There's something wrong with the ink. It's rust-colored, nothing like the quills or ink Lenora used. Some of the words have been scratched out and new ones added over them."

"How do you mean?" Margot asked.

"Listen," he said. "It looks like originally it reads: 'She wanted to meet her fate, but changed her mind.' But it's been scratched out and now reads: 'She wanted to meet *Ada*, but changed her mind *and died*.'"

"What? Why is it altered?" Margot said.

Doreen thought of Eleanor/Lenora, and how she was like the two worlds of the chapel—shifting from one form to another. How the sentences were saying one thing and then another, how they were in one world that seemed to be more like two.

"Miles to go before she sleeps," Doreen said. She walked over to the hole in the middle of the floor. "What if Eleanor couldn't come here without being summoned?" she said. "This is a place that is orchestrated, and that means everything that happens is being done on purpose. It's like there are two sides of Eleanor—the one I met in her home and the other version. What if she's bespelled?"

"So why send us here?" Margot said. "Do you think she wanted us to call her here?"

"I don't know what to think," Doreen said.

"She said she's part of the family," Margot said.

"Only one way to find out," Doreen said.

"What are you two thinking of doing?" Ambrose asked.

"There's a way to call us to one another," Doreen told him. "A type of MacKinnon communication—the aunts used it when we were little and gone too long into the woods. Though I don't know if it will work now, since we've been untied from our line."

"Only one way to know," Margot said.

"*Safe as secrets,*" Doreen said, calling their family motto up, her voice ringing loud.

"*As it ever was,*" Margot replied, her voice echoing in the space around them.

The lanterns in the room exploded, the flames rising high before they shot across the room, creating a bridge of light. The ground creaked, the wind moaned, and the chapel shook before it let loose a bang and the center of the floor caved in on itself.

They scrambled back, over the pews and away from the sinking floor, Ambrose holding on to Doreen, Doreen pulling Margot after her.

One by one the rows of books toppled as the chapel shook, and then finally stopped.

A long, terrifying minute passed. They waited for Eleanor to appear.

The only sound in the room was the swishing of the fabric of a skirt, shifting like a sigh. Doreen turned to Margot to ask her to be still, when she realized Margot hadn't been wearing a skirt. Neither was she, nor Ambrose.

The sound came again, the movement growing closer.

Doreen's heart thumped so loudly in her chest she wanted to shush it.

There was a flicker of a light, and then a rumble deep in the chapel. More candles than the room could possibly hold flickered to life. The land quaked. Suddenly, pages shot from the hole in the center of the room. Hundreds of them, one after the other. They rained down on them, fluttering like petals from a giant flower.

She thought she heard a rush of words from the poem that had pelted their skin once they'd left the castle.

The woods are lovely, dark and deep,
But I have promises to keep,
And miles to go before I sleep.

Briefly, Doreen wondered if those words weren't for her, or even Ambrose.

What if it was all for Ada, or from her? Grief in one of its many forms. Haunting them.

Whispers filled the room, a resonate voice, ageless and tired, and the poem's words tapered off. The words of the pages bucked as the floating pages came together in a whoosh of air, snapping into line between two thick covers. The book dropped directly in front of Doreen's feet, and the chapel fell silent.

SIXTEEN

The chapel Ada stood in was empty. The floor was littered with debris. Covered in wood hunks from the crumbling ceiling, caked in dust so thick it was practically carpeting, while the single tall candle in the room flickered with its black-and-gold flame.

Ada turned jar after jar around, reading the labels, as she walked along the far wall, muttering to herself. She was looking for a box, one she had misplaced hundreds of years ago. Or so she pretended. She was waiting on the shadow of Lenora MacKinnon to return, and the spirit had been gone far longer than it should have taken to assess the situation.

Sending the spirit to spy on the witches should have been as easy as breaking a bone, but they weren't listening. Either their humanity was waning or Ada's hold over them was. She had to believe it was the former because she could not lose the power to control these souls until she had succeeded in finding the one lost to her.

Ada's spirits always ended up unruly—their humanity faded the more she used the bits of their souls, the more of them she took in. Bits of this person and that, a modern-day Frankenstein's monster. Or, to be more precise, the truth of what Mary Shelley had seen when she'd stayed in the wrong castle, with the wrong ghost.

The shadows liked to torture the living, and Ada only cared to control them when she needed them. She'd never wanted children, and having an army of clingy ghosts had reinforced the belief a thousand times over.

She studied the bones on the ground before her, how lovingly they were arranged. She brushed the dust away from the skull, poking the empty eye sockets with her pinkie, waiting to feel something in her own eyes as she probed. But there was nothing. No pain or pinch. The only thing Ada felt was the gnawing ache of a lifetime of loss, and the pinprick of fear that her time would run out.

"Where are you?" she called out, the flame flickering in reply. She walked along the far wall and turned into the corridor, a board on the floor catching her eye. It was tilted up in the corner, and a silver spoon handle stuck out of the raised end.

"Ah," she said, the memory rushing in. Of the box being sunk into the space beneath the board and the ghost storing it there. "That's where you went." She walked toward the board. She should have known Lenora might try to hide the paper. It was a warning. But while Lenora might think she could change the course of Ada's plans, she was still her puppet. Nothing and no one would ever alter that. Ada reached down to pry the board up with the spoon handle, and, when that didn't work, kicked at the board until it popped free. She knocked the raised board out of the way, revealing a dusty box. Ada reached down and opened it, the wood creaking in time with her mismatched bones. She pulled the scroll free and let out what some might call a laugh and others a bellow.

Ada unrolled the scroll and flexed her fingers as she began to read. The ache bloomed into a break, and it took everything she had in her many bones to keep reading the journal entry, to allow herself to look back.

September 1232

It wasn't that I didn't love Hastings. I'd known him as the boy from down the creek for so long, with his bright eyes and a smile that promised trouble. The trouble had always involved a forage into the forest, him telling me to try the next tincture I was afraid to mess up, me believing a little more in myself because of him. That sort of support made it impossible not to adore him. Hastings didn't just befriend me, he saw me.

But he didn't change the way I saw myself. That honor didn't belong to him.

Hastings MacDonald became my best friend the way the leaves change on an oak tree. There are subtle signs, hints of gold mingling with the green, until one day you look up to find the most vibrant red you've ever seen. He was kind too. He brought me a dog when I fell and broke my leg. The resetting of the bones had been so atrocious I was too afraid to walk and spent weeks in bed. Until I had to chase the dog. I went from terrified to running in no time.

In return, I taught Hastings spells to curse his enemies. To mix in a bit of their hair or fibers from their clothes in a tincture of moonwater and pumpkin and thyme, how it would enable him to shift the tides in the autumn when they were turning on him. Soon he taught me ways to bend the wills of anyone who dared challenge me, which I used often on my poor lady-in-waiting.

Hastings and I . . . we were the happiest of companions . . . until our families had a falling-out.

The threat of war over land shifted our dynamic, with the two families at odds, and then there were no more excited grins and delicious mischief. No more star-gazing or foraging. I worried over him when the big war began, the battles growing bloody and fierce.

For a long time, there was only his letters, until those too tapered off. Months passed, a year, two. Then more.

Time had a way of helping me move on. Time and a new friend whose lips tasted of cherry wine and whose voice followed me into my dreams.

Until one day, a new enemy hundreds of miles away cropped up for both our families. The two factions decided to repair the dispute. Decided to bring the two clans back together with a binding that would be unbreakable.

I had thought to reconnect with my old friend. I'd even daydreamed of how we might perform a spell under the new moon, lay a feast for the goddess of remembrance and rebuild what had been broken.

I had been a fool to think such niceties would suffer the folly of rushed men. Instead, it was I who was gifted like a loaf of bread, packaged, and delivered to a doorstep. Promised with words that had not been anyone's other than mine to give.

I was offered to Hastings like I was the second-best mule. Ten years and one heartbreak later, handed off to a boy who had grown into a man who fought his own battles and carried too many scars.

My friend was changed. And in due time I learned

that what was lost could not be found, not when what he wanted was something I could and would never give.

"My love," the shadow whispered, crawling out of the wall.

"I have not called for you," Ada said, refusing to look at the shape lurking beyond her shoulder. She dared not move, lest she reveal the weakness of her heart.

"You always call for me," it said.

Ada waited, knowing it would come to stand before her. Not quite the man he was, but as determined even in servitude.

Hastings MacDonald's ghost was a quiet and irritating thing. It was clear he carried love for Ada, no matter what she had done to him, to them both. He also carried revenge in his bones, and Ada could never trust him because of it. Which was why she had stored the rest of his soul and humanity far away.

He had been with her the longest, and she knew his humanity was dangerous. Hastings could no longer evolve—he was dead, after all—and yet, he had been observing the world for as long as she, watching her. He was always watching, always there, and she could no more let him go than she could give up her search.

"I never call for you," she replied, not meeting his gaze.

"You do," he said. "You call for me even as you seek her."

"Do not think her name," Ada said, her pearl eyes flaring as she finally looked at him.

Hastings flickered before her, the man behind the ghost showing before it shrank back into the thing she'd made him by binding him to her, by feeding on the few remaining pieces of his soul that she kept along with all the others tucked away in the jars of her caves.

She much preferred to imbibe on living souls, but the witches of the MacKinnon line protected themselves now. They were stronger than she had ever been. She had pride over that, over how her blood and Margaret's had made it so. Their oath and bloodletting together bound them, the same as their love—the ties that bind are simple, and for Ada and Margaret they had been true.

The coven had driven Doreen to her, and then cast out Margot. She had two living vessels waiting, trapped.

Ada smiled at Hastings. She could afford to be lenient when she was so close to getting new power, so close to the end.

"Why are you really here?" she asked.

"You have my bones."

"I am not using them."

"No, but the boy will."

Ada stopped what she was doing and looked up at him. "How could he? He gave them to me."

"You're not as clever as you hope," he said. "Send me to him, and I will make sure he doesn't have the chance."

"You would harm your own?"

"I would do whatever was required to protect you. It's all I have ever tried to do."

Ada shook her head. "Too risky, and you can't be trusted. I'll keep an eye on them all the same."

He nodded once, his gaze going to the back wall, where the jars waited. Ada did not see the smile shift across the caverns of his face, rendering him almost human, nor see him flicker in and out one last time.

He faded from the room, shade into shadow into shade. Ada remained lost in the past, her eyes focused on the parchment in her hand and the story it contained.

Eleanor stared at the group in front of her. Ambrose, with his posture somehow both unguarded and upright. He always seemed

ready to go into a battle. He shifted closer to Doreen, seemingly unaware he was doing so, as Doreen glanced at him in surprise. Doreen
was a sloucher, but in a graceful I-can't-be-bothered-to-use-my-
backbone sort of way that reminded her of a cat being petted. She
arched and elongated like a tabby, unlike Margot, who stood with her
feet planted and her hand fisted at her hips. Power radiated off her
in a more aggressive way than how it rolled from Doreen. Together,
though, they were mesmerizing. It was little wonder Ada wanted them
for her collection; she could last hundreds of years off their brightness,
their goodness.

"We called for Eleanor and received a book?" Margot said.

"I think we found what she was telling us to find," Doreen said.

The three sat, pulling the pages out and passing them between
themselves. They could not know these words were the only true
ones in the room. Ada's words, her truth, was here in more than one
place.

"It confirms Ada used her experience in the trials to re-create
what she could remember. To build this place," Margot said, as she
skimmed the page.

Eleanor nodded, unseen by those before her. Magic did not stay
for long in this prison. It shouldn't exist at all, but magic didn't follow
a mortal set of rules. It created its own, and what wonderful magic it
was, to have the two cousins together.

"She can't sustain herself without a tie to this world," Doreen said,
reading over Margot's shoulder. "That was the punishment the gods
gave her for winning the trials and asking for power over a soul. They
granted her request but gave her a set of parameters that would keep
her from tearing the world apart."

"She wanted the power to find the soul of the one she loved." Ambrose gave a small smile. "It never goes as it should, does it?"

"You couldn't have followed me," Eleanor said to him, her mouth moving but no words rising to reach him. "And had you gone, you may not have survived the storm."

"I could survive anything for love," Doreen said, the truth of what Eleanor spoke finding her, though she did not know she was answering Eleanor.

"That's what Eleanor thought too," Margot said. "She was right, and she was wrong." Margot turned to face her cousin. "Listen to this . . .

"Ada would lay down her life a thousand, a hundred thousand, an infinite number of times over to find her. To find Margaret. To reclaim her lost true love, who she assumes is waiting, suffering. We all do her bidding, and the creatures she commands are splintered here with her.

"Eleanor is her puppet; it's the price everyone pays for Ada making her deal with the gods," Margot said. "All of the journals here tell half-truths, and the spirits bound to this world are half beings. Maybe that's why the other journals sound like narrations and this one sounds like her real diary."

Eleanor waited for them to finish piecing the journal together. Then the two women moved from the main room into the antechamber. She sent the last of her power into it, to knock aside the stone in the wall and show them one last thing they needed.

"I am sorry, Ambrose," Eleanor whispered, as she prepared to give him what he needed to know. "The truth can set you free, but it might devastate you first." She crossed to him, lifted her hands to his face, and pulled him close.

Ambrose blinked in surprise, sensing Eleanor, though he could not see her.

Eleanor pressed her mouth to his, soft and unyielding. She poured the truth of herself into him.

Then the candles flickered, Eleanor shifted from Technicolor back into black-and-white, and in the next mortal breath, she was gone.

As Doreen and Margot entered the nearly concealed side room, a large slab of marble tumbled out of the crumbling wall. A light flashed by the fallen slab, and Doreen was reminded of the stone table in the Goodbye Castle that Ambrose had told her was there to honor the dead. As she drew closer, she realized that bones had been resting on the marble, but they were now deposited at the base of it. She went to take a step back, but paused when an object to the right of the slab caught her eye. The marble had broken through the wood in the floor, showing a box concealed there. Doreen reached for it.

Her thumb pricked the edge of the box, a drop of blood pooling there. As soon as it dropped onto the latch, the box clicked open.

"'By the pricking of my thumb,'" Doreen whispered. She opened the box. Another journal lay within. This one did not look like the others. It was soft, the cover green, and it reminded her of a Bible. There was something precious here in these pages, she could feel it. Gently, she removed it and slid it into her pocket.

She glanced over at Margot, who was examining the far wall of the chapel that led outside. A crack had splintered there. It was spreading, reminding Doreen of the lines in the family tree crest at Ambrose's castle. How the limbs of the tree stretched out and curved and looped.

Slowly, then all too quickly, cracks sprouted in the other walls in the chapel, and the floor groaned. Margot spun around, eyes wide. "We need to get out of here, Dore."

The chapel shuddered as the walls shifted. The bones and rock on the ground vibrated, and the far wall groaned as more rock broke free and fell.

"It's ready to cave in," Margot said, panic in her voice.

"Okay, come on," Doreen said, her hand checking to make sure the book was secure.

She hurried back to where Ambrose stood, swaying on his feet. His cheeks were flushed, and his eyes were glazed. She yanked, physically pulling Ambrose from his daze. "It's time to go," she said. "The whole place is going to come down."

"Grab as many bone journals as you can," Margot called, scooping up books from the pews. Doreen and Ambrose seized what they could, keeping one eye on the far wall as it shook and cracked. Doreen made sure she grabbed the books with her and Margot's names before nudging Ambrose.

Together, they all stumbled out and onto the grounds behind the chapel right as it wheezed out a puff of stone and dust, sending debris flying toward them. As it rained down, they ducked, using the books as protection over their heads.

The chapel emitted a sound like an old woman sneezing through a cloud of perfume. Then the building settled, and all was as still as the resting dead.

Doreen and Margot gathered the books scattered around them while Ambrose removed his overshirt. Doreen struggled to focus as she watched him undress. His forearms were as solid as the rest of him, his wrists tapering to lead into hands that belonged on an artist. It shouldn't be seductive, the juxtaposition of strength and elegance, but it summed the man up so perfectly. He was careful and methodical in how he piled the books on his shirt, and she couldn't help but think that he'd be equally gentle and methodical in any activity—until he wasn't. The power banked in him was like a cannon waiting to be ignited, and as she tracked the exposed skin on his stomach when he shifted, her mouth ran dry.

She thought of the journal entry she had not written. Of the truth in those pages.

She wanted him, and that scared her. Doreen wanted a man who was head over heels for a ghost and responsible for her being unable to find love. She could die because of him, and she couldn't stop thinking of how it would feel to slide her fingers up to where the skin was peeking out by his stomach, to inch her fingertips under his T-shirt. She wanted to scrape the scruff on his chin with her teeth, to drag her lips across his wrist and smell the skin there.

She wanted to keep him safe, to make him hers. To win the trials and his heart. It was more than this craving; it was how he made her laugh when she didn't want to, how he had been through hell and still was somehow clever and kind. He believed in her. He didn't try and hide magic from her, but instead showed her how to use her own. Ambrose saw her for who she truly was, and he accepted her.

And more than that, she *wanted* him to see her. She wanted him to want her, to dream of her, to fall for her the same way she was falling for him.

Admitting the truth was like a fire hose blasting across her skin, burning the need into it. Saturating her with a love so heady she thought she might burst. Into tears or fireworks or both.

Doreen had never known this type of love; she had hoped it was possible, but she hadn't known it might feel so consuming.

"Doreen?" Ambrose called, as he finished tying his overshirt into a makeshift bag to hold as many books as possible. He lifted his gaze to hers.

Doreen stared at him, everything about him in sharp focus. He narrowed his eyes, and she looked away, the words and emotions clogged in her throat. She glanced over to Margot, who was watching her with a knowing glimmer in her eyes and a sympathetic tilt to her chin.

Margot could read her like the alphabet. Doreen blushed and pushed the hair from her face. "I'm here."

Ambrose passed the books he held over to Margot. He didn't speak again right away, but he kept those aquamarine eyes on her. Doreen was charged, standing so close to him, terrified to move a muscle. Could he tell what she was thinking; was she wearing her love like a flashing sign across her face?

"We need to go back to the castle," he said with a one-shoulder shrug. "I know the way now."

Then he slung the bag over his shoulder and started walking, his steps sure, his head high.

The ground before them glittered like a field of diamonds. A lone pluck of violin strings rose up and wrapped itself around Doreen, tugging as though connected to her heart. The organ itself knocked three times in her chest, her heart giving a painful thunk as Doreen admitted she was falling in love.

A sense of knowing unfurled and rooted. She was in love with a stupid stingray. As the thought settled, the path to the castle grew clearer in her mind.

Heart.

Without intending to do so, Doreen had completed the second trial. She'd found a love story, her own.

Margot reached out, grabbing Doreen's hand, and gave it a squeeze. Ambrose did not wait for them. He brushed a hand over his lips as he marched on, not bothering to look back.

Unfortunately, she realized her love story was one-sided. Ambrose was in love with a ghost, and Doreen was on her own.

She glanced down, certain the thump she felt was a book dropping to the ground. The journal was still clasped in her hand.

As Ambrose got farther away, and Margot tugged on her arm for them to follow, Doreen realized it had only been her heart plummeting to her feet.

SEVENTEEN

The Goodbye Castle's stark stone walls and climbing lilac wisteria stood out vibrantly against the hazy indigo skies. This time, there were no melodies following the travelers as they made their way up to the arch and moved inside, and the castle's fires flared to life as soon as the three entered. The walk there had been brisk and quiet, save for the loud thudding of Doreen's heart in her chest.

Ambrose had not spoken so much as a vowel as he led them down a path, onto a road, up a hill, and down another path. Doreen had the sense he could have led them in his sleep. He didn't miss a step. He also didn't look at her. Not once.

It was unnerving how she had disappeared from his consciousness. Or so she felt.

"You okay?" Margot asked her, as Ambrose left them in the entry-way of the castle to walk down a hall.

"Sure," Doreen said. "Never better."

"Dore," Margot said.

"Remember when Nick Hargroves was obsessed with you, and you cried for days after you realized it wasn't real?"

"How could I forget?"

"Remember how I didn't say a word, I just brought you Skittles and horror graphic novels of zombies eating hearts?"

"Some of the best stories I've ever read."

"Let's invoke the same unspoken rule now."

"A few years ago you declared processed candy vile and disgusting."

Doreen's stomach rumbled and she sighed. "I would eat my weight in Skittles right now."

"Let's see if we can't find something to eat in the horror of this place. Any idea how we can find the kitchen?"

Doreen shrugged. "No clue." She looked around and had a thought. "Uh . . . Sinclair?"

The slender ghost walked out of the fireplace, and Margot let loose a scream.

"Holy ghosts, don't do that," Margot said, a hand over her heart.

Sinclair dipped into a low bow. "Apologies, I didn't realize we had a lady in the house. How may I assist?"

"Margs, meet Sinclair, Ambrose's valet. Sinclair, is there a kitchen, and can you help us with food? The kind living people eat. I assume you dine on the air of inequity or the sorrow of the masses."

Sinclair lifted a brow. "I prefer to devour the happiness of a quiet afternoon, but I believe I can help with your needs."

True to her word, Sinclair led them to the kitchen in the lowest level of the house. It was a staff kitchen, and it was both large and imposing. There, Doreen and Margot found a fully stocked pantry.

"How is this here?" Doreen asked, studying the various fruits, vegetables, grains, and nuts.

"It stocked itself when you arrived," Sinclair said.

"The food just appeared?" Doreen said.

"It disappeared from the gardens and reappeared here."

"A self-sustaining kitchen," Margot said. "Clever."

"It's tied to the needs of its host," Sinclair said. Her mouth moved, but no sounds came out. There it was—a frozen glitch in Sinclair, similar but different to the one with Eleanor. Sinclair cleared her throat and spoke again. "I do hope it will help. If you have need of me again, you only have to ring that bell, on the far wall, or call my name."

Then Sinclair was drifting toward the bell, and through it.

"That was odd," Margot said.

"The frozen-mouth thing?" Doreen asked.

Margot nodded.

"Did it remind you of Eleanor, and her glitches from black-and-white to in living color?"

"Yes."

"Me too."

They stared after her for a moment before Margot finally cleared her throat. "I think it's time you read, while I whip up something for us to eat."

Doreen nodded. She climbed onto the large stone table in the middle of the kitchen, sat crisscross-applesauce, and opened the green journal, eager to see what secrets it held. After rolling her shoulders back, she nodded to herself and began to read.

Autumn 1289

It started with a kiss.

Or to be honest, it started with a girl. The summer our family came to stay was the summer everything changed. She was my first friend, and the first person I met who I couldn't stop staring at. I tried. I even forced myself to count the minutes when I wasn't looking at her so I wouldn't be tempted to. It became a game. Can I get to one thousand before I allow a glance? How high can I go? What if I count other things, the number of objects in the room that are blue?

It was astonishing how beautiful she was, how smart and funny, and everything about her looked so soft and warm.

She loved the garden. The stars and the sea.

Eventually, she loved me.

It started with a girl, which led to a kiss, which changed everything.

Doreen stopped reading as Margot slid a plate with freshly sliced strawberries, almonds, carrots, and cashews before her. She grabbed a handful and chewed greedily before she registered that Ambrose had come into the room. She swallowed, twice, and put the book down. Margot had placed a mug of water by her as well, and Doreen drank. Ambrose watched her, tracking all of her movements. It shouldn't have felt so intoxicating, but Doreen could barely breathe while his eyes were on her.

"Do we think it's Ada?" Margot asked.

"It sounds like her, and the date is right."

"Ada and a girl, huh?" Margot asked with a nod, tossing a cashew into her mouth.

Doreen nodded. "Can't imagine that would be well received in their time."

"So does this mean we have two of Ada's journals, then?"

"I guess, though I don't know why this one was locked away when her other pages were in the main room."

"I wonder if it was real for them," Ambrose asked, moving farther into the room. "Does the book say?"

Doreen returned to the book. She ate another handful of nuts and vegetables, swallowed, and resumed reading.

Winter 1292

Hastings has returned, bringing with him a storm. Biting winds so cold they freeze the tip of your nose and an unforgiving rain. The wet sinks past all layers of clothing, nipping into the bone. Fire does little to chase it away; the drafts find us without hesitation in and out of our homes.

Our last visit was tense. There is a sickness in her, a gnawing worry about us being caught. She is pulling away. The looks between us don't last as long. When I enter a room, she barely acknowledges me. Occasionally, she leaves as soon as I take up my knitting and sit.

She leaves tomorrow. The clan meeting will soon be over, and I am not sure when she will return.

Hastings haunts the hallways; he doesn't speak, but the looks he gives me are ones I know well. They remind me of the ones I have given to her.

The storm is a warning of what is to come.

I do not know how we will survive it.

How I will win her heart and refuse his.

as Ada married?" Margot asked, interrupting Doreen. "What do we know about the queen of the dead?"

"She was not," Ambrose said. "She was betrothed to Hastings

MacDonald. The handfasting never took place. A feud arose and the MacDonalds broke the arrangement."

"Because of Margaret?"

"Because of Hastings," Ambrose said. "Or that was the legend in our family. They said he only wanted to marry for love and found it elsewhere. He never settled, not even for more money and land."

"And Ada?"

"She lived to the ripe old age of eighty. Ancient in those days. She never married, and her clan remained one of the greats. There was a sister, younger, I believe, who bonded their clan to others."

"What about the marker in front of the chapel?" Doreen said, locking eyes with Ambrose. "Margaret MacKinnon."

"It's possible," he said. "The marker for her was the following year of the last entry you read."

"Shit," Doreen said, skimming ahead.

"Cursed from the beginning," Margot murmured, before eating a grape.

Spring 1294

It has taken me time to look back on what happened. To be willing to crack open the thick oak door with its angry iron fittings and large metal portcullis. There is a thread of knowing, perhaps not noticeable to adults. It's a truth children know, one accessible when you aren't doubting the truth of what could be and what is. I forgot to tap into that knowledge for too long, even with my powers being as great as they are, even with the tether—a very real thread growing between me and her.

The night of the céilí brought music and laughter, and a coil of tension so tight it thrummed through my whole body. Being near them both under the banner of celebration of our three clans coexisting should have left me on a high. However, it was both easier and harder to tolerate the proximity with the candlelight and flutes and bonfires whose ashes floated to the tops of the tree line.

I sat with my feet bare, tapping against the smooth stones. With every other tap, my big toe scraped against the rough patch of boulder. It coincided with the beat of my heart, and the feeling of eyes on me, a prickle of skin to the left of my shoulder blade. I didn't want to look back, afraid the wrong person would be watching. It was amazing how much of my day was ruled hoping for the right person to see me.

Not wanting to stay another moment in the anticipation, I left the courtyard and walked down toward the cliffs. I could have taken the walk even in a night at its fullest dark, with all the stars—every last one—blinked out from the sky.

The ocean drew me to it, in the same way the tilt of her head drew me to her.

I reached the edge, stopped, and waited. It never crossed my mind that I would remain alone at the edge of my world on the lush hardscape of the land my family cared for, the land that cradled our bones long after our lives were lived on this earth.

The truth was, I simply miscalculated who would join me. Hastings's footsteps fell hard and fast. He did not hesitate in his movements. The gait of the man was as sure and determined as the heart of him.

"You are avoiding the world," he said, coming to stand at my elbow. I did not have to look over my shoulder to know how he would be standing, with his legs planted, his chest out. Hastings was born to take up space.

His eyes, however, would remain roaming over the terrain and horizon, into spaces few could ever see in the dark. Danger lurked in every corner for the men and women of our clans. I knew this, but unlike him, I simply did not care. I had power on my side, and enough of it that I had rarely ever been concerned about the things that went thump in the night.

I did not bother turning my head to answer him.

"I cannot avoid it when I live in it."

"Then perhaps you are avoiding me."

"I haven't managed such a feat since the summer I turned thirteen."

"You refused to leave your room. It was a quiet season, that."

"I was sick with fever for weeks."

"You are barely mortal; I don't see how you could be sick." He laughed at the joke, one he loved to make. Hastings saw me as stronger than his mightiest enemy. He was not wrong.

"I experience all the mortal atrocities, I assure you."

He hummed, the sound low and friendly, like a childhood lullaby.

"You know what is coming," he said.

"You are referring to the handfasting," I said, never one to run from a truth. I did not plan to marry him, but I had to discover a way out first. I would not hurt my friend. But I would never betray my heart.

"Yes," he said. "Much will change."

"Change is always coming; it's as constant as those waves beneath us seeking the sea."

He reached for me then, his fingers capturing a loose strand of hair. He brushed through it before releasing it and me. Then his footsteps were receding, leaving me alone with my thoughts.

That's all there is," Doreen said with a sigh. She flipped a few pages ahead and found a page with ten words written across it. "No, wait."

"What does it say?" Ambrose asked.

Doreen looked up, and behind Ambrose was Sinclair, watching them.

Sinclair shook her head, and Doreen looked back to the words.

"'The spell is the truth. The truth is the spell.' I . . . well, Ada said it to me."

"I've heard the aunts say it before as well," Margot said, frowning.

"Another family spell?" Doreen asked.

"Or a spell for sending?" Margot said. "Stella said something similar right before she cast me out."

"So it is a spell for casting out . . ." Doreen glanced up and Sinclair faded away. "Or summoning."

Doreen swallowed, and then she took a breath and spoke the words. The rest of the pages filled in, but with a different handwriting.

I stood beneath the stars, speaking to the earth. Calling the vibrations up into me, sending them back down, a blast into the ocean creating jets that never reached where I stood but called to me all the same. It was our game, and the earth was always ready and waiting.

A spray of leaves rained down and I held my arms up and out, smiling as they fluttered into my outstretched hand. The left one. The one Ada would have held, if we were alone and far enough away from home on a walk to forage.

I knew it was her, and I knew she would need answers I didn't have. There was no future here, and there was no way around any of it. But if you couldn't find a door in a castle wall, you only had to knock out a window. Power had been granted to me, more than any other witch in our family. More than anyone in the family knew. I would find a way to blast through.

"Did he find you?" she asked.

"He always does."

"It's not unlike the way you always find me," she said.

I nodded. She wasn't wrong.

"We can't keep pretending we don't know how this ends," she said.

I turned at that, my hands fisting in anger, until I saw her face. How crumpled her brow and forehead, how deep the frown that pulled at her lips. Then I wanted to shake her.

"How can you not even fight it inside your own mind?" I asked. "If you aren't willing to put up the fight for me before it comes to fruition, it will never work."

"It was never going to from the beginning," Ada said, her voice soft. "You know how I feel. I would do anything to be together, but there is no together."

"Anything is possible; we simply have to find the right solution."

"The right solution is for our families to stay out of fighting each other. It's going well enough. Do you really want to risk a war for us?"

I wanted to snort at the nonsensical idea, but I couldn't.

While I could protect myself and Ada from outside forces, not even my power could stop my family from making rash or stupid decisions. I had tried to bind them before; it was impossible to control the line of my blood.

"I won't let anyone take you from me," I said. "You have to decide if you're willing to fight for us, to run for us."

"Margaret." Ada whispered my name, and it was so full of longing that my knees shook.

Ada wasn't a fighter, but I needed her to try. She met my eyes, and I couldn't stop myself—I reached for her, pulling her into my arms. "Perhaps I have enough fight for the both of us," I said, making it a promise to myself.

When I kissed her, all my worry melted away. Fear ran from me. All that mattered was this moment. Ada. Our future.

"What are you doing?"

Hastings's voice cut through the night like a sword through butter. I let go of Ada, turning to face the fire in his tone, putting her at my back to keep her safe.

The man I faced was not one I knew. He was confused, angry, and staring at me as though I were his enemy.

He wasn't wrong, but he wasn't right.

"Ada Rose, what are you doing?" he said, as she shoved me aside. She stepped forward, her arms braced on her hips and her shoulders back. A goddess rising.

He blinked, as if to clear smoke from his eyes. We were not a thing to blink away.

"I'm sorry," I said. "Hastings, I can't marry you."

He stared, shock centering across his features. "You can't marry me, Margaret?"

I shook my head, and he looked between us. His stance shifted from charge to retreat.

"I won't marry you either," Ada said.

"Do you think you're to marry her?" he said, but I could not tell if he spoke to Ada or me.

It was my turn to stand my ground. I planted my feet wide, fisted hands on my hips. Speaking his language. Our language, the warriors' reply.

"It doesn't matter," I said. "I don't love you in the way you need, and you can never give me what I need."

He looked to Ada, and she said, "You will never be her, and I—I can't keep doing this."

"You have always had too much steel in your backside," he said, rubbing a hand over his face.

"I won't bend, but that isn't a bad thing."

"No? What do you think will happen if the wrong sort sees you?"

"They won't."

"You're so godforsaken lucky it was me to find you, and not your da." He looked to Ada, whose skin had blanched to a white crisper than new-fallen snow. "How would your family take this? Were one of your brothers to find you?"

She shook her head.

"Don't," I spit the word out. "Don't scare her off so you can have your way."

"It's not my way." He ran his hands through his hair. "I've seen how you look for her, you know. Watched you wait, with your eyes on the door. You follow after her like a child trailing their mother's skirt. I know you. I have known you all my life. I didn't realize you were a fool as well as besotted."

"If you knew, then why are you pursuing me?" I asked, my skin hot, my jaw tight. "If you care so much, why interfere?"

"Who else can protect you?" he asked, his hand going to his

belt as though a threat was closing in. "From yourself, from what's to come for you if you keep up with this, and her. Who else could save you?"

I bit back a strong curse.

"And you, Ada?"

"I don't need help," she said, "and those are pretty words crafted to provide the way for you to get what you want." She reached for me then. I found her hand and squeezed. Hastings let out a muffled cry at the gesture.

One beat passed. Two. She pulled her hand away.

I turned too fast, words tripping over my tongue to yell at her for not holding on. For not fighting for us.

A goldfinch chatted, trilling in the distance. The wind blew a soft breeze over our feet. Below, the waves crashed in their constant, set course.

My eyes were pulled from gazing off the horizon.

In a matter of seconds, my feet had sped too quick. The air rushed from me. I had spun the wrong way. Ada knocked into me. My hip connecting with hers, my shoulder knocking hers back. I stumbled once. A small step back, as though readying to ask her to dance.

It was a simple miscalculation. The tiniest of steps.

In an instant I tumbled down, into the deep, dark, waiting waters.

The power to save myself should have been mine. In my veins, flooding my system, I had so much magic banked— waiting there to call the wind and carry me back.

Instead, I did nothing. I waited in disbelief, wanting every-thing to undo itself. As though such a thing could exist. Then I hit the water.

In time, Ada would recognize Hastings was holding her.

His arms tight, his words low and soothing. She was sobbing yet she did not notice. I was screaming but she could not hear. He carried her home. She never felt the earth rise to meet her.

They sent a group to recover my body, though they never would find one. Our love was gone.

With me lost, there was nowhere to go but inside my mind, into a forest so quiet, dark and deep.

For nothing mattered any longer. Nothing ever could. Not now that she was gone and so was I.

The journal, it's Margaret's?" Doreen said, her eyes going back over the words. Rereading the ending.

"How?" Ambrose asked.

"I don't know," she said.

"It's all so horrible," Margot said, accepting a glass of the wine Ambrose had found in the pantry and decanted. "Both heartbreaking and terrifying."

"It was not the way of things," Ambrose said, stopping his pour at a fourth of a glass. "To go against the family in those times."

"She must have felt so close," Doreen said, thinking of Margaret going over a cliff. Unable to think of anything else, to stop seeing it play out in her mind. "Her dream was at her fingertips, and she sent it tumbling into the deep."

"No wonder Ada went dark," Margot said.

"How could this exist, though? If Margaret isn't here?"

Ambrose shook his head. "I don't know, but we're in a prison world that shouldn't exist, run by a spirit who should be deep in the earth. Maybe the better question is what can't exist here?"

"It makes sense she'd rage out, but to go from a strong, oppressed badass to the queen of the dead?" Margot said. "I think I need more wine, and a break from reading. It's devastating, and the words . . . they're hard to hear."

"It's the truth of it," Doreen said. "It's never easy to take in someone else's truth and force it out. I wonder if this is why there are so many journals. If Ada's truth is something she has never been able to accept or make sense of, maybe she's trying to gather everyone else's?"

"Or she's simply psychotic," Margot said.

Doreen snorted as she took her half-filled wineglass and topped it off to the brim. Ambrose made a noise of disapproval, and she shot him a halting look. "Don't you start with me."

The corner of his lip hitched up in the smallest of curves, and Doreen struggled to hide the fizz of bubbles bursting inside her at the sight. She knew what Margaret had meant, about wanting to be seen by the right person, about struggling to take her eyes off them.

"I'll see if there's anything more to discover," he said. "I have too much truth floating inside me. I can't see how one more will topple me over."

Doreen wanted to ask what he meant, but he simply moved around her. She bit her lip instead, trying yet again to drag her eyes from Ambrose MacDonald and stuff one more unasked question down her throat.

He sorted through the books they had brought and found the one that had rebound itself inside of the chapel. The one composed of the hidden pages that had flown at them, the one they thought Ada had written.

He opened it and began to read.

Winter

There has always been talk of the gods of the forest. Of things otherworldly. Our family has pagan roots, no matter the shift in acceptance of one god for another. We are the outcasts, the fringe clan. We were born with power, but I think it's the isle that has allowed it to grow. Every generation becomes a bit stronger, though none have the way of communing with the land as I do.

Premonition through dreams as warnings is what we are known for, while Hastings's people are said to be able to touch another and know their intention. Margaret knew plants on instinct, how to blend them and merge them to make a healing balm or tonic. And how to use them to harm or even kill.

The earth liked Margaret almost as much as I did.

The three clans are the strongest because of our gifts, though I don't know if any of the others know we all have them. I would not have, had it not been for Hastings and Margaret.

I would not have known what to do with mine, had it not been for him. For the story of the gods and the trials had been told to him by his grandfather. No one had ever won them, but I think it was because only men ever tried. I was not fool enough to think I was stronger or smarter or cleverer than the gods.

I won because I was more desperate.

I woke the statues of the sleeping maidens with the truth. I freed the drowning kelpies, and I traded my echo for one of theirs.

They could not refuse me then.

I stood before them in the center of their labyrinthine cage and made my request——never a demand.

"Power to find the soul I have lost," I asked for, my voice ringing clear. "I would give my heart and life for it, if I could bring the soul back to me."

I wanted them to take my life. To send me to her. Instead, they did as I asked. They granted me the power of the lost.

The first ten years were a steep learning curve. I dreamed of the people in Margaret's line. Of those in my line and in Hastings's. I did not dream of Margaret. I scried for her and spoke to the wind. I asked the earth to seek her and bring her to me.

Instead, it brought her kin. To my door, seeking guidance or help with their gifts. It was my prize for winning the trials, and because Margaret and I had shared blood under the new moon when we pledged our love. We had given one another a blood oath, and now my blood called to hers——and those of her line. It was on a sunny spring afternoon that finally I realized what I could do. I sat, listening, trying to be patient for Margaret's sake and to honor her family, when it happened. The young man was speaking of battle and wanting to avoid being injured. He reached out to touch me, and I saw his light. A bright white light scouring through him. Not just in him, but as him. I reached for it, drew it in. I did not know what I was doing, and I took too much. He died on my floor, his soul soaking inside of me, filling up the cold places.

After that, I did not get sick or age for another ten years. I studied the fireflies at the outer edges of the isle, calling them to me from across oceans. I could summon birds, insects, and sea life. A new power, unhelpful in my search, but entertaining. I did not realize I was haunted until the singing started.

A low, solemn note. It was rose soft and sure, low and lonely. It crept in through my open window.

It sounded like Hastings. That was my first thought. Though I had not seen Hastings since I left him by the fireside of his home, so many years before. I had told him I could not, would not, marry him. He did not understand. Margaret was gone, he said. He needed a wife, and the clans needed us to bring them together. He would be good to me, he said. It did not matter. My will was set.

I left him for the trials, and after that, everything was different.

This was not Hastings, however. It was the young man whose soul I had taken, and he was lost now. A shade of himself. I let him in and kept him close. He was bound to me, I soon realized, and until I released him, he would have to serve me. I sent him out into the world to look for Margaret. I knew souls sustained me and made me stronger. Learning I could control them after I took them, guide them to help me find her——it was revolutionary. I could not lose the connection.

It wasn't thought out. It was instinctual. Most pursuits of power are, though, I suppose. I called to the souls in my line, in those of Hastings's and Margaret's. Those bound to me by the loss and my win in the trials.

I did not drain them as I had accidentally done that first time. I siphoned them instead, slowly and over time. It was easy to store the bits of them I needed. A jar here, a box there. The caves beneath my home made it simple, and soon I left the little house on the edge of the cliffs for the caves. I no longer felt the cold, rarely needed food to eat or water to drink. Eventually, I needed nothing at all.

Yet my Margaret remained gone from me.

That's a horrible prize," Margot said. "It sounds as though they handfasted to one another and bound it by blood."

"Blood that tied her too closely to us," Doreen said.

"It would be beautiful if Ada hadn't gone rogue," Margot said.

"If her vengeance weren't happening to us, I might agree. Does she say how she defeated the trials?" Doreen asked, finishing the last of her wine. Ambrose flipped ahead, read, flipped back, shook his head.

"Most of her pages are lines of repeated phrases, dark things that don't tell much other than she was losing her mind. There is one other entry, though." He paused, reading ahead, his face drawn. "It's grim."

"Let's have it," Margot said.

Doreen grimaced but nodded.

The Unending Winter

It is always dark now, always cold. Tonight, I stood at the edge of my cliffs once more. It is forever the edge that I return to. The flowers I planted so long ago bloom still, enchanted and trapped in their youth. The petals are marked by the cold; they have gone soft and blue in their frost, no longer pink and precious. Beside them, I grow beyond old.

I have stood on the edge of that cliff an unknowable number of times. I do not feel the cold, I cannot see the dark. The flowers, which once soothed me, no longer bring me solace nor grief.

There is no reason to deny the truth. The need for more grows. More power. More souls. More time to find her.

It is easy to store what I need. The souls in the boxes in the cracks in the corner of my world. Tucked into the seams of the caves that I call home. Hidden in plain sight, not that there is anyone to see anything any longer.

The spirits are with me. Always. I store them well. Keeping them close and safe. If I cannot fly free, neither shall they. Not until she is home to me again.

The spirits closest to her shall lead me to her. They cannot escape once they are in my hands. She and I will be together, and nothing shall ever stand in our way again.

She hid the souls in the *cracks of caves?*" Margot asked, as Ambrose finished reading. "What the hell does she mean that she holds the spirits in her hands?"

"It's insane how she really has been collecting our ancestors," Doreen said, downing a fresh glass of wine, wiping her brow. "The graves outside, the ghosts trapped here."

"Stealing their souls from the beginning," Ambrose said, setting the book down and moving to stand closer to Doreen. He smelled of wine and cedar and she leaned closer, sniffing as discreetly as possible. It was impossible not to be affected when he was so near.

"We must be missing something," Margot said, walking to the doorway leading out of the kitchen. "Ambrose, where is this ghost of yours? Sinclair?"

"She should be upstairs by the fireplace. You only have to call for her."

"I don't think she wanted us to read those pages," Doreen said, frowning. "Ada, I mean. It's why Eleanor sent us there. We need to use the knowledge against Ada."

Margot nodded. "I'll be back." Then she was striding out of the kitchens, leaving Ambrose and Doreen alone.

Doreen looked up at Ambrose and the words died on the tip of her tongue. She realized, as she stared into his eyes, which had gone as dark and broody as his moods, that she had been fooling herself.

She wasn't going to be able to hide what she felt; she was lost for him. Staring into his eyes, that thread of growing awareness and heat building . . . it was the most potent feeling she'd ever had.

There was no thrall, no forced desire on anyone's part. This was real. Real and petrifying.

Doreen knew she should be worrying about Ada, about the souls and how to break free from this place. But she couldn't think at all when staring into the stormy blue of his eyes, and when he leaned closer, she forgot how to breathe.

EIGHTEEN

Ambrose stared down at Doreen, his mind racing. It was too easy to lose himself in her eyes, in the desire to get lost inside her completely. He was still reeling from the moment in the chapel when he saw a flash of Lenora. Her bright green eyes, her mouth on his. A new and wild truth she had passed from her to him in what he was certain was meant as a goodbye kiss.

As soon as he felt lips brush his, he heard her voice inside his head. "I am sorry, Ambrose. For you never knew the truth." She showed it to him then, and it rocked him to his marrow.

Nothing was what he thought it had been, and he had made so many mistakes.

Staring down at Doreen, he was determined not to make them again. He vowed to himself to love her unconditionally, with honor and honesty.

The feeling was so overwhelming, he had to force himself to look away. To take a step from her side. It was like shoving a boulder along a hillside. He had never wanted to move less, and yet too much was at stake to remain still.

Margot came hurrying back into the room, with Sinclair alongside her. "I found Sinclair," she said, slightly out of breath, her blue eyes bright. "I thought if we want to know about the spirits bound to Ada, we might want to ask an actual spirit."

Sinclair shimmered and shifted, coming to stand before them.

"Sinclair," Ambrose said and rubbed the back of his neck. Of course. They had a spirit before them, one he cared for. Maybe finding out why it was bound to this world would help them to free her. "Why are you here, my friend?"

Sinclair leaned forward. Her eyes closed. Wind blew into the room, rattling the crockery, sending the fruit rolling off the table onto the floor. Ambrose braced himself against it. Sinclair's hair flew back from her face, off her shoulders. It floated behind her as though caught in a storm. She lifted her hands as though she could fly. She shifted, arching as though over something.

Doreen thought Sinclair looked like a woman standing on the edge of the world, about to leap. She had stood in the same position before, when she freed Ambrose, when she jumped from the ledge of the castle to nowhere and into this world. It was a hair-raising place to stand.

"I am here," Sinclair began, and started to shake. A vibration tremored up and down her body. Full, consuming spasms wracked her. Doreen thought of Eleanor, of the spirits being splintered. Anchored and yet not. She reached out, and placed her hand into the spirit of Sinclair, through her.

"Why are you stuck?" she asked Sinclair, keeping her hand steady, holding on to that which she could not see. The light inside of Sinclair pressed against Doreen, a spark of something greater.

The tremors shuddered into submission as Doreen kept a hold of the spirit. Sinclair sighed air she could not breathe in relief. "I stole my way into this place," she whispered. "It is not mine; it is yours. Yet into the woods I crept, the woods so lovely, dark and deep." Sinclair's eyes focused on Doreen, she placed a hand over hers and *squeezed*. Doreen gasped as Sinclair leaned closer. "The old man knows."

"The old man?" Doreen said.

"Nothing here can be anything other than what it is in the real world. Except me. I came and was more than I was; I was the first possibility. Able to transform once I crossed the barrier in the Goodbye Castle, because my bones reside along the veil there. The rules here are hers, but your magic is changing it. Your magic has the power to alter this prison. It is a cage, and all cages are made with doors to be bent, kicked, slammed open." Sinclair shifted closer. Her words flooded out in a rush. "The bones bind this prison world. Her blood. Your family's blood. Her bones. Our bones." Sinclair's voice shifted, the Sinclair from Ambrose's castle coming though, deep and male. "Destroy her. If you do, you will set us free."

Before Doreen could speak, Sinclair shook like a carbonated bottle of fizzy soda. Her form wavered before them. "Follow the song. Through the forest, so lovely, dark and deep. Finish *her* trials."

Then Sinclair rushed into Doreen, knocking her off her feet.

For a moment, Doreen was underwater. Back inside the moat outside the castle walls. She was drowning, dying. She tried to shout, and she was standing in a forest. Sinclair leaned against a tree, beside her. The spirit lifted a finger and pointed into the woods. Tall oaks and pines dotted the landscape, spreading out onto a runway in the night. Between them flickered little lights. Fireflies. A song filled the air, and the fireflies blinked out one by one. *Not* fireflies; these were sparks—bright and luminous.

Souls.

Sinclair turned and pointed in the opposite direction. Doreen spun until she was facing the castle. Sinclair clapped her hands together, twice, and the singing in the forest intensified.

The castle wavered. The one she had come from stood with the moat surrounding it, and then it was gone. Ambrose's family home was there instead. The gardens wild and unruly. She looked up and saw the ledge of the castle, and two forms standing there.

Herself and Ambrose. Holding hands.

Standing on the edge of the world. Preparing to jump.

She called out for them, and the world wavered again. The forests no longer held the lights and trees; instead, row after row of blue flowers dotted the cliffs, blowing gently as the wind swept across them from the sea.

"It's not real," Doreen said, taking in the castles and the forest and cliffs. "None of this is real."

"It is as real as magic can be," Sinclair whispered. "Save him, save yourself, save us all."

Then Sinclair faded, and Doreen was underwater again, spinning and flipping until she landed with a thump and found herself in the kitchen of the castle, in the embrace of Ambrose's secure arms.

D oreen came to, gasping for breath. Her body trembling so hard she couldn't stop it. Every muscle shook, her nervous system revolting from what Sinclair had done. From the things she had shown her.

"We're trapped," Doreen gritted out.

"Yes." Ambrose nodded. "We are aware."

"No," Doreen said. "I don't think we're even here. I think you and I are still standing on the ledge, about to jump." She looked to Ambrose. "I think we're as stuck as the spirits."

"What ledge?" Margot asked.

"When we crossed into the trials, we had to make a leap of faith," Ambrose said.

"I didn't jump off anything," Margot said. "I was shoved." She picked up the berries littering the floor. "The aunts sent me to you."

"The aunts," Doreen said, sitting up. "Maybe they can help?"

"The ones who cast us out? *Those* aunts?" Margot said.

"They don't know about the souls. Their souls will eventually be taken by Ada too, if we don't succeed. We need to tell them what's going on. That our family line is stuck in this world, and if we don't get out, we will all be trapped here for eternity and then we're all screwed."

Margot's brows shot up. "It sounds more convincing when you say it like that."

"Yes." Doreen nodded, and she rubbed at the side of her head, where a knot was sure to form.

"They may try to take him," Margot said, nodding at Ambrose.

He grinned. "I would love to have them try."

"Stop," Doreen said, giving him a look. "Sinclair . . . she also said to ask the old man. I haven't seen any men here besides Ambrose."

"Could be part of the curse," he said. "There is only one old man I know of on the Isle of Skye." Ambrose's hand lingered on Doreen's arm, his fingers trailing up and down, leaving goosebumps in their wake. "Sinclair loved to tell the story of him to me as a child, the Old Man of Storr."

"If everything here is a copy of the real world," Doreen said, "maybe he's who Sinclair means."

"What you're saying," Margot said, reaching for the closest open bottle of wine and taking a gulp straight from it, "is that we need to send a message to the aunts who have excommunicated us and go visit the Old Man of Storr on the Isle of Skye, a freaking rock formation, because we're trapped in a prison of our minds and that is the only way out."

"Pretty much, yes," Doreen said.

"Good, good. So long as we're all on the same page."

Ambrose and Doreen exchanged a small smile, and they all got to work.

NINETEEN

Kayleen and Stella were worried. When they had come up with their plan to send Margot to Doreen, and use Margot as a be-spelled human tracker, they had been under the influence of a new batch of Kayleen's extremely potent moon-bathed jasmine wine. Every-thing Kayleen created was potent; it was one of her many gifts. It was also why they were drunk for three days and didn't sober up until after the cousins left and their house and yard were covered in dried flowers, empty cups, and a raining haze of ennui.

They had not anticipated they would lose track of Margot en-tirely. That when they scried for her and Doreen, using the wisps of hair they cut from them when they were girls, they would come up empty. But there it was, no location, no sign of either.

"It *was* a good idea," Stella said, sitting at the table on the wrap-around porch. She was in the process of filing her nails, studying a star chart, and flipping through a shadow book for spells on how to undo a shitty spell gone wrong. The last one, Kayleen had told her precisely three times, did not exist and no amount of magical thinking would summon it.

"It was a drunk idea. When has a drunk idea ever been a good idea?" Kayleen was leaning into her powers instead of wishful thinking. She was busy making a potion out of reishi mushroom, lavender, and her own highly effective CBD to open her eyes to see what she could not. "We sent your daughter who knows where, neglecting our niece in the process. What were we thinking, turning on Doreen like that?"

"We didn't turn on her, I just suggested we use her as bait."

"Lost bait."

"We're all lost," Stella said. "It's the story of our lives. Lost to everything but our ability to enthrall."

"Thank the goddesses we have each other."

They shared a smile as Stella's Scrabble pieces—she didn't believe in runes, thought they were too clunky—began to vibrate.

"What did you ask?" Kayleen said, leaning forward to stare at them.

"The same thing I've been asking all damn morning. How do we find our children?"

The pieces shifted and flew upright. Like tiny soldiers at attention, they began to march forward, a handful coming up while the rest moved back. Then, one by one, they fell over, revealing a single word.

STORR

The two women looked at each other. "*Scotland?*" Kayleen said.

"I'll grab our broomsticks," Stella replied, her tone dry as she looked to the closest holly tree.

"Last time we took the portal overseas I didn't see straight for at least an hour."

"Good thing we have both our sets of eyes, then."

Kayleen nodded and took off for the tree. Stella grabbed her bag, throwing in the crystals, talismans, Scrabble pieces, and herbs spread across the table. She didn't know what they would find but refused to be unprepared.

As she thought of Scotland, the land of her ancestors and the witch trials, she let out a curse. She had spent her life trying to prepare her girls. She was hard on them, harder than she knew they wanted her to be. But they didn't understand what it meant to live with knowing that those you loved most, the children of your blood and heart, would die if you didn't do whatever it took to keep them tethered to the earth. That they were the thirteenth generation, and that was an auspicious promise. You didn't need a reading or the stars or dreams to tell you that. Doreen's lack of dreams had meant one thing: that she could dream up anything. It had terrified Stella. She knew Doreen would be the witch—particularly with Margot at her side—who could alter everything. Stella had tried to protect her, while pushing her to be independent. To rely on herself, instead of anyone else. It was the only way for Doreen to grow into who she was meant to be, into who she could become. Now, she hoped that Doreen's strength, and her power, would be the things to save them all.

She had little doubt that the two could handle Ambrose Mac-Donald, but the wilds of Skye and the magic buried deep in its lands were another story.

Margot, Doreen, and Ambrose walked along the cliffs as they made their way to the Old Man of Storr. Wisteria, purple and bruised, hung from the trees that bordered the land beside them. They had spent most of the day trying to reach the aunts. Doreen and Margot had tried to use their blood, words, and every timeworn spell they knew to call them. Nothing worked. Finally, they wove a strand of their hair into clovers and threw them with the ogham, while whispering where they were and where they were headed.

It had likely failed, but they'd had to try something before they moved on.

"I saw this," Margot said, her eyes on the flowers. "The wisteria was in my dream."

"Were we lost in your dream?" Doreen asked, kicking a rock out of her path.

"No," Margot said. "You had pearls for eyes and were wearing a crown."

Ambrose lifted his brows. "That sounds like Ada."

"Or it was a warning," Margot said. "That the queen of the dead was trying to steal your soul."

"All our souls," Ambrose added.

"Keep us and eat us," Doreen said. "She's one pissed-off cannibal."

"She's villainous. She's also hurting," Ambrose said, his voice rough.

"Would you be willing to eat your ancestors for Lenora?" Doreen asked. Then she winced. "Don't answer that. You cursed us in a way that's not that dissimilar."

"I took away your ability to find love, not live."

"What is the point of living without love?"

"I . . . I thought I knew, but I was hasty. Yet, I do think it may be better than living and being tortured with no way to escape or die," he said.

"We didn't curse you with the inability to die."

"No, Ada did that when I made the bargain with her. I will live until the curse is broken; isn't that payment enough?"

"You think I want you to die?"

Ambrose let out a soft breath. "I have lived far too long as it is, Doreen."

"You didn't answer my question."

"You didn't stop the torture."

"I *freed* you."

"For your purposes. And I'm still trying to save you."

"I'm the one who keeps saving *you*, Ambrose, so I think you might want to quit while you're behind."

"And I am telling you, Ada is hurting."

"And when I break the curse, you get to stop hurting? Nothing to transform into now, so you're just fine with it?"

"I didn't say that," he said, his voice heating. "I only know mortal life is not mine while I am bound to the curse."

"You're an idiot for making that curse, and Ada is not hurting inside. The only thing she is hurting is people. She is a monster."

"She's broken, Doreen. It's not only the truth, but also how we defeat her."

"You want us to use compassion for the person who has trapped our entire family line?" Doreen said, her nostrils flaring, her voice shaking. "What, hug her into submission?"

"With awareness of how she works, we can look for opportunity."

"It's not the worst idea, but I can't help but take anything he says with a grain of salt," Margot said, her tone dry.

"I am not speaking to you," he said, turning to her, his tone harsh.

"You sure as hell aren't speaking to her like *that*," Doreen said, stepping into his shoulder, glaring at him.

"I speak the truth, especially to one who is new to life and the way of things."

"I've been alive longer than Doreen, and I am not new to magic," Margot said, throwing her hair over her shoulder and shifting forward onto her toes.

"You chose to give up on love, which tells me your magic is lazy," he said.

"I'll show you lazy," Margot said, raising her left palm.

"*Hey,*" Doreen said, stepping between them.

"I don't think you want to push me," Margot said, flashing her teeth.

"I would love to see you come at me," Ambrose said, the muscles in his neck cording as he shifted his stance.

"I have to amend my earlier statement. You're *both* idiots," Doreen said, unsure how everything had escalated so quickly. She was livid with Ambrose, unable to think past him being gone from her. She didn't care about Ada or the curse when it compounded his being dead. Which might have been reckless, but it was true. She heaved a sigh, tired and wired all at once.

She reached over and placed her palm on Ambrose's arm. The change in him was instantaneous. His shoulders relaxed, his chin tucked. He looked to her, and then away. Doreen stared at him as he blew out a breath. After a terse moment, he nodded to Margot in a silent near-apology and walked on.

"He's tweaking," Doreen said to her cousin. "That wasn't okay."

"He's been in her shoes," Margot said, crossing her arms over her chest. "I think it's closer for him, or easy to project onto Ada what that misery is like." They watched him walk away. "Eleanor left him, and he lashed out. Margaret died and Ada lost it."

"You think he's grieving?"

"I think he's a bit mighty on his own thoughts, and I assume his grief is old. But as I said, I didn't disagree. The more we know about Ada, the better off we are."

Doreen rubbed at her eyes.

Margot cleared her throat. "Dore? Do you really believe we'll get out of here?"

"Of course I do." Doreen lifted her chin, studying the retreating form of Ambrose. As though he could feel her, he glanced back. She forgot to breathe, caught in his gaze. His eyes softened, and he turned away, continuing on his path. "Together we can do anything."

"I think you already have," Margot said, quiet resignation in her tone.

"Huh?"

"I guess I just mean you haven't given up yet."

"No." She shrugged. "And I don't plan on it."

Later, they camped beneath the stars, taking turns keeping watch. Ambrose and Doreen sat across from each other, their backs to sturdy oaks. They didn't speak, but she could feel his gaze on her, and it warmed the scared parts of her, giving her a little pulse of strength. Every so often she'd look to the sky. Twice she thought she saw her aunt Stella's eyes, carved out of constellations. Surely a trick of her mind.

She met Ambrose's gaze.

He believed in her. She didn't think she'd really believed in herself before. Even her last-ditch effort to break the curse had been just that—a final push. She'd wanted it to work, to be able to find him and the Dead House. She'd had a month to try. She only had a little time left now. She had thought answers would be forthcoming, like shaking up a Magic 8 Ball and finding the answers there in the palm of her hands.

Instead, she was cut off from everyone but her cousin, had fallen in love with her family's enemy, and was somehow responsible for saving her entire line before she lost her own life to the curse. She thought if she could save them all, perhaps she wouldn't mind dying. Maybe it would be worth it for Ambrose and Margot to live lives with love, even without her. For her family to find peace and the bound souls to be set free. But she didn't want to lose Ambrose. She was selfish, and she could admit it. She didn't want to lose him or anyone. She had—gods, they *all* had—lost enough already.

"Do you think Sinclair was right and we need to complete the trials Ada created?" she finally asked, breaking the silence.

"I do," he said. "There are rules here. Sinclair said this world is like the real world. Ada constructed this world out of her trials. Out of that reality. If we want to face the gods, or in this case Ada, we have to win." He sighed. "We are in two realities. The spirits, the places. Even you and me, our physical bodies."

"The journals?" she asked.

"Yes." He nodded. "They read as true, don't they?"

"Margaret's did. The others read less like a diary and more like . . . like how you might sound if someone emptied your head."

He shifted, crossed his arms over his chest. His thinking pose, Doreen thought. "What do you mean?"

She brushed a fallen leaf from her shoulder. "I've been think-ing about how straightforward Margaret's journal is. It sounds like mine whenever I've kept one. She's trying to make sense of things. But the others?" She reached into her bag, sorting until she found the one she was looking for. "This is one of the other ancestors' books we took, Sera MacKinnon. Listen to this.

"Kindness was the key to Sera's magic, until she discovered she didn't like being kind. Not to the people who were mean to her. She tried hard, harder than most people might ever consider trying, and still she grew sad and melancholic. She thought dark thoughts about leaving the world, so ready to escape the pain of witnessing those whose hearts were turned. Whose greed and lust and sprouted meanness kept them hurting others over and over."

"Sera sounds depressed," Margot said, from where she lay on the ground between the two of them. "Sorry, I can't sleep."

"Hard ground?" Ambrose asked, and his voice was gentle. He was trying, Doreen thought, to be kind.

"Weirdly, too soft," Margot said, flashing a smile. A truce in the turn of her lips.

"Oof," Doreen said, biting back her own grin. "Sorry about the ground, but you're right. Sera's entry sounds like a narrator describing her feelings. Have you ever referred to yourself in the third person, or as melancholic?"

"Her phrasing is entirely observational," Ambrose said.

"And nowhere near a stream of consciousness. Hey," Doreen said, crossing her legs at the ankles and trying to get more comfortable. "Did people used to talk about themselves differently? Is this like the English language before Shakespeare came along to describe the right words for how things feel?"

"I doubt anyone has ever spoken of themselves in the way of that entry," he said, stretching.

"There's something to it," Margot said. "This one compared to the one from the graveyard. One sounds like a journal and the other sounds . . . it's almost like a newscaster. Like someone reporting. My brain is too tired to figure it out."

"One of us should get some sleep," Ambrose said. "Dawn will soon be here and there are miles yet before we reach the Old Man of Storr."

"If we reach him at all," Doreen said, yawning and slouching lower against the tree.

"We will," Ambrose said, and then Doreen's eyes were closing, and the world was blinking out.

She did not dream, for she never dreamed, but when she woke, Ambrose was beside her, his hand wrapped around hers, and she thought it might be better to wake to a dream than to have them in sleep.

In the morning, they washed in a nearby stream. Margot foraged for berries and Ambrose passed around some of the nuts they'd taken from the castle. Doreen and Margot had bespelled the tin they carried them in, so it would continue to replenish from the house's pantry. As long as the castle had food, they would too.

The next few days were more of the same. Hiking across lands so green and lush they looked like something from the pages of a children's storybook. Blooming wild purple wisteria, arching cliffs that rose over frothing navy seas, and paths that wove in and around a constant stream. Ambrose was following the water, and it proved a good resource.

As they trekked, they talked of the journals, of Ada, of Margaret. Ambrose asked Doreen why she had fought so hard to be able to fall in love, and she had stared at him, unable to look away as she answered, "To be loved back, in kind, might be the truest form of magic that exists."

Three nights in a row Doreen was certain she caught a glimpse of her aunt Stella's face in the sky. It was improbable, but it filled her with hope. That perhaps their message had reached her, perhaps for once she might do something for the good of them.

On the morning of the fifth day, they awoke to discover a range of mountains that had not been there before, waiting for them.

"Teeth," Doreen said, staring with a shudder.

Here, in this section of their prison world, two mountain ranges rose from the land. A giant one that looked like a row of distended molars, and in front of it, a small cluster of large stones. Buck teeth before the rest.

The crooked teeth were the Old Man of Storr, and he was waiting in front of the Cirellian Mountain Range for them.

"This place has no boundaries," Margot said, studying the two juxtaposed ridges.

"It's an amalgamation of Skye." Doreen nodded. "Not quite right, but similar."

"I think it's more than that," Ambrose said. "My castle, the chapel, the caves. All of it feels like it's plucked from memory."

"Whose?"

He shrugged. "Ada's?"

"I don't know," Doreen said, rubbing her cheek, trying to wipe sleep from her face. "I was in Eleanor's home. Her house seemed like it was purely Eleanor's creation, not Ada's."

"Eleanor never had a home, outside of her family estate," Ambrose said. "She died before she could."

Doreen shrugged. "Maybe when you're here, you have parameters you can do things in?"

"Or if Eleanor is controlled by Ada, she has certain permission to create as long as she does Ada's bidding," Ambrose said.

"And when she's wearing a certain face, she can do what she wants."

"Which is why she keeps her faces hidden."

"Creepy."

"Yes, okay, any ideas about what we do now that we're here?" Margot said, staring at the rock formation.

Doreen had been thinking about it on their journey there. About Ada, Sinclair, Eleanor, the trials, and the journals. "I might," she said, looking at the head of the stones, and how it looked like the head of a man. She took a fortifying breath. "If we want for him to help, I think we have to wake him up."

TWENTY

The spirits were not cooperating. Ada stood next to the candle with the black flame and tried not to scream. The wax, which for so many centuries had not melted a whisker, was a good three inches less than it had been the day before.

She was, finally, running out of time.

The gods had not granted her eternal life, but rather a way to continue this one while she sought what she had lost. While she searched for Margaret. The souls kept her going. They kept her tethered to reality and gave her time. The bones made her strong. Ada should have felt invincible. After so many years of trying, she had managed to trap not one but two living souls. Plenty of food.

But her strength was waning instead of growing. She couldn't feed off any of the three souls inside her underworld. It was like they were encased in glass. Little lights she could see, who her spirits could follow, but did nothing to satiate her.

Ada was starving.

She had consumed many pieces of souls in the past year, too many, but still they barely dulled the hunger. Her appetite was growing. The bits she had consumed only managed to reduce the ache to a gnawing chasm. She wanted more than a snack. She needed a feast.

"You summoned me?" Hastings said, the last of his shade drifting forward.

"Once again, I really didn't."

"You are fading," he said, his voice a low metronome. A constant ebb and flow, a *tick tick tick* in her head.

She *was* fading. She was also tired of him. Of the reminder of what could have been. Hastings had been a ghost long before he was dead. He had spent all his years in life and beyond haunting her.

She sighed, stood, and walked to the alcove off the farthest entryway into her cave. It held a few jars, a small altar of stones and drawings, and a box. She opened the box, then pulled out another, and another. Ada removed the key from the final one, walking out of the alcove and into the main chamber. She went to the wooden shelves and slid the key into the door at its base. It was rusty and angry but opened.

There, she pulled out a doll.

It was the oldest of the dolls, having been Margaret's when she was a child. Carved of stone with exaggerated etchings, it was a gnarly thing. She pressed her palms to it, leaned down to whisper against its face. Ada wished she could remember how it had felt to hold the doll when Hastings gave it to Margaret, when Margaret had been a girl. Now it was just a stone with a face and a reminder. Of a free, happy, funny light who laughed all the time. Ada could no longer hear the laughter.

Ada didn't remember merriment.

She only knew longing and hunger and pain.

With one last stroke to its head, she looked up to see the spirit of Hastings hovering. He gave her a deep, final bow.

Ada nodded once, and then she leaned down, keeping her eyes on the man who could have been her husband. She pressed her lips to the temple of the doll and its mouth broke open. Wind filled the cave. Hastings flickered. The ground shook and Ada grinned as the last of his soul floated up and out, and she sucked every drop of him down.

Margot knew certain things about magic to be true. You needed to water it every Thursday like you would a String of Hearts plant. You had to honor your ancestors, the four corners of the world where they might be hovering at any moment, and, perhaps most importantly, yourself.

Magic was also unpredictable. It opened the doors precisely when it could.

Finally, if you wanted anything to work, you had to believe. Belief could move mountains. It might even wake one up.

The three witches stood beneath the stones that formed the Old Man of Storr, staring up. The earth here was hard and cold, and dotted with smaller pebbles that made it difficult to walk across.

"How do we want to do this?" Ambrose asked Doreen.

"Maybe we yell?" she said, trying to find her footing.

Margot screamed. Doreen shouted. Ambrose bellowed.

Echoes of their calls rained down on them, but the rock formation of a slumbering man did not so much as shift a pebble.

Next, they spread out, pacing back and forth, up and down, across the stones grouped there. They called his name. *"Wake up, Old Man,"* they said. *"Rise and shine, Mr. Storr."*

The echoes followed, before settling at their feet and fading away entirely.

"That was strange how it ate the sound," Doreen said. "And also ineffective."

"Maybe if we are trying to wake a giant," Margot said, "we have to get his attention?"

"Can't be any sillier than our yelling at him," Doreen said.

Margot gathered a section of rocks and she and Doreen attempted to bespell them, to charm them to move for them. Doreen had seldom felt so foolish as she did saying, "Come on, little rock, roll to your home." They'd thought to use the rocks to shift the tectonic plates under the sleeping rock form.

Slide the man around and see if moving him physically would wake him. It made sense in theory . . . but these rocks rolled together and broke apart, over and over.

No matter how they varied their spells, the ground beneath the Old Man of Storr remained unmoved, and so he slept on.

"This is a waste of time," Margot finally said, throwing a large rock at the mountain range and causing a small avalanche.

"Let's spread out," Doreen said, wiping sweat from her brow. "See if we've overlooked something?"

Day settled into night, and the moon rose high into the sky. They walked the grounds, focused and searching. Doreen murmuring about teeth as she passed Ambrose, while he hummed a quiet melody.

Margot watched them, the way they checked on one another. How Ambrose would reroute his steps to be near Doreen, to provide a hand if he thought she needed it, which she never did.

He did not know how strong Doreen was.

Margot thought of Dean. Of how he seemed to know what she wanted as she wanted it. How he was never overbearing or needy or clingy. He knew precisely what to say and when to say it. He was a perfectly gentle lover, a spot-on gift giver. He never hogged the remote and liked all the same books and movies as she did. He didn't burn the toast or try to guard her from things that could harm her. He would not have stayed close to her like Ambrose was positioning himself to be beside Doreen. She wouldn't have growled at him like Dore did to Ambrose when she noticed.

She didn't really even fight with Dean. Not unless she had the thought that it was time for a little conflict, in which case Dean was more than willing to contribute.

Their relationship was practically perfect in every way.

But as she watched Ambrose and Doreen, she understood it wasn't real. It was an echo of a relationship, built solely off her preferences and her power. The truth of it broke her already fractured heart. She wished with every wish imaginable it would be, could be, real.

Margot turned a corner, nearly tripping over a thorny bush, and looked up. "Oh my," she said, her eyes traveling over the bench in front of her. It was covered in Gaelic symbols, surrounded by flowers blooming in this otherwise barren wasteland of a rock formation.

"I think I found something," she called, looking for her cousin, and found Doreen nearby. She appeared to have found something as well. Doreen stood in front of a chair, or throne perhaps, with similar markings as Margot had seen on the bench.

"I don't know how we move him into the chair or bench," Doreen yelled, nodding at the giant.

Ambrose stood behind Doreen, his eyes drinking in the etchings.

"Can you read what it says?" Margot called back, leaving the bench and moving closer to them.

Ambrose hesitated before his eyes met Doreen's. Whatever they shared, unspoken and unacknowledged, led him to giving a single nod.

Yes, Margot thought, what they had was very different from her relationship with Dean. Here, between the two of them, was a language of their own, and an endless array of possibilities.

"It says that love is like wildflowers, found in the most unlikely of places," he said.

"It's almost a greeting card," Doreen quipped.

"I wonder if it's true," Margot murmured to herself. "There's a bench too, over this way."

The bench was down closer to the foot of the mountain. It read: *View the miracle of a single flower, and your whole life may change.*

"Okay," Doreen said. "Neither of these tell us what we really need to know, though I like the poetry."

"Yes," Ambrose agreed. "They're poetic platitudes. I'd rather not write that beast of a rock man a sonnet if that is what this implies."

They crossed back up the hill, and Ambrose came to a stop in front of a large table made of the same stone as the rocks littered around them. "Here's something. *Tomorrow's flowers bloom because of the seeds of today,*" he read.

"Okay," Doreen said, blowing out a breath. "I don't quite know what that one means."

"Oh," said Margot, and she thought of Dean again, of what she was missing. "It's little bread crumbs. The flowers are the miracle— they can change our tomorrows. Look at the flowers bordering the chair, bench, and table. There are doll's eyes, moonflowers, wolf eyes, and black-eyed Susans. All are flowers meant to bring sight or heal failing sight."

"And we what? Eat the flowers?" Ambrose asked.

"Not quite. I think if we want to wake a sleeping giant, first we have to make sure he can see."

"Of course," Doreen said, looking over her shoulder at Margot. "You can't see without eyes. You can't wake without seeing."

Margot nodded.

"How do you propose we make eyes for the giant?" Ambrose asked. "Carve them into the stone?"

"Stop being grumpy," Doreen said, rubbing his back like a child soothing a puppy.

"It's a logical question."

Margot opened her hands. "We use the flowers of the gods. We make a poultice and smear it in. If you have eyes that need to see, this should help them."

Ambrose looked at the flowers surrounding the table. "Many of these are poisonous."

Margot smiled sadly, thinking of her marriage. "Some of the best things are, Ambrose MacDonald."

The three of them collected the flowers, mindful of the poisonous parts.

Margot hummed as she worked, and Doreen thought of their many mornings in the apothecary. This was Margot's happy place, working with flowers, creating and educating, healing and helping. Her cheeks were rosy, her eyes light.

This will work, Doreen thought.

It was a simple matter of blending herbs mixed with a handful of dirt to bind it, using the words of the ancients to pour into the petals. Then grinding them down with stone and creating a paste. They made the poultice in under three hours and portioned it out. Each witch carried a separate portion. Together, they systematically spread it across the stones. A little fusion here, a dab-dab there.

It took them as long to spread the ointment as to create it, and when they were done, they stepped back to admire their work. Slashes and blots of a dark ointment oozed across the various stones of Storr. It was as though they had given the rocks a very colorful mud bath.

They waited, watching, listening to the steady breeze and constant exhalation and inhalation of their breath.

The stones did not move.

"Maybe we got it wrong?" Ambrose said.

"Or maybe we didn't use enough?" Doreen asked.

"It seemed so straightforward," Margot said.

"I mean, we have done everything I can think of," Ambrose said. "Maybe we need to scream at it again."

"Perhaps we simply need time," Doreen said, standing as her eyes tracked the illumination on the rocks ahead. Under starlight and moonlight, a path arose. A simple path that had not been there before, it went up the side of one rock and down the other, over and around, until it came to the center stone. Here the light split and lit up two deep caverns.

"Are those . . ." Ambrose started.

"His eyes?" Margot finished.

"Have to be," Doreen said.

They crossed to the section and Margot reached into her bag for the last of the poultice.

"Hang on," Doreen said. She stared at the place where eyes could be and thought of Ada. Of how the Queen of the Order of the Dead had eyes that could not see. Pearls for her sight. There was a parallel here, a connection. She reached into her bag and pulled from it a stone.

"I don't have pearls," she said, "but I have something perhaps better."

"Obsidian?" Margot said, leaning closer.

"Once used to restore the soul," Doreen said. "It's a stone from the fire in Ada's cave."

Margot passed her the potion and Doreen rolled the obsidian eye in it, smearing it with purpose and focus.

She carried the eye to the giant and studied it. Ada's words in the cave returned to her. *The spell is the truth, the truth is the spell.* She lifted the eye and sat it into a notch of carved stone, whispering a single word: *"Awaken."*

No sooner was the stone placed than the ground started to rumble, the earth shaking. Doreen stumbled back as the first rip in the soil started. Like a series of threads being snapped with the snip of one line, the large boulders of Storr began to vibrate, and ever so slowly . . . roll. As they rolled, they began to pick up speed.

The farthest two sped in toward the center stone, followed by the other outlying ones. They came together with a thunderous snap before they shifted and righted. The head bowled up the side of the rock body and centered at the top. The eye, black as a single pearl in the center, blinked and opened. A howling cry came from the slit in the center of the face as the Old Man of Storr awoke and came back into one piece.

"Holy hells," Margot said, taking a few leaps back. "Was this really the best idea?"

The three of them continued down the hill as the old man stood and wobbled. They ducked and covered as smaller stones freed themselves and fell over them. Soon a bellowing laugh filled the canyon, echoing off the mountains behind. It looked, for a moment, like the other mountains were laughing, the teethlike peaks quaking, and then all noise came to a deafening stop.

The Old Man of Storr looked down on them and said, "Little witches. I see Ada's time is finally running out. Which of you is here to take my place?"

TWENTY-ONE

Stella and Kayleen had been trying to make their way into the Goodbye Castle for days. It was as though a wall had gone up, invisible and sturdy and refusing them entrance. They could see Doreen and Ambrose, standing on the edge of the ledge of the world. Margot's shadow was just barely visible as well.

When they had gone to Storr, they found a crack in the rocks. Mischief of magic, a wrongness permeating the grounds. The castle had called to them both, each dreaming that first night of the wisteria. They circled the grounds, trying to call the ghosts that lingered there.

Even the ghosts it seemed were frightened.

"We're going to have to cast," Kayleen said from where she stood by a long hedgerow of bushes that made Stella's flesh crawl.

"We've tried that—it's not doing a damn thing."

"Not to get in there," she said, waving a hand toward the castle. "We can't go that way, and I don't want to go through the hedgerow, so we will cast to be open."

Stella stopped and turned. "What did you say?"

"We open up."

"If we open, we could lose ourselves. To be open is to allow ourselves to become lost."

"But we could also be there when the girls need us. They will be able to find us in the underworld."

Stella marched up to the castle and slammed her hands against the barrier. This time, the wards sent her flying back onto her ass.

"Stupid prick of a castle," she snarled at it. "Wake up, Dore!"

The figures didn't so much as flinch where they stood, on the precipice of their lives.

"Fuck it," Stella said. Her fear and guilt were equally stifling. She loved the girls more than she loved herself, and she was failing them. Perhaps had failed them all along.

She thought of Jack, and how she had done what she thought was right at the time. How Doreen had still not forgiven her.

Perhaps they were all cursed to fail one another, over and over.

"Fine," she said, marching back to Kayleen, who sat with her upright posture and ruby-red full lips, not a hair out of place and looking like a fashion model out for a stroll along the cliffs. Stella's own hair was untamed, her clothes wrinkled and her face itchy. She felt as wild as she looked, and hoped Kayleen felt as poised and deadly as she appeared. "Let's cast the circle. But if we survive this, you owe me five batches of that moon wine."

Kayleen flashed a smile full of teeth that came nowhere near meeting her eyes. "Deal."

They came to stand face-to-face. Their hands clasped with the other's, they squeezed three times, and then, with the words of the ancients falling from their lips, they wrapped their arms around one another as uncontrollable blasts of wind gusted through the garden, coming up from the earth and between the two women, bending each of them back as they gripped each other tight.

They looked like a flower bowing as it opened, the petals unfurling.

Rain fell from the skies, but the two women remained in their embrace, hearts open, eyes unseeing, the door between them and their kin cracking open. They were braced and ready if Doreen called, their circle formed. They would be there no matter the cost.

Doreen blinked up at the craggy and crumbly Old Man of Storr. The creature was both human and alien: the face with its odd eye, the mouth a slash of marble.

"Are you a trapped soul too?" she asked, thinking of Eleanor and Sinclair, of the graves before the chapel.

"I'm a punished soul," the old man said, his bright eyes tracking Ambrose's movements like a hawk watching a field mouse.

Ambrose studied the old man warily.

"Don't recognize me, do you, boy?" the old man asked. "Not with stones for my bones."

Ambrose gave his head a slow shake, looking to Doreen. "I don't want to know what he's talking about."

The rocks shook. "You bound me to the queen of the order. Delivered me to the feet of Ada and left me stuck in this world. She had a piece of my soul, but she never had *me* until you."

Ambrose's eyes closed. "Shit."

"Hastings?" Doreen said, her voice a note too high. "You're Hastings MacDonald?"

"Aye, of course I am," he said, sitting down with a crack and a boom that resounded through the canyon. "For five hundred years I have been mostly trapped in these stones, splintered as the bones of the gods themselves."

"Angels wept," Ambrose said, swallowing, his eyes fluttering open. "I didn't know you would be *stuck* here."

"No? Didn't think there would be a cost?" He let out a harrumph that sounded like thunder. "Never thinking, playing with magic beyond your skills. It's the plight of all witches born after the splintering. When the gods took back their power from Avarice, before Ada took too much back from them when she won the trials, it left us cockeyed. Magic is tricky now. Each spell asks if you will be a better man or woman because of it, or if you will let your will and desire corrupt you."

"Did magic corrupt you?" Doreen asked, stepping up to stand at Ambrose's side. Shifting as though she could shield him.

"Nay," he said. "It corrupted Ada, and it was Ada—and my love for her—which corrupted me. It broke my heart after she broke her own."

"When Margaret died," Doreen said.

Hastings shifted, the rocks crumbling down toward them, and Doreen jumped out of the way.

"Yes, when beautiful Margaret went over the cliffs, everything might as well have turned to ash. I have spent a long time waiting, watching, and coming to grips with the truth. Being bound to Ada has allowed me to witness her pain, and to come to a reckoning over the pain I caused her and Margaret. Time is slow to change, but the winds do bring change to us all. Love, at the end, is all I have held on to."

"Can you stop moving?" Margot called up. "You're worse than an avalanche."

He let out a dark chuckle and nodded. "I can try."

"She's punishing you still, isn't she," Ambrose said. "Ada."

"It's what we excel at, isn't it, boy? This world knows what goes on in the other, as sure as the sun rises and sets. We can't help but bleed all over those around us, even when we're wrong."

"What did you get wrong?" Doreen asked.

"I was a child when I met the girls," Hastings said. "Our clans were the three main clans on Skye, and we were in and out of each other's pockets. I never thought Margaret and Ada would grow closer to each other than they were to me. I was the hero of my story, and I couldn't see it coming—that I was just a side character in theirs. We were friends. Then we were ordered to be more, me and Ada or me and Margaret. It didn't matter. The clans needed power, so joining with either family would have worked. I loved Ada and Margaret both, and yet I never saw them. Not until it was too late. I didn't help Ada after she was broken. I went to war to battle my wounds and thought I'd leave her to lick hers. It was wrong of me to look away. She was alone in her pain, and she took the trials of the gods, asking for a power too great. It corrupted her, ate her from the inside out, and she was lost to us as much as Margaret was. Ada was family. We are all family, the witches of Skye."

"Family can harm," Doreen said. "We need to stop Ada. How do we free you and get out of here? How do we leave this world for good?"

"There is only one way out," he said, his voice echoing. "You must go through. You completed the first two trials. You were brave to enter the cave of echoes and save Ambrose. You found your heart not long ago or you wouldn't have gotten far enough to find me. You were strong to wake the rock man of Storr, using the power of your minds over the brawn of your hands. You have to prove your strength, but the cost to continue is high." He sighed, a small and lonely sound. "You must pay the toll for waking me."

Doreen shook her head. "I don't like the sound of this."

"I am free," the old man said, "for you have woken the sleeping giant. There must always be a giant to guard this land, and one of you will have to take my place."

"He's worse than Ada," Doreen said, her gaze going to Ambrose, who took a step forward as though to volunteer. "Don't even think of it, Ambrose. It is utterly ridiculous."

"It's simply the cost," Margot said, stepping up to stand between them. She placed a hand on Doreen's shoulder. Squeezed it hard. "Dore, we know how often there's a cost, and we're so close. It couldn't have been this easy. It's okay. I will pay it."

Doreen spun around to face Margot. "You most certainly *will not*."

"I'm sorry, but I can and will," Margot said. "I will take your place," she said, turning to Hastings, giving him a firm nod before shooting her cousin a determined look over her shoulder. "*You* will get us out of here, and you need him." She bit her lip and looked up at the rock giant. "Tell me it's like taking a long nap."

"It's as easy as closing your eyes," Hastings said.

"This is *ludicrous*," Doreen said, and she stamped her feet in a way she had not done since she was a child and Margot stole her favorite book. "No one is taking his place, least of all you. I need you."

"Then no one leaves," Hastings said. As soon as the words were spoken, a rush of pebbles shifted forward, morphing into a wall of rock that closed in around them. "We will all be trapped in our little cave together. At least this time, I will not be lonely."

The rocks began to wrap around them, snaking up and down. Doreen screamed and called a quick spell to try to blast them back, but they just closed in faster.

"I love you, Dore, and you must trust me and forgive me for doing what is right. I know you can do this," Margot called. Then she looked up at the skies and her voice rang out clear and strong: "With my own free will I give myself in place of Hastings MacDonald; may he go free until those who are mine free me."

Doreen let out a keening cry as the rocks rushed up, surrounding them. As swiftly as they'd rushed in, they fell apart with an abrupt snap. She turned to where Margot had stood, and found her cousin frozen into a statue.

Doreen stumbled over to her, shoving at the statue, trying to slam Margot free. She chanted a dozen different spells as tears streaked down her cheeks.

Ambrose moved to Doreen, his arms coming around her, gentle as he tried to hold her up. She lifted her angry face to Hastings.

"I will *end* you," she said, and without thinking, Doreen dug deep into the magic of the land. She tunneled into the song of sorrow, gathered the threads of the song of longing, and bound them to herself and the hum of the earth. Then Doreen *yanked*.

Light erupted. The air thinned. Doreen pulled magic from the old man, his soul rising up as she did.

It tasted of honey and wine, smelled of cedar and anise, as his truth, who he had been and was, shifted into her. Memories and moments, of Ada and Hastings as children, of Margaret with flowers in her hair. His kindness and wickedness flowed through her.

"Doreen," Ambrose said, stepping in front of her line of vision. "Doreen, *please*."

She yanked hard again, and Ambrose was the one who stumbled. She tasted ale and tears, his sorrow and more—his love for her.

She let go, dropping the threads and gasping. Doreen had reacted on anger and instinct. She'd responded and didn't realize what she was doing. How she was pulling on their magic, their line.

Their souls.

The shock of it left her staggering on her feet.

"It's okay," Ambrose said, his hand reaching for her. She hesitated, and then recalled the love inside him, how it flowed for her, into her. She stepped forward and threw her arms around him.

"I didn't mean to hurt you," she said, relieved to find him whole.

"You didn't. You wouldn't."

"Your stone witch can be freed," Hastings said, his voice riding the wind. "Do not give up, Doreen MacKinnon, or let your heart turn cold as Ada has. Witches are like flowers; the most potent ones don't think about their magic. They do not try to control or change or guide; they simply bloom."

Then Hastings was gone. Margot was silent. Ambrose and Doreen were alone.

TWENTY-TWO

Doreen did not feel strong. She felt broken and exhausted, but if she knew a single thing, it was that she could not stop. The only way out *was* through. They had one trial left: cunning. She found it laughable because all she had left was courage. She had not been clever enough to save Margot—how could she be clever enough to free her now, to free them all? Maybe she was never as clever as she had thought.

"I hate this," she said, as she and Ambrose walked down the hill. She looked over her shoulder every few feet. The form of Margot stood whole, a perfectly beautiful stone statue.

"She won't stay that way," he said. "We will free her, and we will get out of here."

"How?" She bit back a sob. Stopped. Turned again. "I can't leave her there."

"We can't stay," he said, his hand catching hers, his touch gentle.

Doreen looked to the horizon, her feet heavy, her heart aching.

"If we don't move on, we will lose the light and the path," Ambrose said, as night grew darker under a thick cloud cover. "Without it, I do not know that we will find our way. There will be an obstacle Ada sets for us—we should be ready, and the light is at least one way for us to see."

Doreen forced herself to walk, one foot after the other. It was a trudge, and as she moved, her heart hardened. At being stuck in this world she never asked for, at how her fingers itched to touch Ambrose, at how she had failed Margot, at how she was failing herself. She didn't know what she was doing. They were trapped, and she was exhausted.

The road was winding and twisted. It was a long journey, and when they paused and attempted to sleep, they slept fitfully, Ambrose shifting to her and holding her in the night. Then it was another day and another night of dreamless sleep and a breaking heart. Following the path and not knowing if it would lead them to the final trial, or if it would lead them into a trap. Finally, the following afternoon, they made it to the edge of a forest.

A forest Doreen knew.

"Sinclair showed me this," she said, looking for the lights of the souls but not finding any. They walked alongside it, down to its edge. "When she pushed me into seeing the truth, I saw this forest. I think this is the end of this realm."

Ambrose nodded. "Lenora showed me as well."

Doreen turned and looked at him. "What? When?"

"When she kissed me goodbye," he said.

Doreen lifted her brows. "What are you talking about?"

"She showed me what had been and could be," he said, his hands shifting to his pockets. "In the chapel, before it came down. She showed me herself, Eleanor and Lenora."

"What all did you see?"

Ambrose looked up, to where the stars were starting to dot the sky. "I was wrong about so many things." He didn't meet her eyes, and his own were misting.

"You're scaring me," she said.

"It's a Möbius strip of repeating folly," he said. "Our families, the curse, the losses. I had it so wrong. Doreen, I never loved her. I never really loved Lenora, didn't understand what love was, and she never loved me."

Doreen stepped closer, forcing him to meet her eyes. He was shaking. "I don't understand."

"When her lips met mine, she took me back. To before. To when I met her, and how lonely she was. You have strong magic, Margot does, everyone in the MacKinnon line does. Not because you're the thirteenth generation of witches or because Lenora was the ninth. You are all powerful because of who you are, and Lenora was no exception; she was simply untrained. She learned how to spell by accident, and she cast one of her most complex spells when she was lonely. She wove a love spell around me, an enchantment. One where I would fall so completely under her thrall, I lost myself."

"She bespelled you." Doreen swallowed around the lump building in her throat.

His nod was slow and measured. "*She* cast the curse I unleashed upon you all. It was what Ada gave back to me. She plucked the spell I was under and cast the net wide. It doesn't matter." He took a breath, looked at her. "It's broken now. You are free."

"Free?"

"Of the curse."

"I don't understand." Her eyes locked in on his form, checking for harm. "Are you dying?"

"No." He let out a low laugh, both warm and devastated. "I broke the curse the moment I stopped being able not to care about you. Lenora simply freed me to see it, to know the truth." He stared into her eyes, his filled with pain and something so bright it stole her breath.

"I don't know what love is. I couldn't. I don't know if Ada knows, if the love she has for Margaret is real or is another compulsion. I can tell you I did not love Lenora, because I know what I felt for her was nothing like how I feel about you. Because as maddening as you are, I would do whatever it takes to help you, to support you."

Doreen thought her heart might have stopped for a moment. It was painful, this kind of wanting. "Is this really the best time to confess your feelings?"

"You can't deflect from this. Not here, when we are at the end of things. I am not under your spell," he said, with a quirk of his lip. "Though you are bewitching. I think I may have fallen a little bit for you the moment you pulled me from my cage. If I am lucky, I will love you every day for the rest of my life. However short it is."

"Ambrose . . ."

"It doesn't matter," he said, shifting closer so they were nearly chest to chest. "You have saved me over and over. Margot sacrificed herself for us, because she knew you would need something deeper to keep going, because she understood."

Doreen shook her head, fear lodging in her throat.

"The trials are a balance of the scales. Eleanor made it clear. Ada's spirits are watching; she is waiting. Ada must be defeated and the souls released, so we may all rest." He brought his forehead to hers. "You are the most cunning of us all; your magic is clever, inventive, and you are brave and strong."

"I feel like you're saying you love me when you really mean goodbye," she said, a sob in her throat, her heart racing in her chest.

"I am saying you can do this. The sacrifices are worth it."

He tilted her chin, and his lips met hers. As he kissed her, Doreen saw everything Eleanor had shown to him. She saw the future and what it might be. The curse lifted, Ambrose and Doreen happy, Margot in love, their world one of peace and joy. She tasted freedom: lavender tea, sweet apple cider, shortbread cookies.

They kissed for minutes, hours, days. His tongue met the seam of her lips, and she gasped as he nipped her mouth open. Then Doreen took over. She pressed into him harder, his hands gripping her hips as she tilted her head and took the kiss deeper. She fisted his hair tight in her hand, tugged him to her and moaned as she greedily drove the kiss. She writhed against him as he groaned and the thickness of him dug against her hip.

She cried his name, and thunder erupted into the night.

They broke apart, panting, their eyes drugged, their mouths ravished, both craving so much more.

Lightning splintered the sky. Rain fell. Mist rose up from the earth.

Doreen wiped her eyes clear of the rain, and she discovered she was standing at the edge of a cliff facing Ambrose . . . but he was no longer her Ambrose.

He wore the face of Hastings, and he was crying.

"How could you lie to me?" he said, his voice wrong.

"I didn't lie," she said, the words floating out before she recognized them—before she understood that they were not hers, but Margaret's. Something had happened when she kissed Ambrose, when they admitted what they were feeling. The past was coming to life, and they were inside it. "I fell in love."

"You said you loved me," he said.

"I didn't know better," she said. "What I feel for her isn't the warm kindling of the heart I feel for you."

"Can you . . ." he asked, trailing off. "Is there any world where you might one day love me?"

"Not in this world, nor any other."

Ambrose reached for Doreen then, his hand wrapping around her fingers, pleading in his eyes.

She didn't hesitate; she jerked away and stumbled back a single step. Her arms flew out, her motions going wild. She spun in a single circle and smashed back into Ambrose. He lost his footing, his eyes crazed, his hair blown back from his face.

"Doreen," he said, the word a strangled, anguished cry, as he went tumbling from her and over the cliff.

D oreen didn't move. For a long, heart-wrenching moment, she couldn't. She was stuck in the loop, playing it over and over, trying to break free. Then she screamed and the spell broke. She tore off running down the cliffside, her eyes tracking over the water. She thought of diving in but feared hitting the jagged rocks. If Ambrose hadn't smashed into them, it would be a miracle.

She and he had relived the moment Ada lost them both. She understood that. Margaret had gone physically from her, and Hastings had instigated a tragedy of his own making—one she could not forgive him for.

A flash of red appeared ahead, and Eleanor stepped out from between the trees. She was there and not there, a faded version of herself.

"Don't give up on him or us, Doreen," she said, twitching back and forth from Technicolor to black-and-white before she fizzled out in a stream of smoke, her voice trailing off. "Don't . . . give . . . up . . ."

Doreen raced on. She tore through a clearing and ran straight for the sea. As she crossed the boggy ground, the terrain bucked. The sandy shore shifted, and large stones—obsidian and imposing—rose from the depths.

Beyond, Doreen couldn't see anything but a void. The skies darkened, the wind howled, and lightning flashed once again across the skies.

The obsidian stones continued to shift and break apart into single circular steps.

They spun out into a labyrinth, a beautiful and cruel maze leading to where Ambrose had dropped.

Doreen jumped onto the first step, and it shook and crumbled beneath her feet. She hurled herself from it, landing back on the shore.

She tracked the stones and realized each was inset with a carving. Doreen's eyes couldn't keep up with her mind. She studied each one, and it clicked—these had symbols etched into them that looked just like the ogham Eleanor had given her.

Doreen closed her eyes and took in a breath. One, then another. She replayed what Eleanor had told her about the ogham markings. One for her wise counsel, one for Ambrose, one for the sisterhood of her family.

Her heart was with Ambrose. Her holly king. She looked until she found the stone with the marking for the holly on it and jumped.

One after another she leapt onto the stones.

When she finally reached the middle, she found three stones waiting. Something was on top of the three stones. Not symbols from the ogham, but something bigger. As she drew closer, they came into focus—the frozen stone forms of Margot, Ambrose . . . and a grouping of her ancestors—the spirits of this world.

All were encased in stone, all waiting—a representation or the real thing, she did not know. It didn't matter. She knew what would be asked of her before it was.

The wind howled up and a single word whistled down: *Choose.*

"Choose what?" she called.

Choose. One.

The forceful wind pushed her forward. She started to lose her footing. If she didn't move soon, she would stumble off and down into whatever waited below, and all would be lost.

She had to fight to keep the tears back. She was failing. She didn't want to give up, but she didn't know what to do. She couldn't choose only one of them to save.

She refused.

Doreen looked up and the lightning struck again. She blinked and stared. Her aunt's eyes flashed before her. They were in the night sky, the constellations drawing them out. The same flicker of a vision here again. Was she dying? Could this be it?

The lightning split the sky again, and she saw her aunt's entire face carved there, calling something to her.

Was she saying "clever"? Was her mind forcing the illusion? Did she really think Stella would taunt her if she could see her, in the hour of her demise? The stars overhead shifted, and the words repeated across the sky.

Choose.

Doreen was always the clever witch, that was what Margot said. The cunning one by her very nature. She looked at her feet, at the stones beneath it. She thought of each trial. Courage, heart, strength, and cunning. She looked back to the constellation of her aunt. Mouthing a single word.

Not saying *clever*. No. Saying . . . Doreen focused on her aunt, reaching for the door between them. She cracked it open, and Stella's voice rushed in. *Forever.*

Doreen looked back to the stones and beyond them to a small grouping of flat boulders in the center of the labyrinth. Beneath them was a clearing in the water. Doreen could see all the way down to the ocean floor where a single stone waited. This one was carved with a different symbol.

The Pictish Beast.

She knew as she stared what the outcomes would be. She could step on the holly stone, and it would free Ambrose: her heart's desire. She could step on the stone with her family, and it would lead her to

Eleanor and all the other souls trapped here. Or she could step on the one for her counsel, her wisest friend, and it would free Margot. The stone at the bottom, the forgotten one with the symbol of the beast, was the worst choice possible.

Forever. That's how long Ada might remain in this world. It was certainly how long she would wait for her true love.

Doreen loved Ambrose. Perhaps she had been in love with him since the moment he first smiled at her, the twitch of a lip and the promise of an adventure and something real. She loved how he believed in her, showed her she could do anything she set her mind to. How he sacrificed himself for her, because he knew she could do this.

She would have searched for him forever too.

Which was why Doreen said the foulest curse word she could summon before she dove past the three stones representing each of her heart's desires and plunged into the depths of the ocean. She swam
into the
    lovely
   into the
      dark and deep
        the dark and deep
          the dark and deep

It was like diving through Jell-O, Doreen thought, for no matter how hard she swam, she barely inched forward. When she finally saw the stone waiting at the bottom of the ocean, her lungs burned so painfully she didn't doubt they would implode at the pressure.

Until her hand slammed onto the surface of the stone.

Light flooded in and the doorway to Ada, the beast who was neither living nor dead but made of many bones and souls, burst wide open.

TWENTY-THREE

The pressure was gone. Doreen shot up like a cannon, the water bursting through the stone like a geyser. She blasted out of the water and was tossed onto the shore, where she coughed and gagged and tried to claw her way up.

As she rolled onto her side, she found herself on the shore by the sea, and ahead of her was a cave. To the right was a set of cliffs, and to her left was a meadow. All four corners of the world, all at the edge of the world.

"I didn't realize how coarse the sand is," a voice said, sounding amused and irritated. "Who knew?"

Doreen looked up to see Ada sitting on a washed-up tree trunk. She looked different. Her bones were in the right place, and her eyes didn't shine like sunken pearls. She was more human than Doreen could recall ever seeing her before.

"Aha," Ada said, smiling at Doreen. Her mouth stretched twice as wide as it should, and Doreen swallowed her revulsion. "You did it."

"Did I?" Doreen asked, looking around for Ambrose or Margot or a door to anywhere else.

"Yes. Congratulations on beating the trials. It's a rare rite of passage." Ada tilted her head and then it twitched. Once, twice. A jerk that was far too robotic to be real.

"What are you?" Doreen asked.

"I am the queen," the robotic Ada said. "What are you?"

"I'm the witch," Doreen said, and lifted her hands. "The spell is the truth, the truth is the spell. *Eviscerate*."

The Ada that was not Ada exploded into a thousand fragments. She rained down around Doreen, splashing into the ocean.

"Nice trick," Doreen called, brushing her hair—heavy and laden with clumps of sand—from her face. "Scared to face me?"

Eleanor MacKinnon strode out from the cave. She was no longer in Technicolor or black-and-white. Eleanor was a sepia dream. A beige-and-tan perfection. She wore a dress Donna Reed would envy and a beehive that had Doreen wincing for her scalp.

"I take it back," Doreen said. "No one needs to face whatever this is."

"Clever witch," Eleanor said.

"Not as clever as a witch with the ability to wear every face it has ever stolen."

Eleanor grinned, and then she tore at her own face, ripping it free. The grim bones and pearled eyes of Ada remained.

"Like I said," Doreen said, terror clawing up her spine, "clever. Though not as clever as the ghosts you impersonate."

Ada rolled her neck, her bones cracking and shaking the sea. "You think they have autonomy? That they weren't working at my behest? Who do you think told Eleanor to befriend you, to help you, to tell Ambrose the truth? Who do you think encouraged you to keep going, not to give up?"

Doreen swallowed but didn't shift a muscle.

"Sinclair showed you the way, helped me get you here. Even Hastings, fool that he was, played the part. His love had him rolling over for me. Begging me to pet his belly one last time. All of it led you to me."

"You didn't need the trials to trap us," Doreen said. "We've been here all along."

"Yes, but your will wasn't. You were doing what you could to break the spell." Ada smiled now, a real one that was so sweet it terrified. "Cut off from me even as you stood in front of me. Lenora cursed Ambrose to love her against his will, and he cursed you all to never find true love. To reconcile the two, someone from each of your lines had to fall in love with the other. The curse is broken, but soon you will be nothing but a broken doll for my collection."

Ada launched herself at Doreen and pinned her down. She held her arms over her head as she leaned in, her eyes sinking deeper into her rotting skull.

"You found your love," Ada said, "what you always wanted. Now you are open. It's time for me to claim what I have been looking for."

Doreen burst out laughing, exhausted and near hysterical, and *broken*. Ambrose was gone, as was Margot. Any love Doreen may have had Ada had destroyed. Ada snarled at the laughter, slamming Doreen so hard against the ground she saw stars. Ada curled a bony finger and reached toward Doreen. She tugged, and Doreen gasped as her pulse stuttered. A spark, bright and true, lifted from her mouth.

Ada began to sing.

A lullaby, haunting and sweet.

Tears rolled down Doreen's cheeks as her soul shifted, a splinter pierced her being, and she could feel her spirit being pulled apart.

This was how she would die, then. She would become another ghost, bound to this monster, to this cruel prison of a world.

The stars flickered overhead, and Doreen thought of Stella. Of her aunt telling her *forever*. She thought of Kayleen and the others, of Eleanor, Sinclair, Sera, Margot, Ambrose, and Margaret. Of all the family she had and did not know. Finally, she thought of her mother and how she'd defied Ada. Her soul was not willing.

Not willing. Doreen could be unwilling too. Ambrose had told her that the memory of spells would be in the land here. She had poured magic into this earth; she had wielded it from others as well.

Doreen furled her hands, and then unclenched them as Ada pulled at her magic, at her soul. She opened herself up and called to those lost souls in the prison world.

Awaken.

The water from the ocean splashed by her feet, and she reached to it and called out in a broken whisper the spell Margot had used to save them when they were children and had been in the lake with the dogs chasing them, the spell Doreen mimicked when she and Ambrose had been facing the kelpie. This spell was theirs, and she would use it with the last of her strength to draw in her ancestral line, to heal the damage and pull those souls to shore.

> *"Into the water*
> *You will go*
> *To gain your strength*
> *And save our souls."*

Doreen did not call the kelpie monster of the Goodbye Castle's moat.

This time, she leaned into the door she had opened to Stella, and she threw it wide. Doreen called her family. She called the *willing* souls to come to her and help her fight.

The pages from every journal kept in the prison world washed onto the shore, one after the other, flooding the shoreline with bits of paper and ink that bled into the earth. The words hit the shoreline, racing across the sand toward Ada, and the voices behind the written words rose like the ascending notes of a redemption song.

When the first line from Margaret's journal slammed into her, Ada screamed.

The next line, then the next, tumbled from the page and straight into Ada. Soon the other voices and words were rising up and cascading over Ada's skin, piercing into what was left of her soul.

Doreen lifted a hand as the words rained down on them, mouthing along with the singsong refrain that rode the wind: *"The woods are lovely, dark and deep, but I have promises to keep."*

The violin's strings warbled into the night, combined with a layer of tension from the guitar's most melodious notes, and beneath it the heartbeat of a steady drum.

Ada rolled off Doreen, curling up, trying to fight the words away. "Make it stop," Ada cried, writhing.

As the words lifted, they shifted into bright sparks of light. These weren't words, but bits of souls, taken and stored. Doreen wondered if Ada even knew about them, if she knew the journals existed, or if this was something else. If this was a recording, a narration of their humanity, stored and now freed.

Souls had to go somewhere, and Doreen hoped letting them out would be enough. The words continued to bind to Ada, constricting her movements.

Doreen knelt beside her. "It wasn't you," she said. "It was them. They called for help. When you devoured their humanity, it was downloaded into the prison world. You thought to keep them caged, but you couldn't control those bits of goodness. They stayed, and now they are free."

The waves lapped at her feet, and Doreen looked down to see a single journal waiting. On the spine was the name *Margaret MacKinnon*. This one was not like the other one—this was in a hard black binding, and when she opened it, she realized it was new. The story whole and complete.

"She was never in this world, was she?" Ada said with a sob. "Margaret was never here. She never could be."

She set the book in Ada's hands. "Her story is written. She moved on."

Doreen's heart broke as she studied this sorry excuse for a soul crumpled on the shore before her. Brittle and broken, misshapen and ruined. "It is time for you to move on, Ada. The truth is the spell. The spell is the truth."

The reality of all the souls being freed, of Margaret's soul departed, rained down on Ada in a final storm. The thunder rolled and the lightning crashed against the rocks. The words of those Ada had tried to take rushed into her, all the souls lighting her up from the inside, hollowing out the dark, and sending the last of Ada Rose out of the bones she had stolen and into the night's sky.

Doreen stumbled into the cave and collapsed. The truth hit her hard as she tried to crawl her way into a seated position.

Ada was no longer. Her bones were ash, and the souls of this world were free.

Doreen could rest.

She closed her eyes and thought if she had to go now, it would be worth it. She did wish, however, that she could have told Ambrose she loved him too.

The sea went quiet, the air turned sweet, and Doreen breathed in magic. Golden, bright, and happy. She opened one eye, and thought she saw the woman from the gardens of Ambrose's home. The lady of the Goodbye Castle, who had haunted near the cliffs. The one who had helped her.

"You're not Eleanor," she said, her eyes fluttering closed again.

The same warmth rushed into her, and then a lullaby. The same one Ada had sung, but this time it wasn't perverted into the dark haunting melody. This was bright and free. It was hopeful, gentle.

A thought struck her, and she managed to crack her eyes open one last time. "Margaret?" she whispered, and then darkness took her completely.

TWENTY-FOUR

The smell of lavender struck her first. Followed by clove and rose. A blend of tea her aunt made when she had been sick as a girl. As she came to, she realized she was lying on soft cotton, not the hard sand of a beach or in a grave, dead, as she had expected. She shifted, groaning when every muscle in her body screamed.

"I had hoped," a voice said, deep and groggy and ridiculously sexy, "that I was finally going to save you, and yet, once again, you saved me."

The smile broke before she opened her eyes. When she did, Doreen found Ambrose lying beside her in the bed at her aunt's home, the one she had slept in as a girl. He was every bit as bruised and scraped as she felt, but his eyes twinkled, and his hand was slipped around hers.

"How are we not dead?" she asked, her throat tight, her voice strained.

"You're very lucky," Stella said, entering, "that your aunt and I were able to reach you and keep you both from jumping off the ledge.

Took every bit of our strength to stay open and hold back your spirits when they tried to do something stupid."

"Our spirits?" Doreen asked.

"You never left this world," she continued. "Your mind entered the prison world, and so your bodies were stuck in the rain and elements for weeks. Thankfully they were bespelled, but you're incredibly lucky. You called for me."

"You're welcome," Doreen said, shifting her gaze to her aunt's. "For, you know, killing Ada and freeing the trapped souls, and making sure you didn't end up there when you went tits up."

Stella sniffed and smiled. Doreen laughed, and then coughed.

"You did marvelous. Safe as secrets. As it ever was," Stella said, her eyes shifting to Ambrose. "He hasn't left your side in days."

"And yet, you're in the room together," Doreen said.

"I . . ." Stella cleared her throat. "I had amends to make. I was wrong, and my actions were unconscionable. Ambrose has been so distraught he simply waved me away and continued panicking over you. He was quite insistent we keep a minute-by-minute watch over you and that he be the main guard."

"You've forgiven her," Doreen said. She could see it, even if he could not say it, or wasn't ready to admit it to himself.

"Losing you is all that mattered," he said, before flicking a glance at Stella. "Don't need to kill you until she's better, witch," Ambrose said, though the corner of his mouth twitched.

Stella rolled her eyes. "I would deserve it, though I can guarantee I am not one to go without a fight. After all, my niece takes after me." She placed a cup of fresh tea on the table for Doreen, pressed a kiss to her forehead, and whispered another apology. This one rang deep into Doreen's bones, and she swallowed around the lump in her throat. She nodded to Stella, who gave her arm a tight squeeze before she walked out of the room.

"You're really okay?" Doreen asked, reaching up to touch Ambrose's face. He brought her hand to his lips and his kiss lingered on her fingertips.

"I am free, and I am in love," he said. "I am the best I have ever been."

"You're not . . . dying?" she asked, wincing as she said it.

"I am dying," he said, his tone cheerful. "As you are and as Stella is, though I think she will go faster. I will die years from now, after we have had a love for the ages, you and I." He grinned, then stopped, glaring at the wall. "Together, I mean. Not that you will have one without me."

She laughed, and her heart felt as though it might burst from the hope building there. "Margot? She's okay?"

"She is waiting downstairs. She and her mother were braiding clovers. She said they had to write a new spell to rebind the whole coven, the living and the dead, and that when you woke, I was to bring you down straightaway."

"Sounds like Margot."

"She sent her Dean away," he said, rubbing the back of his neck. "With the curse broken, she swears he needed to be free. He isn't taking to it. Has been calling day and night, but she thinks the curse is delayed for him."

"What do you think?"

"I think Dean may have a bit more to him, but time will tell."

"Hmm," she said, reaching for the tea, finding she wasn't quite as sore as she thought. She drank it down, and then she turned to Ambrose, her hands finding his face again. "I think my strength is returning," she said, relief and desire coursing through her as her power flared bright and brilliant in her veins. He laughed and his lips found hers, until Doreen didn't bother to think at all.

Ambrose's hands slipped into her hair as her hands slid into his shirt. She gasped as he took the kiss deeper, and she pressed against him before she leaned back and yanked his shirt up and off. He murmured her name, and the sound vibrated across her skin. Every nerve ending on her body lit with desire, and Doreen's mouth turned greedy as it sought his. Soon it was a clash of tongues and lips, and the occasional scrape of teeth. Every angle brought the need higher, and soon their hands grew as rough as the sounds they made.

Ambrose lifted her up and over, so she was straddling him. He was careful in his movements, treating her as though she were more precious than a promise, as he removed her clothes in the time it took mortal men to blink.

Doreen explored his chest, biceps, and collarbone with her teeth and tongue. Ambrose's moans steamed the room, and Doreen had never felt more powerful as she took control. Their forms aligned, and as she lost herself in the ecstasy of his body, it was even better than Doreen could have dreamed, had she been a dreamer.

After a nap, and another round of discovering new angles of Ambrose—he was wonderfully ticklish under his left knee—Doreen sent him downstairs as she showered. She was eager to see Margot, to thank her and hug her, and to help with the binding of the family.

It was right, and it was time for new beginnings for all of them.

She finished toweling off her hair and looked into the mirror before she turned to shut the light off and leave the bath. She stopped, blinked, and swallowed.

A faint outline flickered behind her. The image of a woman, there and gone.

The ghost had touched her eyes, then pointed at Doreen.

The lady of the Goodbye Castle, her scent of moonflower lingering on the air. Doreen shook off the shock and smiled to herself. Margaret had been saying goodbye. Doreen hoped she was free now too.

"May you be free, and may you finally find peace," Doreen said to the space where she had been. "Thank you."

She flipped the light off, and starshine drifted in from the open window.

Doreen looked up into the mirror again as she went to step away, and this time her breath caught. Her cheeks were flushed, her skin was rosy from the shower, her smile was tender, but her eyes . . .

"The spell is the truth, the truth is the spell," she whispered as she stared into her own eyes, which now glowed in the dark, a bright and luminescent shade of pearl.

ACKNOWLEDGMENTS

The life of a book is a multilayered journey and collaboration. I am beyond fortunate to have worked with so many amazing people who lent their hearts and knowledge to the shaping of this book.

Top of my list of gratitude is my editor, Vicki Lame, and assistant editor, Vanessa Aguirre. Talk about a dream team! It was such a delight to work with you both on *A Circle of Uncommon Witches*. Thank you for encouraging me and inspiring me throughout the process; you made it utterly delightful. I am also extremely thankful to have been able to work with the following team at St. Martin's Griffin/Macmillan: Publisher: Anne Marie Tallberg; Creative Director: Olga Grlic; Jacket Designer: Olya Kirilyuk; Designer: Gabriel Guma; Managing Editor: Chrisinda Lynch; Production Manager: Jeremy Haiting; Marketing: Rivka Holler and Brant Janeway; Publicist: Sara La Cotti; and Production Editor: Layla Yuro.

None of this would be possible without my incomparable and exquisite agent, Samantha Fabien of Root Literary. Sam, thank you times infinity for all you do. Having you by my side means everything. (And thank you to Team Root for being such a freaking fantastic team!)

To the Porchies, whose generosity and belief in me are one of the truest treasures, I give heartfelt gratitude to Helen Ellis, Ariel Lawhon, J.T. Ellison, Patti Callahan Henry, Laura Benedict, and Lisa Patton. You are some of the strongest, most wonderful, and most capable women I know.

J.T., thank you for fielding all my questions and making me laugh, loving me as I am, and never failing to champion me. Laura, your willingness to read for me in a pinch, and cheer for me always, means the world. I see you, and I am in endless awe of you.

While I'm no longer at the coffee house with my Nashville crew, I carry your hearts in my heart—each and every one of you.

Myra McEntire, I love you to the moon and back again and again and again. Erica Rodgers and Alisha Klapheke, it's not an understatement to say I would not show up to the page without the two of you. In life and in creating story and researching and storyboarding, I couldn't ask for better friends or sisters. Always.

Megan Bell, bookseller and owner extraordinaire, your notes were invaluable, and your friendship is just the icing on a scrumptious cake. I know how lucky I am to have you, Josh, Patience, and Sandra in my corner.

Amy Mass, you are a gem of a human. Thank you for your story and plot walks and talks; they are the cat's meow, just like you.

Whitney Price, thank you for being a beacon of support and love, and I'm sorry (not really, hee) that I named a cave ghost after your gorgeous, brilliant child.

Toni Trucks and Lee Trucks, thank you for all the research help! I would have struggled if not for your photos, information, Scottish tour guide connection, and stories. You are such amazing friends and souls.

Adrian, thank you for the resources, support, connections, information, and kindness. You are a delightful human and hands down the best tour guide I have ever had the immense pleasure to know.

Kayleen McAdams, thank you for letting me borrow your beautiful name. Though to be fair, the gratitude really goes to your adorable parents for such good naming skills! Thank YOU for being such a brilliant and kind friend.

Megan Niedzwiecki, thank you for being such a precious soul and friend, and for helping me brainstorm all the things. You are a goddess.

Margot B., there is a reason Doreen has a Margot and because of her she is never truly alone. If ever I feel lost, I know I only need you, me, and a creepy-ass lamp to find my way home. I love you, beauty.

Heartfelt thanks to Jewl, Margot, Casey, Celisse, Jeff MT, and Marcus for answering my various and at times endless music questions. Also big hugs to the Grateful to 'Be band for so often providing my writing soundtrack!

Sara and Katy, I love you more than words. Melon and Juby, thank you for having my back for so many (manyyyy) years. Dali, you are the bravest badass I know, who is making it a better place on top of it all. Ya-Ya!

I have a brilliant and beautiful sisterhood in my corner of the world. I would be lost without them, and I am so thankful they let me be myself unapologetically, and with total (kinda weird but wonderful) acceptance.

So much love to: Nell, Whit, Melody, Steph B., Steph H., Toni, Rachel G., Jen B., Rachel M., Kayleen, Megan, Meagan, Morgan, Court, Mandy, Ames, Dorothy, Lady Elaine, Jess, Vanessa Ga, Sophie, Vanessa Gu, Mary, Kara K., Kara N., Kim B., Kim, Christina T., Christina E., Linds—we have come to the point where I realize we are legion and I am forgetting quite a few people and how is that possible and I love you all so please forgive me and I will gladly hug any and all members of our girl gang and I apologize but now I must add a period here.

I am so thankful for the many years of cheering me on by my dad, Ken McNeese; my stepmother, Amelia McNeese; my brother and stepsiblings; and my three incredible nieces and my nephew (and their parents too). I'm also the luckiest to call Lynne Street my mother-in-law.

Marcus, I really couldn't do any of this without you or our two amazing and wild and wonderful children. Thank you for never doubting me for a single moment. I would wait forever for you.

Thank you, dear reader, for showing up, for reading, and for allowing me the gift of being with you in this story. I hope you never doubt for a moment that you are magic.

ABOUT THE AUTHOR

Paige Crutcher

Paige Crutcher is the author of *The Orphan Witch*, *The Lost Witch*, and *What Became of Magic*. She is a former journalist, and when not writing, she prefers to spend her time trekking through the forest with her children, hunting for portals to new worlds.